The
I.M.P. Master

(Book Two in the
Ghostwalker Tribe Series)

by

Kevin Robinson

Copyright © 2017   Kevin Robinson
112 N 12th Street – Box 148 – Tampa FL 33602
johnghostwalker@yahoo.com

ISBN: 978-1-62967-090-4
Library of Congress Control Number: 2017901324

10 9 8 7 6 5 4 3 2 1
First Digital Edition

Acknowledgements

This book was unique for me in several ways. First, I "fed" it to my wonderful first readers two chapters at a time, like an old magazine serial story. Why they agreed to this madness, I'll never quite understand, but it helped immensely to see potential reader problems right away and sort them out as I went along. Having said that, I'll never try that approach again!

Second, I never imagined having so many volunteers! Many thanks to my "Alpha Readers:" Dick Todd, Jody Drake, John Mutrux, Denise Toy, Ellie Apuzzo, Melissa Weaver, Bar Scott, Kevin Wohler, Barbara Spegal, Brian Allman, and Alicia Milan.

Also, my deepest thanks to my two amazing copy editors and friends, Pamela Dawes-Tambonino and Denise Low-Weso. You are both great authors in their own rights, and even though it might not look like it in first three or four manuscript passes, you have graciously and patiently taught me ever so much!

My "computer guy" and high-tech book builder is a very cool human being out in California who led the way for self-published e-bookers like me who were raised to fear the "vanity press" scoundrels. Brian Schwartz makes it easy and affordable for low-tech writers to publish a professional looking and easily readable book in both paperback and e-reader formats...even though I'm still clueless as to how he does what he does! Thank you, Brian!

At home, I blathered on, pondered aimlessly, and cried out loud over this story. And my best friend always listened patiently. Thank you, Ellie. I love you more than I can express in words.

Foreword

My last four novels were relatively easy to navigate, for both the writer and the reader. There weren't that many characters, the plotlines were simple, and the bottom line was fairly straightforward. The first three were standard mysteries, and the fourth, *The Ghostwalker File*, was a contemporary novel and the simplest yarn yet. It was (hopefully) a warmhearted character study, a romantic coming-of-age story about a fish-out-of-water baby boy found in a cardboard box who is adopted and raised by a community of Miccosukee tribal members on their reservation just west of Miami. John Ghostwalker was my opus. Everything I might know about humanity in general, and "lost boys" in particular, poured out in that book. I was certain it was my last novel, and sure that it was the real me—along with whatever worthiness I might have as an author.

Then that notion of being finished was recently overshadowed by a dream I had about a woman who took a great job that turned out not to be so great. In the morning, the concept felt like a high-tech thriller, and it seemed a bit out of my bailiwick. But I woke up the following morning startled again. I turned to my dear Ellie, and said: "Damn! It's a sequel!"

I don't think you need to have read *The Ghostwalker File* in order to enjoy *The I.M.P. Master*. But if you did watch John Ghostwalker grow up in my last novel, and if you love those characters only half as much as I do, I expect this one will mean all the more to you.

But, this book is—like most thrillers—a tad more complicated. It is inhabited by a larger cast of characters, and there are often several sub-plotlines happening simultaneously. Yes, at 65 years of age, I had to create a cheat sheet in order to keep all my new imaginary friends straight in my head throughout the year it took to write *The I.M.P. Master*. It seems only fair that I pass my crutch forward to you—enjoy!

Characters of Some Note

John Alden – real life legendary sailing yacht designer during Miami's heyday in the 1940s & 1950s

Joseph Allen – Rad-Corp security guard and former 101st Airborne military acquaintance of Phillip Crowe

Dave Bartlett –legendary humorist, author, and longtime columnist for the *Miami Herald*

"Bronx Billy" – Miami pushcart pretzel man who surreptitiously started the kiosk mall under the Rad-Corp building

Peter Bloom - a member of Rosie's team at Rad-Corp

Chris Tosh –NBA superstar with the Miami Heat

Barry Cole - a member of Rosie's tech team at Rad-Corp

"Spray Ray Colors" – noted Miami tagger, artist, and busker

Ted Connors – the "Sultan of Sleep," Miami's largest mattress retailer

Phillip Crowe – Rosie's direct supervisor at Rad-Corp, former Army "Gunny" Sgt. with the 101st Airborne

Mr. Drake – owner of the Bradford Group, a hotel/resort conglomerate set to build a new resort & spa on the Grand Flamingo Hotel block of downtown Miami

Lou Garcia - a member of Rosie's tech team at Rad-Corp

John Ghostwalker – Miccosukee tribal member, Dan Stone's only child, highly acclaimed architect, and visiting professor at Haskell Indian Nations University in Lawrence, Kansas

Professor Hastings (a.k.a. "Dr. H") – college prof who saw Rosie's potential and mentored her at New York University

Hemingway – Sherman Kanz's beagle mix

I.M.P. – Individual Micro-robotic Personnel (a bee-sized micro-drone)

Abraham "Abe" Jacobs – owner/operator of Jacobs & Associates, a successful Miami architectural firm, and director of Space Station, LLC, a high-tech micro-housing manufacturer

Patty Jenkins - a member of Rosie's tech team at Rad-Corp

Sherman Kanz – Pulitzer Prize winning reporter for the *Miami Herald.*

Representative Ellis Keith, a.k.a. "Kicks" – African-American, Muslim U.S. Representative Congressman from Minnesota's 5th Congressional District and childhood friend of Seth Lowenstein

Joe "Walking Fish" Lamont – Miccosukee tribal elder and mentor

Benny Lopez – director at Filling Empty Houses, Inc., a non-profit corporation providing housing and job training to Miami's homeless families

Katie Lopez – Benny's daughter by his first wife, Stella

Mary Lopez – Benny's second wife and everyone's favorite cook

Louisa – Miami Latino food truck owner/operator

Isaiah "Izzy" Lowenstein – Seth Lowenstein's father

Seth Lowenstein – master of disguises, security specialist, oft-times private investigator for Baltimore law firms, and a former Navy Seal.

Sean "Mac" McKnight – professional (freelance) corporate headhunter and John Ghostwalker's significant other

Hector Nuneo – formerly homeless Miami teenager whose family works with Benny Lopez and Filling Empty Houses, Inc.

Capt. Jay O'Connor – Captain, Miami Fire Station #12

Rad-Corp – a shadow corporation specializing in military electronics, most notably, drone technology.

Grandmother Renee – highly respected Miccosukee elder and "everyone's grandmother"

Sally Roebuck – senior local news editor at the *Miami Herald* and Sherman Kanz's boss

Rock Bottom Remainders – real life classic rock band composed of some of America's foremost writers, including Dave Barry, Roy Blount Jr., Scott Turrow,

Stephen King, and Amy Tan, along with others through the years (Google their 2010 "Wordstock Tour")

Maybelle Johnson – co-owner/co-operator of Shorty's Ribs in Minneapolis, MN

"Shorty" Johnson – co-owner/co-operator, Shorty's Ribs in Minneapolis, MN

Dan Stone – Miccosukee tribal member, John Ghostwalker's dad, director of Personal Space, Inc., a non-profit corporation providing high-tech micro-housing to homeless individuals

Linda Ulrich - a member of Rosie's team at Rad-Corp

Eddie Vogel – Rad-Corp security guard working the ground floor entrance desk alone during the Save the Grand Flamingo Sunday event

Howie Wales – director of the University of Miami campus bookstore

Sandy Wales – Howie's wife

Marlene Weathers – Rosie's late mother

Robert Weathers – Rosie's late father

Rosemary (Rosie) Weathers – protagonist, brilliant PhD. recipient in micro-robotics & micro-electronics engineering

Chapter One

Rosemary Weathers stood in her bathtub. She teetered on top of a pile of old reference books, with her elbows on the tiny windowsill, letting the moist, salty air caress her face. The little crank window was screened, and even if the screen were removed, a large house cat would have trouble squeezing out. The cast iron scroll work on the outside seemed like overkill, not to mention the twenty-story drop to the Miami sidewalk below. She had been living in an exciting fantasy world, but it was starting to get to her. "It," of course, was reality.

"Rosie girl," her father often said, "before you can remedy a thing, you've got to understand what kind of a thing it is."

This strange twice-daily habit at the little bathroom window was now a ritual, and it always made her remember her first day in the glowing Miami high-rise. The outside appearance was *Nuevo*-Art Deco, the windows reflected the brilliant south Florida sunshine, and from the front, the twenty-seven story structure almost fit into the city's picture postcard persona. If passersby paid close attention, it might occur to them that (unlike every other high-rise in Miami) there was no obvious front entrance. Not long after she moved in, Rosie began to see the hulking modern monolith as darker, more ominous somehow—at least on those rare occasions when she saw the outside at all. Rosie actually left the building only a dozen or so times during her years there, catching quick glances as she boarded one of Rad-Corp's long black Mercedes Sprinter excursion busses.

The view of Biscayne Bay from her miniature faux balcony would have been magnificent. The sunrise lit up her bedroom and living room like a theater stage nearly every morning. But the sliding glass door was as faux as the balcony, and so, like her bedroom window, there was no means by which it could be opened. Though no one had said so, Rosie believed with all her heart that the glass was both hurricane *and* bullet proof. The evening traffic far below was always steady, but only on nights when the Miami Heat had a home game, did the cacophony rise 20 flours and remind her of college days at New York University. If she could have transported herself to Times Square, or Washington Park, or anywhere else far away, she finally understood (at least mostly) that it would be for the best.

The concrete stilted Rad-Corp building's ground floor was a wide-open maze of kiosk carts which included stylish mini-boutiques, Cuban coffee baristas, and several ethnic eateries, but she had only shopped there once. She had copies of numerous restaurant menus from throughout downtown Miami, however, and Rosie could call out for delivery anytime she wanted. However, this convenience required her to ring up the security office on the house phone and place her order with one of the silver-blazered guards whose office made up nearly the entire first floor. She was a team leader, but that carried little weight. Non-administrative employees of Rad-Corp surrendered their cellphones, laptops, and any other electronic devices on day one. Only after a major series of promotions (it was rumored) did anyone's cellphones get returned. There was no internet access, and both her newly provided personal computer and her office computer were restricted to whatever reference resources the in-house system contained. Those resources were massive, and more than adequate to her work, but she still missed Facebook and Google.

Even television and movies were subtly restricted. Movie nights in the cafeteria or recreation levels on the 27th and 26th floors were fun, and no expense was spared. But over time, it became apparent that crime shows, high tech thrillers, and military us-versus-them films were getting shown more often than anything else. High tech television shows were obviously popular, and nearly everyone turned out for *Scorpion* night viewer parties, but Rosie missed Charlie Rose and her daily fix of *CBS This Morning*. Fox News was the only choice on the Rad-Corp in-house system.

Security was everything at Rad-Corp, and it was not surprising that her unseen bosses liked to boast (but only through the department supervisors) that "none of our employees have ever been compromised."

"Why would anyone want to go outside in Miami, Rosemary? I mean, really..." her supervisor had quipped when she posed the question. "It's too damn hot out there, everything costs a fortune, and there's nothing to see that we can't see better from the Cloisters!"

Calling the high tech high rise "the Cloisters" was an inside joke that only seemed funny to the supervisors and the security team members. On a good day, it seemed too much like a dormitory at a yuppie boot camp, and on a bad day it felt like a cross between a military boarding school and the world's fanciest prison. The top floor cafeteria was staffed by talented chiefs, and was open 24/7. The views, in all directions, were stellar day and night. The 26th floor rec center, gym, pool, and spa complex was undoubtedly superior to anything in Miami. There was a virtual driving range, an outdoor track, basketball, racquetball, tennis courts, and even a putting green on the roof...encircled, of course, in heavily tinted eight-foot high plexiglass.

But the promotional pitch for signing on with Rad-Corp was certainly true when it came to personal expenses. Literally everything was free: prepared food (from within or outside of the complex), groceries, grooming products, clothes, furniture, everything—as long as you ordered in via delivery and didn't request an excursion pass. But, as

Rosie's late father was wont to say: "Free usually comes with a high price tag." Despite the perks, the complex had never felt like cloisters, but only recently, and only to herself, did Rosie dare whisper her own name for the place. Rosie called it "the Hotel California."

★ ★ ★

The headhunter had called Rosie during her final months of grad school at Massachusetts Institute of Technology. That was years after NYU. She had put off her engineering graduate work and taken night school classes in nursing. This interruption in her career trajectory came because both her parents—retired in a quiet Miami suburb—were fighting cancer. They couldn't afford a nursing service or a live-in caregiver, so Rosie quickly memorized the Licensed Practical Nurse curriculum, breezed through the practicals and exams, and took over their care. When her father died first, she took work at Miami facilities like the Veterans Administration hospital through Miami Medical Staffing, thinking to build a nest egg for when she could get her life back on track and return to school. Those were bleak and complicated years as her mother lingered, and with the exception of a brief, but doomed, love affair with a stunning tall, dark, and handsome local, it all seemed like an unintentional side trip that would never end. Rosie had always been alienated from her parents, not only because she was a genius, but because she was an only child and came as a complete surprise to her folks, very late in their lives.

Neither of her parents had attended college. They were working class folk, getting by pretty well when it was just the two of them. Her dad was the youngest of five brothers who grew up in a ramshackle house on a high bluff along the Mississippi River in Wapello, Iowa, before he joined the Navy. What he lacked in formal education, he more than made up for in common sense and raw work ethic. Though he and his wife couldn't understand most of the subjects Rosie loved reading and talking about, they were determined that she get a proper education. Both had maintained employment into their eighties when their smoking habit finally caught up with them. Caring for them had created a bond that hadn't existed before, at least on her part. Rosie would always feel both happy and sad about that time of reconciliation and deeper understanding.

"Life is like my old backyard in Wapello," her dad told her at the very end. "Every year a little more of the river bank gets washed away. When my oldest brother Jack was born, our house was a hundred yards from the bluff. By the time I left home for the Navy, we could toss a rock in the Mississippi off the back porch...and watch it hit the water. I reckon the house went in shortly after, but I was the only one left, and I didn't want to watch it go. Rosie girl, stay as far ahead of the erosion as you can."

When her mother died, she finally reached Cambridge, Massachusetts and registered at MIT. She felt like the honorary mom to all her young grad school classmates. She flew through the coursework with honors. Five years later, Rosie was completing a doctorate in miniaturized robotics. Her specialty was downsized drone engineering aimed at replacing the seriously endangered honey bee with a motorized equivalent.

No one wanted to state categorically that this might be the only viable future for so many vital fruits and flowering plants, but among the experts on the plight of the tiny pollen mixologists, no one was forthcoming with any data suggesting that things were even marginally turning around. Every new report on the waning honeybee population was more catastrophic than the last. Rosie's redirected air-flow designs led to the project's first successful cross-pollinations. The previous drone prototypes were light enough, fast enough, and even collected enough pollen. Unfortunately, by the time the tiny four-propeller drones reached the next flowers, most of the pollen had shaken loose and blown away. Her design solved that problem, and she was granted a patent for her Corrugated Propulsion Scoop design. When Rosie's work was published, the project's grant money began flowing in, slow but steady, just like honey.

Whenever she recalled the day when the young specialist from a "large corporate placement service" arrived at the MIT lab for her interview, she chided herself for paying more attention to the way he was dressed than the way he walked and stood. His clothes might have said "business," but in hindsight, his posture said "military," or even "spook." She felt a chill every time she remembered his opening the laboratory door that day. There were a dozen other co-eds and female staff in identical white lab coats throughout the room, yet the striking young man had walked straight to her without hesitation. She had assumed it was because of her advanced age. It was not. Her vetting process had undoubtedly been impeccable to the extreme.

"Is there somewhere private where we can talk, Ms. Weathers?" he had asked.

"Sure," Rosie had answered, "there's an empty classroom right across the hall."

"I won't keep you long," he replied as he followed her out of the lab, "but this is a unique opportunity for you. This kind of job is only offered to the most brilliant, unattached, and patriotic Americans."

The irony of that statement was now like a splinter in her finger that was buried too deeply to dig out with tweezers.

"I know you've done leading-edge work, Ms. Weathers," the recruiter said, "but at Rad-Corp, the leading edge is considerably farther out on the envelope."

The way he had almost whispered, leaning forward, and drawing her in, was only obvious long afterwards. And slipping the heavily coded word "unattached" in between two positive and flattering descriptions reminded her of an article she'd once read about writing a termination letter: "Always begin and end your letter with short, positive paragraphs, inserting the bad news in the middle." Everyone at Rad-Corp was, like herself, profoundly unattached. No one ever mentioned friends or family on the outside. Rosie now called herself and her fellow detainees "the lonely hearts club band."

But the young recruiter's promise of high pay, great benefits (including room and board), no budget constraints, and state-of-the-art research and development resources had garnered her full attention. The signing bonus didn't hurt either: automatic repayment of all her college loans. Rosie had never heard of anything like it. At her age, she was already anxious about competing with much younger candidates in an exclusive field and a shrinking job market. The recruiter sealed the deal by suggesting that most employees at firms like Rad-Corp worked for a decade or more before receiving the security clearance she would start out with. Her work on the drone bee technology had awed the board members and the CEO, according to the serious young recruiter, and thus she would head a top secret team and work on a project which was "far more crucial to our nation than replacing the honeybee."

There would, however, be certain inconveniences necessary when working on such a highly classified project. It was all spelled out in her contract. She actually read it, word-for-word, but the salary, the posh south Florida location, and the freedom from years of college debt danced in her head like sugar plum fairies. The contract made no mention, however, as to the true nature of the work she had committed herself to, or the impact on her personal sense of honor once that matter became clear. The slick young headhunter was a natural, and between the lines, he had convinced her that she would be an unsung hero, one the good guys. But the recruiter had lied. And so it was, that every morning, and every evening, Rosie stood on her tip toes in her bathtub, letting the smell of freedom and tropical salty breezes salve the weariness she felt in her soul.

Chapter Two

Moving into the commanding high rise building had been another in the long list of firsts for Rosie. Rented trailers and heavy lifting were, for the first time in Rosie's life, not required. She wasn't even involved. A Rad-Corp crew went to her Cambridge apartment while she was taking a company jet to Miami, packed up everything, cleaned and repainted the apartment, sold her car, and drove the remainder of her belongings from Massachusetts to Florida while she spent two nights in a penthouse suite at the Biscayne Bay Marriott thinking she could really get used to Miami again--especially this neighborhood.

Rosie remembered those two days fondly, and she still ordered dinner from Mama Leona's in the adjacent mini mall at least once a week. She also suspected that it was highly unlikely she'd ever dine there in person again. Some employees came and went occasionally, but Rosie couldn't stand the ever-hovering security escort. They never talked to her; instead, they stared. During one of her few private outing experiences, at a café in the open-air kiosk mall under the building, the solemn guard sat directly across from her and stared at her face. It was as if he suspected she would blink out security secrets in Morse Code if he took his eyes off her for a second. That was just too intense.

On the other hand, her office in the lab was beyond cool. Drones were apparently Rad-Corp's top selling item, and her specialty was their ticket to the next level in drone technology. She would design, and her team would build, the first Rad-Corp I.M.P. (Individual Micro-robotic Personnel) from the ground up; based on her revolutionary work at MIT. Her six-person team had been hand-picked from other drone-related departments, all the best at their specialties.

Every member of her Project I.M.P. team, including her supervisor, Phillip Crowe, also had apartments surrounding the lab on the 20th floor. Each team member's apartment door led directly into the lab. Her door, and Phillip Crowe's, led to their individual offices first, and then a second glass door led into the lab. Rosie's office desk was state-of-the-art. Its legs rose and lowered electronically so that she could work sitting, standing, or presumably, sitting cross-legged or lying on the floor. In her adjacent apartment, she had an efficiency kitchenette hidden behind her bookshelf, but there never was much reason to cook. Her elliptical exercise machine overlooked downtown and Biscayne Bay in case she wanted to work out there rather than with other staff members on the roof. Above the small laptop computer in her apartment, there were three flat screens on the south wall so that she could monitor several sets of lab results or demonstration tests in real time...without actually stepping through the door to her office in the lab.

The passenger and freight elevators were located next to Phillip's office, and the elevators only opened their doors when an appropriate key card was swiped. Rosie's security card permitted her to ascend to the media and entertainment floor, the cafeteria floor, and the roof recreational area--but nowhere else. To attend a meeting on the third floor administrative level or to travel to the ground level lobby for an excursion, every employee housed in between needed a security escort. She sometimes referred to such an elevator journey as "The Green Mile," but only in her head.

Laundry was the best. Rosie simply placed it all in a black nylon bag with her apartment number sewn on in gold embroidery, set it with everyone else's in a bin by the freight elevator, and within 24 hours, the sanitized bag, filled with clean laundry, was sitting just outside her lab door. Items requiring pressing or dry cleaning would be hanging on her door in a clear plastic covering. Easy-peezee.

Fire codes generally require an alternate escape route should the electricity fail, and so—behind a locked door—there was an emergency stairway passing through the center of each floor. Like the elevators, it travelled to the ground floor lobby. There, after passing the guard desk (accompanied by their personal guard), a set of red metal doors finally led employees to the center of the open air commercial kiosk mall amid the building's thirteen massive concrete stilts.

"Each level's fire door," Phillip had assured her on her first day, "will unlock automatically in the case of a real emergency."

Rosie hoped that was true.

"And these are the secure lockers where your prototypes will sleep," Phillip Crowe had said with a chuckle. "Each work station has all the same tools on their racks, and all the same component inventories in the drawers below. Anything you need to do on your job, Rosemary, you just fill out a requisition and forward it to me. Almost everything arrives overnight—or we find a new vendor." His tight smile suggested her tour was not high on his priority list; or perhaps he'd done it too often.

Her first few years at Rad-Corp were pretty thrilling, enough to at least put off any deeper considerations about her situation. Her first employee excursion made her feel like Elvis Presley or Michael Jackson when she realized that Rad-Corp had rented Disney World for three entire days. Employees were issued salary and investment account debit cards to use during excursions outside the building. These were connected to in-house accounts, the balances and debits showing up on personal account pages in the company's on-line database. And no one ever suggested there was a spending limit on the cards.

Apparently employees were free to borrow against future earnings and owe the company store. On that first excursion, Rad-Corp's fleet of black Mercedes Benz Sprinter vans sat alone in the vast Disney parking lot, and each employee could pick the in-park hotel of their choice. There were no long lines, no noisy children, and no pushing crowds. Everyone had a front row spot for the evening parade and the fireworks.

Her second group excursion had been similar; only this time, an entire cruise ship and Paradise Island in the Caribbean had been rented for the duration of their exclusionary company retreat. When she'd taken a more intimate Rad-Corp excursion to Paris one year, Rosie had expected their hotel to be reserved, but was shocked to find the Eifel Tower barricaded off with "Under Construction" signage on chain link fencing when their black van dropped them off beneath its shadow. Each historic site they visited had seemingly needed refurbishing just prior to their arrival...but they were all ushered through the "Construction Crew Only" gates. Yes, at the beginning, it's hard not to love living like a rock star.

There was an excursion to Dubai every year. Phillip Crowe had confided in her, in almost a conspiratorial kind of way, that Rad-Corp had its international headquarters there. She'd seen Dubai on TV and on the internet years before, but the magnitude and scope of it in person was breathtaking. Less inspiring was the obvious chasm between the super-rich folk who owned and toured there, and the working class poor who served them with either utter devotion or well concealed fear. Each Rad-Corp employee might as well have been super-rich and was assigned a personal servant who waited on them hand-and-foot, acted as tour guide, and even laundered their clothes.

★ ★ ★

On the job, Project I.M.P. was everything the young recruiter had promised, and more. Rosie headed up a team of young geniuses who believed, as Walt Disney had, that "if you can dream it, and draw it, we can build it." In the beginning, she believed that the Individual Micro-robotic Personnel units they were creating in her lab were a game changer, with the capability to do worlds of good on a global scale. Over time, however, the company's project priorities began to trouble her.

"It is crucial, Rosemary," her supervisor kept reminding her, "that these drones not look like drones." Phillip tended to pace behind his desk whenever he called her in for a meeting, never quite meeting her eye.

"But Phillip," she always argued, "we lose so much additional capability with a more inefficient design."

"You will create multi-use marvels on future projects, I'm sure," Phillip said with a patronizing pat on her shoulder, "but an I.M.P., first and foremost, must *never* be recognizable as a drone if someone should happen to notice it. Imagine creating a real honeybee, but even smaller. Your honeybee drone at MIT—elegantly amazing as it was—looked nothing like a honeybee. It looked like a wonderful toy, and would be scooped up and carried off by every child—and most adults—who happened to spot it."

"Yes, I can see that," Rosie nodded, "but it seems a waste of great technological capability."

"Not wasted, Rosemary," her boss assured her, "just saved for our team's next world class project."

As he said this, her boss was staring out into the shop, and something about his body language later made Rosie begin to doubt his veracity. But still, looking forward to those "next" projects kept her going for years, and I.M.P. was plenty of fun to develop, even with its harsh restrictions. Rosie and her team had two primary rules: (1) the drone must not attract any unwanted attention; and, (2) if and when an I.M.P. ran out of battery power and fell to earth no one would cast a second glance at it--even if someone stepped on it.

"And if and when some civilian does step on one," Phillip insisted, "the crushed remains must be as innocuous as the insides of a cigarette butt."

Within two years, Rosie's team had working prototypes that looked, for-all-the-world, like bumblebees. Their insides were cleverly painted to look like insect guts, and a tiny sac of green goo was used to cushion the electronics within the carapace. It pained her to let Phillip Crowe step on the first prototype, but the results were eerily realistic. She and her team, at least according to Crowe, were company all-stars.

Chapter Three

"That's great, Linda," Rosie said as she walked around the conference table in her lab. Monday morning was her weekly Sketch Seminar. For the first hour on the clock-- accompanied by Starbucks coffee and a tray filled with breakfast pastries--her team sat around the table sketching furiously. "Don't forget to show us a little sketch of how you see that propeller opening and folding up." Linda Ulrich nodded without looking up.

Rosie laughed out loud when she passed Barry Cole's seat. "Barry, leave it to you to come up with a cocktail drone! Show them." Barry held his sketch pad up and panned the fruity drink umbrella/drone drawing for his co-workers. Everyone laughed, but never stopped sketching. That was the rule. "The altered helicopter approach has proven itself very workable," Rosie said, "but everybody loves playing with a cocktail umbrella, especially kids."

"What about turning it into a mushroom?" Linda said as she poked Barry with her elbow. "That's innocuous enough, isn't it?"

"Maybe when pigs fly, mushrooms will too," chimed in Peter Bloom, never lifting his pencil from his sketch pad.

They could talk, if they kept sketching, but aside from sipping and munching, Rosie insisted that they just keep drawing, no matter how silly and/or ludicrous the result. Sometimes, well, most times, she enjoyed being team leader. This exercise was Rosie's first big team idea, and it always went over well, stimulating more friendly chat among the otherwise largely myopic tech heads. She had been to a writing seminar many years past, and the instructor had attempted to differentiate the nature of right-brained people and predominately left-brained people. He did this by exposing them to two very different timed writing exercises. The class had been told to raise their hands when they'd imagined a protagonist, a plot, and a place or setting for a possible short story. When the last hand went up, the instructor told them they would have exactly five minutes to write a first paragraph that successfully introduced the reader to each of these three crucial story components.

"During those five minutes," he had told them emphatically, "you will NOT stop writing. No pausing, no posturing, and no pondering...just a continuous stream of your words to paper. GO!"

Rosie remembered the terror she felt. Her brilliant mind was frozen, the words she was scribbling were just so much nonsense, and it was the longest five minutes she had ever experienced.

"STOP!" the instructor finally shouted. "Turn over your paper, think up a new person, place, and plot, and put your hands up." When they had all raised their hands, he said: "Same rules, no stopping, but this time you have five minutes to create an outline of what that opening paragraph will be. You know, Roman numerals, capital letters, numbers, and small letters--GO!"

That exercise was easy for Rosie. She loved lists, and she always outlined every essay or report before she began writing her assignments out. Her outline flowed naturally, almost effortlessly, and she was finished long before the instructor shouted "STOP!"

"About half, or slightly more, of any random group of people are apt to be predominantly left-brained, linear/logical individuals," he told them. "But you signed up for a writing course, so odds were good we'd have more right-brained, creative types in here. Put up your hand if the first exercise was more fun for you than the second."

Most of the hands around Rosie went up, while she, and a paltry few other obviously left-brained students, looked at each other with an expression that said something like: "They're all fucking crazy, those guys." But she learned a lot in that seminar, especially that being left-brained did not mean you couldn't be creative. In fact, she'd taken away a dozen great ideas on how to tap into the creative side of her brain.

"The best thinking, the best writing, and all the most significant creations throughout history always require that both brain hemispheres play well together," her instructor had said, "but sometimes, like an old Jewish matchmaker, we have to provide a non-threatening environment where they can get acquainted with each other."

Of course, Rosie had researched that intently, discovering more ways to become a more creative "whole brain" person. So now, at Rad-Corp, she shared what she'd learned. Every Monday morning, she steered her geek squad of left-brainers away from their lists, their inventories, their outlines, and their test results data, insisting that, aside from the many insect-inspired drone designs already being discussed, nothing was off limits. This, she hoped, would lead to a breakthrough, a drone so uniquely innocuous that even a master drone manufacturer would never suspect anything--even if it flew right in front of their security cameras every day. Whether she realized it then or not, she was already thinking ahead.

Chapter Four

For some time, the two opposing aspects of her job and life existed on a teeter-totter, see-sawing back and forth between the joys of discovery and invention, and the security restrictions and isolation. But, in the end, the reality was undeniable. By almost anyone's definition, Rosie was a prisoner. From time to time, a Rad-Corp employee stopped coming to the cafeteria or the entertainment gatherings, and when Rosie asked after them, no one seemed to know anything. Phillip Crowe's stock answer was: "They probably retired. At the rate you're going, Rosemary, you'll probably retire early too." But there had never been a single retirement announcement or party in all her years there, so Rosie secretly suspected that her job was a life sentence. No phone, no internet, and every letter written by an employee had to be screened by the security office. If a letter passed muster, they would mail it out at no cost to the sender. Having a Rad-Corp salary account, funded with money she had few ways to spend, seemed somehow worse than prison. Convicts could at least buy a pack of cigarettes.

It was her August monthly sit-down with Phillip Crowe that had finally pushed Rosie past all her personal denial and fear, and hurled her over the edge.

"I'm not supposed to show you this, Rosemary," her supervisor said as she took the only seat across the desk from him, "but you're going to be moving up anyway after Project I.M.P., and, well, it's the first big win I've ever had with one of my teams."

He spun his flat screen desk monitor around to face her, clicked his mouse, and came around the desk to join her. "Watch this," Phillip said, "it's just too awesome!" He was pacing faster than usual.

The video showed maybe a dozen or so poorly dressed Hispanic men, day laborers perhaps, lined up at a folding table where three casually dressed, but militarily groomed white men were handing out pesos, and saying "*media ahora, medio después de la prueba.*" Her Spanish was very rusty, but she was pretty sure the men passing out the money were saying "half now, half later." In tiny grey text near the time code at the bottom of Phillip's monitor, it said: "Domestic Crowd Control field test: DCC-13." When the last man took his pesos and said "*gracias, senor,*" one of the three men at the table picked up his cell phone, thumbed it quickly, and said: "It's done. Go."

One of the Individual Micro-robotic Personnel units her team had developed would not have made a sound loud enough for the camcorder to pick up, but Rosie recognized the faint, high-pitched murmur as the sound she had heard when several drones were running in the lab at one time. In an instant, in near perfect unison, all the Hispanic men slapped at their necks, bewildered, and collapsed to the ground still as corpses. One of the three Rad-Corp men threw a handful of pesos on the ground where the unsuspecting test subjects had fallen, then turned to help a companion fold up the table and the three chairs. The third man walked up to the camera, reached below it, presumably to collapse the tripod, and Rosie saw the dancing picture spin past the first two men folding up the table and an upside down black Mercedes Sprinter van as the third man hefted the rig to his shoulder and hit the On/Off button.

"A thing of beauty," Phillip Crowe exclaimed. "Those were your A-3 bumblebee I.M.P.s, Rosemary, but the bosses downstairs renamed them 'A-3 Stingers.' Wait 'till they get a load of your A-4 model!"

Rosie nearly threw up right there on Phillip's desk, but choked back her emotions as best she could and tried to nod. She dared not try to talk, and fortunately Crowe was just getting amped up, so she let him expound in his moment of glory while she got herself back under control. This image of those still bodies on the ground would not fade from her memory. In that moment, Rosie Weathers decided that she had to take whatever measures might prove necessary to get this horrible news out to an unsuspecting public.

In her wildest dreams, amid all the life-saving and hunger-ending uses Rosie had imagined her I.M.P.s might be put to, domestic crowd control would never, *ever*, have occurred to her.

★ ★ ★

Determining to act is one thing, but her Hotel California existence was designed so that employees and/or information could never leave. Her drones could prove useful, but the only person who could leave the lab with one was Phillip Crowe, and he, only when accompanied by a Rad-Corp security guard. Crowe personally counted each working prototype and locked them up at the end of each work day, so getting one back to her apartment was not a very reasonable goal.

She was staring out her bathroom window that night, taking deep, slow breaths of the warm salt air, when she began humming an old Johnny Cash tune her dad said he and his brothers used to like singing at family gatherings. It was the humorously sad story of a Detroit GM factory worker who built Cadillacs by day and knew well that he could never afford one. His dilemma was solved when it occurred to him that maybe he could sneak himself out a long black Caddy *"One Piece at a Time."* Rosie smiled and sang the chorus quietly to the traffic 20 stories below.

– Kevin Robinson –

*"I'd get it one piece at a time,
and it wouldn't cost me a dime
You'll know it's me when I come through your town
I'm gonna ride around in style,
I'm gonna drive everybody wild
'Cause I'll have the only one there is around"*

Chapter Five

The lynch-pin epiphany came on a Monday in late September. Rosie was filing the Project I.M.P. team's sketches when she spotted something on one of Peter Bloom's whimsical drawings. It was a mini-morphed dragonfly, almost dragon-like, with graceful rotating wings and a long tail, a subject Peter returned to often, but it was the sketch's backdrop that caught her attention. The hastily drawn tree had scribbles for leaves, but the tree itself looked just like the great maple which stood outside her old apartment in Cambridge. Every year she had been fascinated when the double seed pods whirly-gigged past her windows in the wind. The sidewalks were littered with them for a month or more, and passersby never gave them a second glance. The air of Rosie's youth was often filled with soaring seeds, from fluffy dandelion fairies to the tiny fluttering flakes from the evergreens in their backyard. Maybe this was something she could work with.

That evening, standing in her bathtub, Rosie used her binoculars to give the familiar neighborhood a closer look. The little window faced north, but by leaning to the left, she could see the north end of Bayfront Park and a section of Biscayne Bay that ended at the marina near the shopping mall. Moving to the living room, and switching off the lights, she could look directly across Biscayne Boulevard from the Rad-Corp building.

There were numerous trees in Bay Front Park, but between the setting sun and the scattered lamp post lighting, only one species looked promising. Its leaves were so tiny that, even with the binoculars, it was difficult to distinguish one from another as they fanned upwards, side-by-side, in sort of a triangular shape that came to a point at the branch tips. But the long, almost flat, seed pods caught her interest at once. Some were still green, but many had turned brown, and those all seemed to be twisting lengthwise as they dried out. These looked almost like the pictures she'd seen of those vertical wind generators with one continuous blade which was twisted around a vertical pole. There were a few pods scattered on the ground nearby, but it wasn't windy enough at that moment, and fall--such as it was in South Florida--had barely begun.

"Wild Tamarind," she read aloud when she finally found one in the Rad-Corp computer database. "*Lysiloma latisiliquum*...I will be watching you."

Every morning, and every evening, Rosie watched those trees. And as the breezes off the bay became brisker by the day, the fallen Tamarind pods could be seen father and farther afield from the two closest trees at the edge of the park. But until she saw one sailing, Rosie hadn't known exactly what flying characteristics she would need to mimic with her I.M.P. Watching a single Wild Tamarind seed pod gracefully spin out over Biscayne Boulevard was more thrilling than any of the Rad-Corp movies she ever watched upstairs.

★ ★ ★

Every night she sketched different variations of those Wild Tamarind seed pods, and every day she took one or more turns at one of the four 3D printers in the lab. Her team was always designing parts, the gears and pins and carapace pieces required for their various prototypes, and the waste bin near the printers was full of their unusable cast-offs. But unlike the precious flying prototypes, no one from the security floor had ever thought about the actual parts and/or wasted tiny bits. And so if Rosie occasionally printed and palmed a little something, as she only feigned a look of disgust while flinging her arm toward the waste bin, well, everyone on her team tossed their failures several times a day.

The tiny bits were easy to drop into her lab coat pockets, and the book-holding shelf which she occasionally used while taking a bath worked well as a workbench when set across her bathroom sink. The lighting was good, she loved creating something new, and the slow-but-steady progress filled her with hope.

Within a couple of months, Rosie felt sure that her first personal I.M.P. pod would fly. To prove that, she would need to either build herself a drone controller, or smuggle one through the door from her office to her apartment without giving herself away on one of the security cameras. There were four mini-cams out in the lab, and only one visible camera mounted in her office, but the three lab-side office walls were glass from the waist up. She'd seen no visible cameras in her apartment, but she was too smart to take any comfort in that. Nothing at Rad-Corp would ever surprise her again. Whatever naiveté she had unwittingly brought with her from Cambridge was now gone for good.

The drone controllers were the size of a large cellphone, each was switchable to a dozen different frequencies, and all six of the lab's units generally lay scattered around on desks or tabletops--all in full view of at least one camera. Getting a drone controller onto her desk was easy enough; one was just as apt to be there as anywhere else in the lab complex. But getting one through her apartment and into her bathroom would take a bit of luck, and building one from scratch would take a great deal of ingenuity and patience. Rosie had no lack of either. As it turned out though, she didn't need to build a drone controller.

Rosie had gone over her bathroom thoroughly, and puttied up every crack, crater, and cranny with toothpaste--just in case there was a camera hidden within. She scrutinized these spot repairs each night, sure that if she had restricted some security guard's view, her work would have been undone the second it was discovered. The same housekeepers who came and went through the labs cleaned the employees' apartments as well, so Rosie knew enough to be extra careful when she stored her high tech contraband.

The answer to her smuggling dilemma came from the kitchen. Not her kitchen, but rather the one on the twenty seventh floor. Upcoming social events and/or excursions were posted on digital flat screen message boards in the common areas on each floor. An entirely new event caught Rosie's attention. "Be ready to party!" the yellow digital flyer said in lime green lettering. "Our first annual Monday Night Football Mexican Madness Party will feature all-you-can-eat Mexican cuisine and ENDLESS margaritas! Come join the madness...next Monday night!"

Rosie had learned a thing or two about both herself, and her fellow nerds: overcompensation for one's social awkwardness is only heightened by alcohol. Somewhere out in the world, Rosie had a son born of her lack of restraint while desperately trying to be "normal." That tall, dark, vet with the great smile had most definitely gotten her attention—and gotten her pregnant. So, she also knew from personal experience that too much alcohol *and* too much Mexican food comes with a different kind of price than her romantic night with her patient had led to. Everyone turned out on Monday night, and Rosie was delighted to see that the security floor was heavily represented. She enjoyed a small plate of the delicious Latin fare, nursed her margarita throughout most of the football game's first half, and slipped off to her apartment at half-time.

Like day following night, Tuesday morning's corporate indigestion/hangover was a thing of beauty. Every member of Rosie's team, including Phillip Crowe, was dragging around quite pathetically throughout that hectically miserable morning. By the end of the day, none of the few team members remaining in the lab were in any shape to know or care that there were only five drone controllers scattered throughout the complex. Rosie hoped that the same could be said for the security guards at their monitor screens downstairs as well. At mid-afternoon, she tossed her lab coat on the desk before sitting down to catch up on paperwork. When Phillip Crowe began dismally gathering up the prototypes and shutting down the lab, Rosie scooped up her lab coat, along with the drone controller which had been resting on the desk beneath it, shouted "good night" out to Phillip, and retreated to her apartment. Provided the sixth controller was always on her desk each day--should anyone require it--she thought she'd be safe.

That evening in her bathroom hermitage, she didn't need binoculars to see that Wild Tamarind pods littered the sidewalks and much of Biscayne Boulevard below. In Bay Front Park, smatterings of brown spotted the bright green grass. Rosie linked frequencies between the drone controller and her personal prototype. It was time to test her little facsimile seed pod. Would it twirl and soar gracefully like the real ones she'd been watching, or would it spin out of control and self-destruct there in the close confines of her bathroom? There was a tiny pair of pincers at the pod's base, and though it had other intended uses, it served well as a handle. She held the wrinkled pod up in front of her face with her left hand, re-inspected her paint job of mottled browns and shaded veins, and smiled as she thumbed the power button on the controller in her other hand. Tiny slivers of sky blue plastic emerged from razor thin openings around both the top of the pod, and from around the bottom, just above her pinching fingertips. When these tiny rotors spun, they seemed to disappear, leaving only a slightly blurry distortion in the air around them.

Rosie grinned as she felt the push of air against her fingers, and laughed quietly when she felt her creation tugging as if to escape her grip. She eased back on the power control, and released her fingers. Her I.M.P. leaned slightly, the rotors pivoted to accommodate the tiny gyros built into the device's core, and her robotic Wild Tamarind pod hovered quietly and ever-so-gracefully before her, patiently awaiting her next command. Rosie, still smiling, flicked a tiny switch on the drone controller, and a very close-up video image of her nose appeared on the controller's LCD screen. Scrolling the focus wheel with her thumb panned the shot back until she could see her entire face. What she saw on that face was hope--glowing, smiling, blessed, and desperate hope.

Chapter Six

Glancing at the timer and the green power bar as she flew the pod around the bathroom, Rosie tried to calculate how long the miniature battery would last. Her drone weighed slightly more than the bumblebee prototypes, but they had no glide capability. She sent the pod to the ceiling, cut the power suddenly, and the rotors soundlessly disappeared in truth. Instead of a dead drop like her bees would have evidenced upon power failure, the pod spun as it descended, traveling leisurely from side-to-side until it slowly, and ever-so-gently, came to rest on her fuzzy blue bathroom throw rug. It behaved even more gracefully than its real-life twins. Wind would also be a factor, and not always in her battery's favor. That variable could cut both ways. A light breeze should prove a blessing, but in a strong gust, all bets were off. On average, Rosie decided after test flying the drone all over her apartment, the pod could count on 45 minutes of flight time in optimum conditions. That would be tested more strenuously in the real world outside her little window, but one way or another, it would have to do.

"Okay, Podrick," Rosie whispered, "it's time to leave the treehouse." After removing the window's screen, she fingered the controller, and her newest creation, named after a squire in *The Game of Thrones* books, rose lightly off the floor, tilted slightly toward the tub, and eased its way up and out into the warm evening air. Rosie sat on the toilet seat lid and focused all her attention on the little LCD screen. "Free at last," she breathed. "Free at last."

★ ★ ★

Over the next weeks, Rosie and Podrick explored the neighborhood together through the tiny camera lens. She wasn't sure exactly what she was looking for, but prayed that she'd know it when she saw it. Podrick performed flawlessly, even in the sudden gusts sometimes encountered when passing between buildings. As much as she chided herself for wasting batteries, Rosie couldn't resist flying her toy seed pod into and through Bay Front Park. It struck her profoundly then, how much she missed walking through trees. In both New York City and Cambridge, her favorite study breaks were solitary strolls through the park areas nearby. During her freshman fall semester at NYU, Rosie got lost during her first hike in Central Park, and she loved every minute of it. Those memories flooded back as she flew around Bay Front Park, watching the stroller pushers, the dog walkers, the power walkers, and the hearty joggers pass by beneath her drone without ever giving it more than a passing glance if she got too close.

★ ★ ★

On one of her morning flights, Rosie took Podrick east around the corner of her building, south a few blocks, and then turned west along the Miami River Walk and Biscayne Boulevard Way. The views were breathtaking as she floated above the palm trees between the famous walking path and the busy street. Once Podrick turned the corner west, she noticed a huge hole on the crowded city landscape. There on Southeast 3rd Avenue across from the Marriot Marquis, the foundation of a new building was being dug and sump pumps were fighting to take water out of the hole so the excavation could continue. At odds with everything else about the downtown neighborhood, an ancient and run down hotel-like building—tiny compared to all the behemoths around it—was sitting alone in the southeast corner of the otherwise vacant block, cordoned off with orange plastic fencing and yellow CAUTION tape. There appeared to be picketers on the sidewalk. As she flew Podrick north across Biscayne Boulevard Way for a better look, she could read the placards. Some said: "Save the historic Grand Flamingo!" Others boasted black and white photos of Dwight Eisenhower, Jackie Gleason, and Milton Berle posed in front of the hotel in its prime. The building's old front doors faced the water, and Rosie tried to imagine what it might have been like to look out on Biscayne Bay in its early 1950's heyday.

Something told her that the structure wasn't long for this world, and yet an unusual looking crew of men and women began filing out the front doors carrying paint cans, ladders, and large black construction-sized garbage bags. These folks were dressed like very regular citizens, not construction workers, and they loaded their equipment and themselves into a long white Ford passenger van with "Filling Empty Houses, Inc." printed on the side. When the van drove away, Rosie took one last pass at the protestors as she checked her battery bar on the controller. The green band had turned yellow, but she lingered. It was obvious that one man on the sidewalk was definitely not a protester. He wore a Miami Dolphins cap, a beige-colored sports coat, and waved at the Latino man who drove the white Ford away from the curb. He was talking earnestly to a placard-holding woman, while scribbling madly on a small spring pad. Rosie took Podrick up and over the small crowd and turned back south to look at them from behind so she could see the scribbler's face.

"Yes!" she said aloud. "I found what I need."

Her excitement died quickly as the man nodded thanks to the woman, turned away, and headed east up the sidewalk. Rosie and Podrick had stumbled upon a Pulitzer Prize winning reporter for the *Miami Herald*. She remembered vividly the series in the paper about Medicare fraud in Miami. She'd read it every day while tending her dying parents. And she even remembered his younger looking face on city busses after he'd won the coveted Pulitzer for that investigative series. But right now, there was less than ten minutes left on Podrick's battery, and Sherman Kanz had disappeared around the corner, probably heading for his car. To have come so close, to have hope blossom and fall away so quickly, felt devastating, but something about the ongoing protest would surely provide an opportunity. She had to believe that. Rosie scanned the protesters' faces one last time before flying Podrick back east to the corner, one eye fixed on the battery bar. As she navigated the corner to head back north on Biscayne Boulevard, Rosie nearly dropped the controller. There, directly beneath Podrick, a beige jacketed man in a Dolphins cap walked up the front steps of the huge apartment building on the busy corner, swiped a key card, and entered the front door.

"Son of a bitch!" Rosie squeaked. "You live there, just a couple doors down the street. You don't know it yet, Mr. Kanz, but you and I are going to become friends."

Every morning and every evening, Rosie watched the entrance to the high rise down the street. Oh, she flew Podrick through Bay Front Park every day, buzzed around the corner from time to time to check on the Grand Flamingo, but her prey was Sherman Kanz. Still, the feeble seeming "Save the Grand Flamingo" protesters were a noble, if small, band of brethren. She wished them well. The unusual crew from Filling Empty Houses, Inc. was obviously being relentless in their renovation of the doomed building. They sparked her intellectual curiosity. "Curiosity, after all, is a difficult itch to ignore, Rosie," her dad used to say. More often than not, her dad was right.

Between Rad-Corp's data base and the occasional *Miami Herald* Phillip Crowe brought into the lab, Rosie learned more about both the protest and the non-profit group headed up by one Benny Lopez, a notable Miamian in his own right. According to Sherman Kanz's reporting, the Save the Grand Flamingo campaign needed an unlikely miracle, but every reference to Filling Empty Houses pointed to a booming success. The crews she saw going in and out of the old hotel were, indeed, every day people, voluntarily renovating the place, regardless of its likely demise. All over Miami, unoccupied homes and buildings that were not finding buyers, or sat waiting on a wrecker's ball, were being spruced up by volunteers so that Miami's poorest could have safe shelter, at least for a while. When the building sold, or the wrecking crew arrived, Filling Empty Houses just moved the family or families to another newly renovated home. According to the accounts Rosie found, no property owners had filed charges after finding their property had been lovingly improved.

Chapter Seven

Sherman Kanz loved the old Grand Flamingo, and wished its would-be saviors well, but the building sat on a piece of Miami's most expensive real estate. It was too old and too tall to move. Even if some rich fool wanted to take it apart and rebuild it somewhere else, the salt-ravaged concrete block was crumbling away. Spalling was what the pros called the disintegration of old south Florida concrete. Back in the day, local sand was cheap and nearly limitless, and no one stopped to think about what the sand's super-high salt content might do to the iron rebar which reinforced it, or to the concrete itself. Spalling repair in south Florida was a billion-dollar-a-year business.

Sherman's grandfather had proposed to his grandmother in the old Grand Flamingo hotel's chic restaurant, and they vacationed there from New York City throughout their 45-year marriage. Grandpa Kanz left Sherman a dozen signed photos of famous Grand Flamingo guests posing with his grandmother. Sherman copied several of the old photos and gave them to the protesters to use on their flyers and placards. Grandma Bertie was a looker in her youth, and even at 80, she was just too damn cute to ignore. When they danced, even near the end of their lives, people stopped to watch. As a boy, Sherman thought their romance magical. Three failed marriages later, he knew it was a fucking miracle--bigger even than the one the old hotel needed right now.

Sherman Kanz was no longer all that thrilled about having won the Pulitzer Prize, or at least he wished it had happened later in his life. His series of investigative reports in the early 1980's had sparked a nationwide Federal investigation, and that investigation ended up ranking Miami as the country's far-and-away leader in Medicare/Medicaid fraud. He'd first discovered a handful of major medical equipment dealers who were deliberately miscoding their invoices for Medicare/Medicaid reimbursement. Simply by changing a few digits on the forms, a $35.00 procedure or item could pull in $3500 in federal reimbursement. Then, while Kanz was interviewing employees from medical supply houses all over the city, he stumbled onto rumors of a ring of rogue local sales techs who had banded together to undercut their own bosses.

Medical supply salespersons were called in regularly by physical therapists at the local hospitals and rehab centers, and their job was to help the therapists fit the patient to the most appropriate equipment, and set it up properly when it arrived. They were paid a small commission on each device they sold for their supply house, but it paled in comparison to the high mark-up profits their bosses made on each deal. When one of them discovered that certain supplies like wheelchairs and other high-priced adaptive equipment could be purchased for a fraction of the price if the invoice showed delivery to one of several South American countries, the Saturday night poker game among eight competing Miami medical techs morphed into a shadow corporation. They wrote up deals, told their bosses one of the others beat them out, and paid one of the group member's cousins to intercept the crates when they arrived at the Port of Miami for their supposed cruise south. It was a gold rush in the millions and drove several of the Miami medical supply houses out of business (or their owners into early retirement) before the Feds could bring down their hammer.

The great story almost fell in his lap, as some good stories do, but good stories suddenly seem less so once you've won a Pulitzer Prize. Sherman Kanz had filed hundreds of good stories since those heady days, but it was somehow obvious that he was no longer filing *great* stories. Oh, sure, he got to bypass lines at several of the finer Miami eateries, passing through the kitchen doors for a chat with the chef before dinner, and the local television stations occasionally called him in as a "Pulitzer Prize-winning consultant," but he felt like he was now a decent beat reporter who could never again live up to the expectations of his readers, his bosses, or himself. It had been fun seeing his face on the Metro buses and trains, but Sherman Kanz had long ago been replaced by zoo animal cartoons. He lived alone, kept at his job, and faithfully walked his dog, Hemingway, but he knew his best days were behind him.

But Glory Days aside, Kanz loved Bayfront Park. His mornings were filled with phone and computer research, and he did his best writing in the evenings, so his lunch break was the perfect time to cross Biscayne Boulevard and walk in the park. Most days, he'd ease out on the rocky sea wall, pull off his shoes and socks, and let Biscayne Bay lap up and over his gnarled feet. His old mostly beagle mix, Hemingway, loved Bayfront Park too, eagerly chasing leaves, thrown sticks, Frisbees, or any moving object that called to the hunter within. Each time they settled onto the sea wall, Hemingway renewed his love-hate relationship with the salty waves. When he successfully bit an incoming wave, he danced away like the victor in a primal death match. But whenever the wave successfully cast salt water up into the little hound's nose, Hemingway sputtered, sneezed, and snarled simultaneously.

★ ★ ★

Rosie Weathers was enjoying a rare mid-day respite, eating lunch at her favorite window seat on the twenty seventh floor of the Rad-Corp building. Her busy lab team often had their lunches delivered, but this day she had ordered them out of the lab with assurances that they could all use a break. Some slipped into their apartments to order lunch and play video games, while others joined her on the elevator to the top floor. The South Florida sunshine sparkled on the bay, and all manner of marine craft could be seen heading towards, or returning from, the inlet. The pre-winter tourist season was in full swing, and so Bayfront Park was crowded. Even from a distance, it was obvious that the little brown-and-white dog was having a blast playing in the water, but it was the man holding the leash who held her attention. From high across the street, Rosie would have needed her binoculars to be certain, but the rumpled beige jacket and the Dolphins cap were too much of a coincidence to be ignored.

"I am the I.M.P. Master," she breathed, "and you are my prey. I will have my way with you, Sherman Kanz."

"What was that, Rosemary?" Phillip Crowe said as he stood over her with his tray. "Mind if I sit here?"

"Oh, of course not, Phillip," she said. "Sit. I was just remembering a little blessing my dad would say before meals."

"Good, good," Crowe said. "There just aren't enough God-fearing folk in the scientific community. Ah! You got the rigatoni too."

"Yes, yes I did."

"Should be good," her boss said, nodding toward the kitchen. "One of the new cooks is Italian. She makes the pasta by hand."

Chapter Eight

"It's not paranoia," Rosie whispered to herself when she sat shaking in her bathroom that night, "not if someone's really out to get you."

Was it her imagination, or was her boss/handler, Phillip Crowe, watching her every move that afternoon in the lab? It seemed that every time she turned around, Crowe was studying her through the glass walls of his office.

"How much did he hear me say?" she asked herself over and over. "What will he do?"

She was too rattled to send Podrick out the window that night, but she eventually settled down enough to think back on what she saw down in Bayfront Park.

"Sherman Kanz has a dog," Rosie thought, "so he has to walk it more than once a day. Surely he takes it out when he gets up and just before he goes to bed."

Some inner logic told her that her best bet was evening. Her right-brained, creative friends in college all had trouble with early classes. They were more social than she, gathering for drinks, pizza, and live music any night any one (or all) of the three were readily available. Sherman Kanz wasn't a fiction writer, but still, he was a writer, and a bachelor by all accounts, so he was apt to be sleeping in while she was already up and at work in the lab. "But when does he go to bed?" she said. "It doesn't matter. I will find out one of these nights—no matter how long it takes."

She still hadn't decided how to actually approach the reporter, but she was working on it. Podrick could carry an ounce or so of cargo in his little electronic pincers, and a single sheet of toilet paper would accommodate a decent amount of text if Rosie kept her printing small. The warm, damp, and salty air would wreak havoc on the ink, so she palmed a couple of the little zip-lock baggies in which all the lab's tiny electronic components arrived. Dry delivery, but what would she say?

"How can I convince him I'm not crazy?" she whispered. "What if he comes or calls here to check on me? They'd make me disappear. Patience. I must have patience."

Rosie smiled despite her anxiety level. "Never pray for patience, Rosie girl," her father loved to say. "God teaches patience through tribulation. And when God sends tribulation, he expects his people to tribulate."

"Well, trust me on this one, Dad," she said. "I've got the tribulatin' part down pat."

★ ★ ★

Crowe's oversight at the lab that week felt like a storm brewing over her head. He was most definitely watching her. Rosie was sure of it. He went out of his way to be near her, to make awkward conversation in ways he had not done before. When he asked her to join him for lunch again, she panicked. Thinking her face must be showing that panic made Rosie panic even more.

"It's a beautiful day to look out over the park today," Phillip said. Rosie thought maybe he was trying to smile, but it wasn't quite working. "Perhaps we could have lunch together?"

After what seemed to her like five minutes, Rosie found her voice and said: "Sure." For the rest of the morning, she obsessed about whether or not she had blinked even once during that horribly long pause, and whether or not Crowe was toying with her like a spider might with a fly stuck firmly to its webbing.

Phillip was already at the same window table where they had sat together before when Rosie got off the elevator. She picked up a tray, got in line, and tried not to let her hands shake. She tried even harder not to glance up at the security camera she knew was just above her head. As she walked to join her boss, Rosie suddenly began to laugh nervously. She had done the same thing in junior high school when the meanie girls surrounded her and threatened to beat her up if she didn't give them her lunch money.

"What's the matter, Rosemary?" Phillip said, rising and waiting for her to sit. "Something funny?"

"Oh, ah, no...well, yes. I'm so distracted today that I picked up a dish of Brussels sprouts."

Phillip's smile seemed genuine this time. "And that's funny?"

"Yes, it is," Rosie said as she sat down. "I hate Brussels sprouts."

"Here," Phillip said, pausing half way back into his chair, "let me take them back. What would you rather have? I took the carrots."

"No, no." she said, motioning him to sit. "I'll eat them— just as a lesson to myself to pay more attention next time."

"You're one-of-a-kind, you are," Phillip laughed and seemed almost giddy. "It's that narrow-focus that makes you dangerous."

"Dangerous?"

"Well, I mean really good at what you do. Rad-Corp's never going to let you go."

Rosie nearly gagged on a Brussel's sprout and glanced toward the elevator, fully expecting to see a security detail piling out into the dining hall. Fortunately, Phillip Crowe was staring out the window.

"Look, Rosemary!" he said. "It's that little dog that likes to chase those seed things."

Rosie couldn't breathe, but looked out over Bayfront Park, knowing what she'd see before she could turn her head. There was the man in the Dolphins cap, and his beagle was leaping after a fluttering Wild Tamarind pod like its life depended on snatching it out of the air, stretching his self-rewinding leash to its limits.

"He's a hoot, that mutt is," Phillip said. "I see him out there almost every day.

Rosie reminded herself to do one thing at a time. She couldn't talk if she couldn't breathe. She couldn't breathe if she couldn't swallow. She couldn't swallow if she didn't chew her Brussels sprout. So, she chewed. Her heart rate might be thudding at a decibel level nearing a nearby human's capability to hear it, but one thing at a time. Rosie loved lists.

"Hell of a job here, Rosemary," Phillip said, fixing her with an intently sincere look. "I mean, as crazy as it is, I never fit in anywhere else before Rad-Corp. Well, except the Army. I was nerdy, but in a very uncool way, and nowhere near a smart as you and all the wiz kids around here. I'm really good at only one thing. I can trudge. Long after everyone else gives up, I keep after it...until it's done. That's why I was such a good soldier, and that dogged determination and follow-through was what eventually moved me up the ranks to Master Sergeant. That got me noticed in higher circles, and eventually by Rad-Corp. They eat that mentality up. Now I'm heading up a team with real skills, and demonstrable results."

Phillip took a breath, and, finally, Rosie did too.

"My boss called me downstairs again yesterday," he went on. "I wanted you to know. He can be a scary son-of-a-bitch, that one, but I think he finally believes in me. Anyway, his chats always end with a 'mission,' and his mission this time was short and to the point: 'Don't let anything, or anyone, get this team of yours off track.'"

Rosie had chewed, swallowed, and breathed enough, but she still couldn't find her voice. The seconds felt like minutes.

"So," Phillip said, reaching toward her briefly before pulling his hand back to his lunch tray, "I just wanted to say 'thank you,' Rosemary, I know you're the reason I'm still here. You're my fourth team leader, and I don't think I have any more second chances left. It's imperative that I don't get canned."

Chapter Nine

All afternoon in the lab, Rosie struggled to reconcile the seemingly nice and semi-normal boss with the scary-as-hell boss in her mind. Phillip Crowe was either extremely straightforward or extremely sly. Then again, perhaps he was both. Had he been threatening her, or begging her, or warning her about something? There were mixed messages there. She was sure of it. Her dad's sage country wisdom came back to her again.

"News is what actually happens. But the minute we start makin' up stories about what it means, why it should or shouldn't've happened, and how it will or won't affect our lives, well, that's what educated folk call 'drama.' Don't ever let 'em kid you, Rosie girl. Drama's just another word for bullshit."

She would, she decided, move forward, working one day at a time with what she thought she knew to be true now, not what she feared might come. She must get away.

★ ★ ★

A few uneventful days later, Rosie was working at her desk when she experienced a very unusual interruption.

"Rosie, look!"

It was Linda Ulrich, the truly shy and quiet one on her team. Maybe the youngest too. Hearing her voice in the lab was a rare occurrence.

"What have you got there, Linda?" Rosie said, walking over to the work bench where Linda stood beaming like a child.

"I'm filing the circuitry order that just arrived. Watch those yellow capacitors when I close the drawer!"

Rosie watched the plastic bin of tiny capacitors as Linda slid the drawer closed, but nothing was happening.

"Squat down!" Linda insisted. "Look under the table's edge into the drawer as it closes. Isn't that cool?"

Just as the drawer passed into the shadow on the work table's top surface, the drawer lit up, flashing thin beams of yellow light before the drawer closed fully. Rosie opened the drawer, picked out one of the capacitors, cupped it in both hands until it was completely engulfed, and then parted her thumbs just enough to peek in with one eye.

"See," Linda said with a delighted smile, "it's phosphorescent! If they dip more of their components with that kind of wild paint, we can decorate the lab with them next Christmas!"

"Well," Linda laughed, "maybe we could light up a gingerbread house, at least. Nice catch. How's the supplier been lately? Anymore nasty notes?"

"Yes, they're 'just reminding' us more often, but why would Rad-Corp not pay the vendors on time? I mean, with these guys, it's like a year," Linda whispered, "and Rad-Corp couldn't really be broke or anything, could they?"

"I doubt it," Rosie said, "but if they don't get paid soon, the paint they use might be radioactive next time." Linda seemed startled by her joke. "Just kidding, Linda, but I think I will mention it to Phillip again."

As she walked away, she tried to imagine being a Rad-Corp vendor trying to collect on a debt. How many options could they have against this kind of wealth and power? No good ones that she could imagine. And, worst of all, no matter what capabilities Rad-Corp might have had prior to her tenure, her A-3 Stingers gave them unlimited power over any individual, anywhere, with almost no risk of detection. Their sporting and entertainment camera drones were famous around the world, their bomber drones were infamous around the world, but the drones she gave them were something else again. Living with that was untenable, so any risk to her own safety was a price she was willing to pay.

★ ★ ★

When Rosie returned to her bathroom/flight control center that evening, and began to retrieve Podrick from his hanger behind the medicine cabinet, she balked. Every night, when she put the drone away, she replaced the four screws which secured the cabinet in a very particular pattern. There were two screws on each inner side panel, and they anchored into the sixteen-inch-on-center wall studs on both sides of the fourteen and a half-inch medicine cabinet. Rosie always tightened the top right screw so that the flat-blade screw slot ends stopped at the twelve o'clock and six o'clock positions. The bottom right screw slot stopped at one and seven, the bottom left at two and eight, and the top left at three and nine. One of the four screw slots wasn't pointed in the right direction. It wasn't off by much—but it was off. She tried to remember the last time she flew Podrick out the window. What was she thinking? Had she been distracted?

As she carefully removed the screws, she looked for any other signs that someone had tampered there, but the screw heads were not nicked up, the white paint around them was not scratched, and there was no sign of drywall dust on the sink or the floor below. Rosie was meticulous about cleaning that up each time, but there was no reason to believe that a Rad-Corp cop couldn't be equally meticulous. She found Podrick lounging in the envelope she'd glued to the back of the kitchenette's drywall, and both appeared as they always did.

"I was just distracted," she told herself. "Too much going on and I get distracted. I'll be more careful tonight."

★ ★ ★

Each day Phillip Crowe seemed more attentive, even if not particularly more threatening. Each evening Rosie flew Podrick fifteen or twenty minutes later than the night before, hoping to catch Kanz walking his dog, even if the last walk was much shorter than their lunchtimes at the park. If Rad-Corp suspected her, even if they were on to her, there was nothing to do but keep trying. All she had to work with was now.

This night's I.M.P. flight began at nine forty-five, and when Podrick's battery bar turned yellow at twenty-five after ten, Rosie made a last quick circle above the park before heading back toward Sherman Kanz's building. She gave him every opportunity to step outside before she had to bring the drone in, and on this night, he rewarded her diligence. Knowing how long they stayed out would help a lot, but her battery called the shots. If Rosie lost Podrick, she'd have to start all over.

Sherman had no hat on, and from above it was clear that his uncombed salt-and-pepper hair was thinning. Rosie watched him, through Podrick's eye, cross the street with his dog, swooping down to follow at a safe distance, but just as she thumbed the joystick to turn homewards, the little pooch spun around, looked up, and darted back onto Biscayne Boulevard with its beady eyes fixed on Podrick. As Kanz spun around, fumbling with the leash retractor to stop his dog, Rosie raced home as fast as her drone could fly.

"Well," she said as Podrick slipped in through the bathroom window, "you learn something new every day. Maybe Joe Public can't hear a micro drone coming, but a beagle sure as hell can."

Chapter Ten

The next morning, Rosie hit the bathroom early, but not for her usual ritual. Within an hour, while still in her pajamas, Rosie flushed away over a dozen squares of toilet paper, all covered with tiny lines of text, hand printed in blue ink. Her fingers ached. When her watch beeped its call to breakfast, she flushed her latest half-finished epistle and hurriedly threw on some make-up, slacks, a blouse, and her lab coat. She never missed breakfast.

"What I need," she thought as she headed for the door to her office in the lab, "is an SD card." She realized she'd not seen an SD card or a thumb drive in all her years at Rad-Corp. The toilet tissue thing might break the ice and start a dialogue, but it would never cut it when she had to turn over real data. At least now she knew part of what she wanted to say in her initial contact with Kanz. Trading national secrets for a twenty dollar SD card wasn't going to make her rich, but it might save her life.

The work day went smoothly, but that didn't mean Phillip's attention had waned. Several times she was sure he would approach and say something, but he always hesitated, nodded shyly, and went on about his business. Despite his curt comments about going outside during her first weeks at Rad-Corp, Rosie often wondered whether Phillip took advantage of the ever-available security escorts and stretched his legs out in the city. Now that he seemed to be confiding in her more often, perhaps that was worth exploring.

★ ★ ★

When Podrick soared out into the warm air that night, there was a baggie dangling in his little electronic pincer clip. Outside in the darkness, the tiny clear packet glowed with a faint yellow light, so Rosie kept it well above the traffic and the treetops down below. She flew the drone right into the treetops above where Kanz's beagle loved to do his business, set Podrick to hover there, high and out of sight, and waited. Sherman Kanz was late, but barring a sudden thunder storm, she had time to be patient.

Hidden in the palm fronds, she could only look up or straight down, so Rosie prayed that the reporter wouldn't vary his routine. She needn't have worried. Before she could see Kanz in the small clearing below her, the little beagle burst in all aflutter and leapt straight up at the drone as if the fifteen feet between them was of no consequence. Podrick had no sound system, but it was obvious the dog was barking its head off. Kanz's face was staring upwards when he came into view, and Rosie was counting on the fact that while Podrick should be almost invisible in the dark canopy above him, the faint yellow glowing capacitor in the baggie with the single sheet of toilet tissue folded in fourths would command Sherman's full attention. It did. When she teasingly lowered Podrick towards him, Sherman instantly reached upwards, and his dog damn near ran all the way up to the reporter's throat before falling back to earth. Rosie backed off while Sherman Kanz scowled at his torn shirt buttons and tried to calm his pet.

They played this painfully coy game twice more before Kanz signaled "wait" with his palm and disappeared from sight. When he returned seconds later without the dog, Sherman held his hands out to his sides and shrugged sheepishly. Rosie liked his intelligent yet boyish smile. His shirt front was shredded, his gray-haired chest was covered with scratches, and yet here he was grinning up at her, holding his cupped hands out in front of him like he was expecting a communion wafer from a priest. Rosie laughed quietly. She then bobbed Podrick up and down several times, hoping Kanz would raise his hands a bit higher; there was no sense exposing her drone if she didn't have to.

The reporter responded immediately, falling to his knees in mockingly prayerful obedience, bowing his head, and dutifully raising his cupped hands over his head. Rosie chuckled, dropped the baggie into the reporter's hands, and flew Podrick back out through the treetops.

"I like this guy," Rosie said as Podrick flew home. "I hope I get to meet him someday."

★ ★ ★

"What the fuck?" Sherman said as he got up off his knees and looked at the unlikely delivery. "I haven't had a drink in three days. Did I really just get approached by a damn drone with a story lead?"

Hemingway was barking himself hoarse, and trying his best to pull the nearby palm tree up by its roots. "First things first," Sherman said as he began to place the baggie in his now dangling shirt pocket. "Shit!" He stuffed it in the pocket of his cargo shorts instead, untied Hemingway, and walked home shaking his head. "And I thought I'd seen about everything!"

As he swiped his key card at his apartment building's front door, Kanz remembered that Hemingway hadn't done his business. "Oh what a night...," he sang as he dutifully turned around and walked back across Biscayne Boulevard, "late December back in '63. What a very special night for me..." He was no Frankie Valli, but Sherman Kanz knew a story when he smelled one. "I'll remember what a night."

Back at his apartment a half an hour later, the reporter carefully opened the baggie out on his balcony table, looking intently for signs of powder or residue. He emptied the contents into a plastic refrigerator storage container, carefully using the blue lid to be certain a gust of wind didn't blow the folded tissue off his deck. He sniffed at it all tentatively, half expecting it to burst into flames like a piece of magician's flash paper. When it appeared that the strange delivery wasn't going to do anything of the sort, Sherman sealed the container and went inside for a couple of pencils. When he returned, he carefully used the pencil erasers to gently unfold the tissue. "Shit!" he said. "It's just a piece of toilet paper."

The hand-written message was brief: "*I want to tell you a story, Mr. Kanz. But I need an SD card. In exchange, I might just give you another Pulitzer Prize. No, I don't want anything but to see you break the story. Well, to be honest, I would like to get out of this alive. Same place, same time. Raise your baggie hand high if you swear to tell the truth and nothing but the truth. I do. Yours etc., Scheherazade .*"

Chapter Eleven

"I was in a London bookshop," Rosie's dad had told her a few months before he died, "you know, a bunch of sailors on leave, seeing the sights. But I wandered off a bit, across the street from the pub where my buddies were drinking. This bookstore, it just looked so, well, quaint and European-like. I had school books and such as a kid, but always had to give them back. The ship had a library, and we all read to pass the time, but I had never owned a book of my own. Not one. When the tidy looking store clerk asked me what I was looking for, I laughed at myself and just said it straight out: 'a book.'"

"'Of course, sir,'" he said to me very politely, "'but what sort of book did you have in mind?'"

"'Why not an adventure book? Or maybe a travel book? What about a book full of great stories, you know, something to keep me occupied while I sail around the world?" I asked him. And that's when I confessed to never having actually owned a book. I felt a little ashamed I guess."

"'Very good, sir,'" he said, just like a butler in the movies. "'I believe I might have just the thing.'"

"The dapper little guy disappeared into the back room, Rosie, and then he came out with a very old looking book— Marlene! Where'd you put my book?"

"In the safe, Bob," Rosie's mom said from the living room. "Same as always."

"Safe?" Rosie had said. "You have a safe?"

"Well, honey," her mother said, taking her by the arm, "your father likes to call it that."

In the garage, her mother began twisting a large white PVC cap fitting that was half way down a five-inch thick PVC pipe that ran up from the floor and into the ceiling.

"Mom!" Rosie had shouted. "Stop! That's the sewer line to the upstairs toilet!"

"Well, not exactly, honey. Your father just installed an oversized cleanout fitting over the sewer line, but it doesn't connect to anything." The cap came off in her hand, and she reached into the dark hole and pulled out a small package wrapped in brown grocery bag paper. "Here. This went around the world with your father more than a few times. He was going to leave it to you anyway. Your father read these stories to you every night when you were little."

"I don't remember that," Rosie had said as they returned to the kitchen.

"Of course you don't, honey. Your father always got home from work around midnight. You were long since asleep."

Now, so many years later, those memories brought Rosie comfort; and, in this case at least, an alter ego: Scheherazade.

With Podrick back in his hanger behind the medicine cabinet, Rosie sat in her reclining massage chair and held the old book against her chest. The famous tales of *The Arabians Nights* were first translated into English by a bigger-than-life, hell, crazier than Hemingway, 19th century Brit named Sir Richard Francis Burton. Rosie had looked him up, and had trouble believing half the stories about his life as a soldier, spy, explorer, linguist, and something of a pain-in-the-ass. That a British shop keeper had gifted a young American sailor with the old copy was, in and of itself, a bit hard to believe, but throughout her father's last days, Rosie read the stories back to him that he had so lovingly read to her.

And now, many years later, she had become Scheherazade. Rosie was just as much a captive as the young storytelling virgin had been, and only the most engaging of stories could possibly save her life...not to mention the lives of Americans whose future public protests might anger or threaten the rich and powerful. "I still have both my cheeks!" she said laughing to herself as she remembered the picture she'd discovered of Sir Richard Burton which showed ugly scars on both of his cheeks. His expedition had been attacked by 200 African natives, or so the story goes, and though his party lost all their gear and several members, Burton fought on, leading the remnant away to safety, all with a native's thrown spear sticking in one cheek and out the other as they ran. Rosie shook her head. "I guess I'm OK so far." She breathed deep, let the massage chair do its magic, and soon fell fast asleep with the old book in her hands.

★ ★ ★

Two blocks down the street, Sherman Kanz was pacing. He'd already wiped a 32 gigabyte SD card and loaded to it a text file that simply said: "I do too." He put that in the baggie with the glowing capacitor, zipping it closed with great care. Hemingway had settled down earlier, but as the reporter began pacing, he too picked up the anxious, excited vibe Kanz was putting out. Perhaps his slow-witted human regretted not letting him hunt down that bird with the annoying whine. Surely, working together, they could kill the damn creature. But alas, that was apparently not to be.

"Hemingway, go lie down," his human said. "It's a blessing you didn't catch that thing...oh, and you owe me a new shirt."

Sherman finally collapsed on the sofa and put one of the Jimmy Buffet Parrothead pillows over his eyes. He always thought better with a pillow on his face. But he also slept better with a pillow over his eyes, so he woke up the next morning with a Parrot on his face and a beagle's nose poking him in the ribs.

"OK, Hemingway, I'm up, I'm up."

As they walked through Bay Front Park together, the sun was well up above the horizon, and the waters of Biscayne Bay sparkled and danced. When they stepped under the small canopy of trees, Hemingway became more vigilant and tugged at his leash.

"She's not coming now, Hem," he said, looking up anyway. "We've got to wait until tonight. And then we'll see. But, jeez, you've got to get hold of yourself, boy. If you keep going bat-shit like that, somebody's gonna call the cops on us."

He'd seen drones, even played with a few, but as Hemingway did his business and Sherman placed a doggy bag on his free hand and inspected the canopy of Palm, Seagrape, and Wild Tamarind branches looming overhead.

"How the hell does a fat-ass drone fly in and out of that shit in the dark, Hem? And how come you could hear it and I couldn't? I can hear those things when they're a hundred feet over the park."

Hemingway never answered, but their bond was such that neither cared. As Sherman Kanz and his drone hunting beagle walked home for breakfast, he couldn't stop watching the sky, and there was only one person on his mind.

"And, another thing, Hem, her name damn sure isn't Scheherazade."

Chapter Twelve

Phillip Crowe was fidgety the next morning, displaying more nervous energy than ever. Rosie had a premonition that he'd be confronting her instead of backing off, by the looks of it. And, sure enough, out of the corner of her eye, she saw him square himself and head for his office door. Whatever was coming was on its way.

"Can we have lunch together today, Rosemary? There are some things we need to discuss."

"Sure, Phillip," she said.

The lab was as cold as ever, and the man was sweating. He nodded firmly in obvious satisfaction and strode back towards his office. Rosie stayed busy, checked on team members, filed paperwork by rote, and hardly thought of anything but how to not give away anything by her words or her actions.

She nearly screamed a few hours later when Phillip gently touched her arm from behind and said: "The elevator's here, Rosemary, let's grab it while we have the chance."

His eyes were twitchy, scanning like a cornered gerbil looking for an escape route from the family cat. "Sure, Phillip," she said, handing Linda back the order reacquisition data pad she'd just signed. Her boss herded her into the elevator car and hit the cafeteria level button. As the doors closed, Rosie felt waves of tension as Phillip slipped one hand into his far jacket pocket. A split second later, the elevator staggered, the overhead lights and the red camera light blinked out, and she felt Phillip's other hand push into her lab coat pocket.

"Don't touch that note until you're back at your apartment," Crowe's voice whispered in her ear. "I used an old prototype static interrupter unit Rad-Corp developed a couple years ago, but I must turn everything back on quickly, Okay?"

"Yes," was all the whisper Rosie could manage. The lights and camera blinked back to life, and the shuttering elevator car resumed its smooth climb to the top floor.

"Well," Phillip said, "that was unusual. Are you okay, Rosemary?"

"I am," she said, trying to play along. "Do you think the elevators are safe?"

"I'm sure they'll get a thorough looking over after that spasm," Phillip said. "Well, at least we made it to lunch safely," he said with a smile as he motioned Rosie to go first in the cafeteria line.

Confusion and anxiety waltzed in Rosie's brain as Phillip chatted about inventories and test data over lunch as if nothing had happened. She had no idea what a static interrupter was, except that it could obviously mess up an otherwise routine elevator ride. Whatever her supervisor had put in her lab coat pocket seemed to be radiating some loud alarm signal she was sure others could feel or hear or something. It was all she could do not to look down and slip her hand into that pocket. It was going to be a long afternoon.

★ ★ ★

Sitting in her bathroom almost five hours later, Rosie was a mess. One half of her brain was fixated on whether or not Sherman Kanz would return to Bayfront Park later in the evening with an SD card; the other half of her brain was terrified at the thought of reaching into her lab coat pocket to retrieve her boss's dramatically secretive deposit there, and still another more ethereal part of her brain was just standing in a cloudy karmic bathroom somewhere, hands on both cheeks like Kevin in the movie *Home Alone*, screaming at the top of her lungs.

When her heartbeat no longer felt like a jackhammer trying to escape her chest, she took a deep steady breath and let it out slowly. There was no putting it off, and, despite her reservations, first things must come first. Rosie withdrew the piece of folded up paper from her lab coat pocket, noting as she did so how its every edge appeared perfectly aligned. When she unfolded it, there was no mistaking Phillip Crowe's carefully marshalled script.

Dear Rosemary,

If I were Steven Hill, or Peter Graves, or even (Lord help me) Tom Cruise, this note would self-destruct in 5 or 10 seconds. But I am not, and this is not Mission Impossible, so I must ask you to destroy it yourself when you have finished reading it.

As I have suggested to you (as discreetly as I could under the circumstances) the top brass has recently shown an even greater interest in you. As you might imagine, here at Rad-Corp, that is not always a good thing. Oh, I thought it was at first, their intense interest in you, but now I'm not so sure. I'm so sorry if I alarmed you today, but while I am not as smart or as skilled as you and your team, I do know something about hierarchical organizations. I have a feel for the pulse. Even though the brass tends to write me off as a grunt in the machine, I usually sense when something's up. I just felt compelled to warn you. I have no real facts nor advice to offer you, except please be careful. That is all I can think to say. If I learn more, I will attempt to communicate like this again.

I also mentioned to you, Rosemary, that my nerdy character has never been remotely close to the "cool" kind. A man well into his 50's who has never been married, nor even enjoyed a serious relationship, must admit this to himself. I have done so long ago. Still, there are things which must be said, regardless of the all-but-certain consequences. Please excuse me for my awkwardness, and if I cause offense, please try to believe that is not my intent. The truth is, that my profound gratefulness and my sincere respect for you has turned into something more. I have fervently tried to reject and suppress my strong feelings of fondness for you, but I cannot. Yes, I certainly understand how awkward this must be for you. I am truly sorry. If you do not respond, if you do not have similar feelings, I will never mention the subject again. My respect for who you are is far too deep to permit any unmannerly behavior towards you, not in any way. I simply had to speak my truth. That much dignity, I have maintained, despite all else.

Your secret friend & humble admirer,
Phillip C.

Chapter Thirteen

Two blocks down Biscayne Boulevard, Sherman Kanz wasn't in much better emotional shape. Each hour in his day thus far had felt like six. His anxiety stemmed from his oldest fear: the fear of failure. Well, it was actually the fear of more never-ending, ongoing, not-another-human-interest-story, slow death failure.

"Hemingway," he said while scratching the beagle's ears, "hope is another name for disaster. You get your hopes up, and you're bound to get shafted. How many stories have we thought might lead to another Pulitzer? Twenty by now, don't you think? And this, whatever this is, isn't even real. Hell, this is insane. What are the odds, Hem? You take a shit while I get a Pulitzer Prize story from an invisible drone—right?"

Hemingway looked up with one eye, but didn't say a word. Best to let his high-strung human work out his own drama.

"It's almost time, Hem. Now you remember what I said about barking. Jesus, Mary, and Joseph, all we need is the cops tonight. Well, let's get to the park."

Hemingway always reacted to the word "park" by raising both of his eyes and ears. He knew his human needed validation more than most, but he tried not to hold that against him. So, he bounded to the apartment door. And, because he felt generous, he threw in some tail wagging for the old man too.

They crossed Biscayne Boulevard under a gleaming, nearly full moon without seeing a single moving vehicle. Bayfront Park seemed empty, at least where the light was good. Sherman usually kept to the lighted areas when they walked at night, except when Hemingway insisted on the dark little grove of tropical trees. And Hemingway always insisted. They'd surprised romantic couples or homeless folk there on several occasions, but never experienced anything dangerous. But nothing seemed safe about this night.

"Is it my imagination, Hem, or are we all on our own out here tonight? All things considered, I suppose that's a good thing, but still, keep your trap shut, okay?" A half hour later, a lonely taxi cab cruised by on the street, but there wasn't another soul in sight. The bay was slapping quietly against the rocky shoreline just to the east, and the little forest of miscellaneous tropical trees loomed just in front of them. When they entered the darkened natural sanctuary, the reporter looked at his watch, paced about on the crunchy brown Sea Grape leaves and Wild Tamarind pods underfoot, and then looked at his watch again.

"I know I told you not to bark, Hem," he said, nervously patting the beagle on the head, "but do you hear the drone yet? Maybe just a yip or two to let me know it's getting close, how about that?"

Hemingway just shook off his human's sweaty hand and went back to foraging among the dead leaves that always got missed by the landscaping crews. He knew the truth, even if his human was too dense to see it. His ferocious display the night before had obviously frightened off his prey, and why his deluded human thought it would return was quite beyond him. The only enemy ever brave enough to face him repeatedly was that toxic water-like substance over by the rocks. Just thinking about how bad that galling stuff tasted made him shiver. When he found just the right spot, Hemingway turned around in place several times and squatted. Some years back, his bizarre human had begun collecting his natural refuse in small plastic bags. The reason for this bewildering behavior eluded Hemingway from the beginning, but like day following night, out came the bag once again. He didn't mind being watched, but taking the stuff home seemed extreme—even for his strange human.

As Hemingway finished his business, Sherman bent down to collect it, resigning himself to the fact that someone had pulled his chain. He'd obviously been "punk'd." At least that's what Ashton Kutcher called being played. This charade was probably all on camera and would be played on the big flat screen wall monitor at the next *Miami Herald* office party. Damn that Dave Barry, he was the mastermind behind this prank—no doubt about it.

Suddenly Kanz fell forward with Hemingway's leavings in his right hand and the leash spooler in this left hand.

He tried to straighten back up, wondering why his hat was on the ground in front of him and why his head and ears hurt terribly.

Down he went again as an insanely angry beagle jumped up and down, howling madly, on the middle of his back. Sherman barely rebalanced himself, wobbling there on all fours. Each time the startled reporter started upwards again, Hemingway came down foursquare. The racket was deafening.

"Hemingway," he managed, "this just won't do." Sherman couldn't hear himself, so he knew that his words couldn't possibly reach the rampaging little hunter, but it had to end. He let go of the plastic baggie, dropped rolling to his left, and then sprang to his feet as Hemingway lost his own footing and fell into the leaves. "Gotcha!" he declared, feeling his right ear and the back of his head. Sherman's right hand came back bloody, obviously, the result of Hemingway's scrambling paws. "You really owe me now, Hem," he said, wiping his right hand on his cargo shorts. He tied off Hemingway's leash to a tree, shook his finger briefly and futilely at the baying beagle, returned to the center of the little clearing, and looked up.

"Damn!" There, dangling above him was another tiny plastic baggie, with another tiny yellow glowing capacitor, highlighting another tiny folded square of toilet tissue. As he tried to mime "trade?" with his hands and shoulders, Sherman held up one empty hand and another holding his own little baggie in his fingertips. The moonlight was poking through the canopy here and there, and he suddenly realized how much better he could see than the night before. Above the affirmatively bobbing delivery was what looked like a Wild Tamarind seed pod. He puzzled over this while steadying his empty left hand, into which the strange drone deposited its load. He could feel the backwash of its invisible rotors on his wrist, and he was amazed. Holding up his right hand, he watched as the tiny pincers gently grabbed his baggie and tugged it from his grip.

"Wow!" he mouthed to the camera, even as he wondered how the hell a Go Pro camera could be manufactured small enough to be camouflaged as a flat and skinny seed pod. He thought about those fiber optic camera "snakes" the cops used to look under doors and in through air vents. Maybe it was something like that. He shook his head in wonder and admiration, waved goodbye to the little flying machine with both hand and smile, and moved to untie his yammering beagle.

Walking back to his apartment, he noticed that Bayfront Park was still empty. He also noted that while no cops had been alerted, he had left Hemingway's business, along with his used baggie glove, back in the trees.

"Well, it isn't really littering, Hem," he laughed. "Not if we pick it up in the morning. Right?"

Hemingway was sullen, not having any of it. He had been so close to catching the whistling little dervish, and then his human had fallen over like a klutzy lummox. Could the man do nothing right?

Chapter Fourteen

Rosie laughed so hard that the drone controller shook on her lap. Tears rolled down her cheeks and splattered on the LCD screen. The spontaneous cathartic release was so overpowering, Rosie banged Podrick into the outside wall and the cast iron window grill twice before she managed to take a deep breath. Poor Podrick's cam view looked like what drunk drivers might be seeing when they can't walk a straight line for the police officer who pulled them over. The shaky movement, of course, was all her fault, so Rosie steadied herself mentally and emotionally. She brought Podrick in more gracefully. "I needed that laughter," she said between breaths, "Lordie, but I needed that tonight. It's been a long time."

She put the returned baggie in her lab coat pocket, placed Podrick safely away behind the medicine cabinet, and cleaned up the drywall dust that inevitably escaped each time she opened up the wall. "You might not save my life, Mr. Kanz," she said, "but you'll probably make me laugh right up 'till the end."

When she was finished, she sat back down on the closed toilet seat and retrieved the baggie from her pocket. She might have preferred an SD card with a larger capacity, but since she probably had the only SD card on 25 of the 27 floors in the Rad-Corp Cloisters, she just grinned as she turned it over and over in her hand. It was time to tell a third story to the man in whose hands she had placed her future.

★ ★ ★

While Hemingway sulked in his bed, Sherman Kanz lay sprawled out on the sofa, reading the hastily scrawled toilet tissue note for the third time.

Dear Mr. Kanz,

From this moment on, my life depends on whether or not you believe me. I am too smart to pretend I can make you do anything you don't choose to do, so I must rely on your curiosity to prevent you from saying or doing anything that would end our relationship immediately; and trust me, one untimely word from you, in the wrong ear, would likely be as dangerous to you as it would be to me. In order to tell you my story truthfully, even though I name no names, I must tell you things that will—as a byproduct—give you the necessary clues as to where I am and by whom I am employed. As you might have guessed, I designed and built my illicit drone (His name is Podrick) right under their noses. Should you carelessly mention what you've seen, there is no one else but me for them to suspect.

My employers are extremely powerful and like to brag about the fact that none of their Miami employees has ever been "compromised." I am compromising myself, freely, and am more than willing to pay whatever the price might be for doing that—just on the off chance that you are smart enough to handle this story properly. As to that problem, I have no advice other than that you be extremely wary. I believe that I am being watched more carefully than usual, so if I do not make contact when I said I would, you can safely assume that my part in this story is at an end. Perhaps tomorrow night you could bring me another SD card so we can swap back and forth? This stationary sucks...

Yours etc.,
Scheherazade

"You know, Hem," Sherman Kanz said, getting up for another nightcap and to put more Neosporin on his scratches, "this mystery lady fascinates me. I mean, I know she might not be a woman, but I sure hope she is. "

Hemingway snored on, though anyone looking at the beagle's face could not miss the displeasure on his usually happy face.

"I think she's a scientist, certainly a genius if she really did cobble together a drone like that without getting caught. And where the hell does she work that she can make and fly drones in this neighborhood?" As Scheherazade had suggested, the answer was easy once he said it out loud.

"Damn, Hemingway!" he said, startling the surly pooch. "She's got to be one of the black Mercedes Sprinter van people! I still got it, Hem. And don't you forget it, Buddy."

Hemingway snorted sarcastically and settled back into the warm spot where he'd been dosing peacefully only seconds before. His human stretched back out on the sofa, pulled a Parrothead pillow over his face, and let the Captain Morgan's spiced rum sail him away to sleep.

The next morning, as he and Hemingway toured Bayfront Park and recovered the doggy bag from the night before, Sherman made a mental list of the things he wanted to accomplish before the guys came over for their monthly poker night. He needed to buy a couple SD cards; stock up on snacks and beer; file copy on the Grand Flamingo hotel and the South Miami storm drain stories for his editor; and he wanted to chat with Benny Lopez before tonight's game.

"There's no time like the present, Hem," he said, dropping both baggies in a trash bin and turning toward the Miami River Walk. "Wanna go see Benny?"

Hemingway genuinely perked up at hearing Benny's name. It wasn't exactly a case of human envy, but Benny was cooler than most humans—certainly more so than his own—and besides, who else but Benny always secretly shared his poker night snacks? Just thinking about Doritos and cheesy nacho dip put a new spring in Hemingway's step.

"That got your attention, didn't it?" Sherman laughed. "Don't think I don't know about you and Benny. I'm nobody's fool."

That's insulting, Hemingway thought. If my human is nobody's fool, that would make my name Nobody.

As they strolled west along Biscayne Boulevard Way, Sherman was relieved to see Benny's white Filling Empty Houses, Inc. van parked across the street out in front of the old Flamingo Hotel building. There was only one protester present so early in the morning. He was an older man, sitting in a folding beach chair reading the *Miami Herald* with his Save the Flamingo sign propped up against the orange plastic fencing. A green thermos rested on the ground nearby. When he noticed Kanz approaching, he jumped to attention and took up his sign.

"At ease!" Sherman shouted as he and Hemingway crossed the street. "I'm not here on business." He waved for the man to sit and led Hemingway up the stairs and into the old hotel. "Benny!" he called from the dusty lobby. "Are you up there somewhere?"

The ceiling was two stories high, and the second-floor rooms all had doors that opened into a hallway skirted by a railed balcony. The balcony looked down on the lobby below. Benny Lopez and his daughter, Katie, popped out of one of those rooms, each with a spackling trowel in one hand and a wet sponge in the other.

"Come on up, Sherm," he called down, waving toward the stairs with the pointed trowel.

"Hi, Katie! "Sherman said with a wave. "Helping dad today?"

The young teenager held up a spackling knife and made her best "Doh!" face. "Yes, Mr. Kanz, but you can take over if you want!"

"Not today, kiddo," Sherman said with a laugh, "but I do need to borrow your dad. Benny, I'd rather you came down if you can spare five minutes. Can we chat in your van?"

"Sure, *amigo*. Just give me a minute." Benny disappeared back into the door he'd just come out of, then reappeared and descended the old curving staircase. He motioned toward the front doors. "My private mobile office awaits!"

Benny was carrying a battered lunch bucket, and Hemingway's tail waved expectedly at the spicy smells wafting along between them.

"*Si*," Benny said, ruffling the beagle's head, "I thought you might like a treat!"

When they were settled in the van—while Hemingway gulped down a *tamale* and busied himself sniffing all the tarps, tools, and orange buckets tucked under the passenger benches—Sherman broached his topic as carefully as he could.

"Benny, I may have latched onto a big story, and it may be dangerous. It definitely has to be kept a secret."

"You know I got your back, Sherm. What's up?"

"Well, that's the crazy thing—I have no idea yet. But, hypothetically speaking, if my source isn't blowing smoke up my ass, I have a damsel who needs to be rescued and made to disappear safely. You and Dan are the only guys I can think of who might know how to arrange such a thing."

"Well, shit, brother, that does sound intriguing," Benny laughed. "I guess this chat means we can't brainstorm around the poker table tonight."

"Hell, no!" Sherman said. "After a couple of beers, Dave Bartlett would go home and write a damn humor column about it and get us all killed."

"Killed?" Benny whispered. "I hope you're being overly dramatic to make a point."

"I hope I am too. I'll tell you more when I know more. Oh, and if I take a little longer walking Hem tonight, you watch my poker chips. I swear Dave rips me off every month."

"*Si, si*." Benny looked at his shoes, grinned mischievously, and crinkled a bag of Doritos. Hemingway pounced.

Chapter Fifteen

Rosie tossed and turned deep into the night. Now that she had her SD card and had seemingly hooked the *Miami Herald* reporter, she could no longer put off thinking about Phillip's strange note. What on earth was going on? Why was Phillip Crowe so hard to read? Was he really that awkward around women, or was he hardcore military issue—a man with a plan?

"He's a company man from the top of his head to the soles of his boots," her father had once said of a very unpopular work colleague. "If I were to so much as fart in the general direction of the boss, he would feel honor bound to report the offense. Another name for that kind of *honorable* person, Rosie, is 'brown-noser.'"

That seemed to apply to Phillip Crowe near enough, but Rosie couldn't help wondering about the man's peculiar admission of affection. It seemed so out of character, not to mention... She stopped herself. What word did all the meanie girls in high school use whenever a nerdy boy worked up enough courage to ask one of them to dance? "Creepy." It was the universal description of an introverted boy's best first effort to grow up where girls are concerned. Any unwanted advance was, when it came to awkward and uncool guys, "creepy." It hadn't seemed fair then, and Rosie did not want to be a meanie girl, especially at her age. But if Phillip was sincere, might he protect her, even help her perhaps?

That thought seemed manipulative. The only reason a meanie girl ever accepted an uncool boy's invitation was to humiliate him in some way.

"We are adults, for God's sake. Old, even!" Rosie thought. "And to think that it's not even possible for two adults to have a private adult conversation without shutting down an entire elevator system. Surely this must weigh on Phillip now, even if it never occurred to him before."

She knew that employees hooked up, visiting each other's apartments. Some even lived together openly. The idea of Rad-Corp surveillance technology in their apartments must surely have crossed their minds? Perhaps they simply didn't care. She was far older than most, and sex merely for recreation was not what it had been cracked up to be—once she had finally tried it, that is. That thought stopped her in her tracks. It always did.

Was her brief dating experience and her one night of intimacy with that wounded Vietnam vet so many years ago really only motivated by a desire to be sexually liberated? She had told herself that it was only that for years afterwards. It was an immature crush, the sudden impulse of a young nerdy woman no one else had ever noticed before. And spending the night with him was just as much her right, her freedom, her adventure, as it was any man's. Looking at it that way, it struck her suddenly, was just a way to avoid thinking about her true feelings— and his. Two very different men had now expressed affection for her. But to be honest, the young soldier, a man of few words and a sincerely attentive listener, had used the word love. Rosie could not help remembering his eyes, his calm demeanor, the matter-of-fact way he had bared his heart to her. Not before sex, but after.

Truth be told, his declaration had terrified her. She had run from that honest admission of love (and that amazingly beautiful night together) as if it were life threatening. Now, comparing it to her circumstances with her boss at Rad-Corp, she could no longer deny that it had never been dangerous at all. Phillip might actually be interested in her now, or be a terrible threat to her wellbeing, but that young man she had first nursed at the V.A. Hospital, the man who fathered the baby boy she bore nine months later, had spoken truth. Rosie felt that truth in a way she had never allowed herself to before. He was, as he had quietly told her, in love for the first time in his life.

Whatever happened with Phillip, she would not be such a coward again. And here at Rad-Corp, hurting Phillip could amount to far greater damage than a broken heart. Before his dramatically delivered note, the idea of compromising his office computer for the Domestic Crowd Control trials video footage gave her little or no pause— other than her fear of getting caught. But if there was a chance that his affection was sincere, she could not subject him to job loss, prison, or worse. There had to be another way; and since she couldn't sleep, she got up to make coffee and think on her feet.

Rosie's apartment was on the northeast corner of the 20th floor. It was three rooms: a small full bathroom, a fair-sized open plan living/dining/home office space, and her bedroom, right in the corner. A deep set of shelves ran approximately eight feet along the same wall as both the bathroom and bedroom doors until it reached the solid west wall of her apartment. That wall bordered someone else's apartment.

These shelves were functional, and she kept books, pictures, and knickknacks on them, but the clever design feature not obvious to her until it was pointed out was that the shelves were nowhere near as deep as the unit itself. There were six castors under that shelving system, and it was hinged to the west apartment wall so that by grabbing the east end of the unit, you could walk the whole thing over across the laminate flooring--just like opening a large barn door--and press it flat against the west wall. Rosie grabbed the built-in handle in that movable wall and literally opened up her kitchen.

Rosie's books and things were no longer visible, and the new section of the unit now exposed to the living area was actually kitchen cabinets and counter space. Here was her microwave oven, toaster oven, coffeemaker, her dinner and silverware, along with enough cupboards for mugs, glasses, cereal, cookies, Ramen noodles, and spices. Rosie needed coffee.

Back along the now exposed wall bordering her bathroom was a tiny, RV-sized stainless steel sink, a small oven with a two-burner range, and a motel room-sized refrigerator. As she filled her coffee pot at the sink, Rosie looked at the painting of a tropical island she had hung on the wall in front of her. Behind that picture, and the drywall on which it hung, Podrick rested in an old envelope she'd taped up behind the bathroom medicine cabinet on the other side. Rosie hoped that was still a secret only she knew about.

When her coffee was ready, she poured a cup and paced her living space in the light from the kitchenette. In the back of her mind she knew they could listen, watch, even trace her movements with infra-red technology rather than fiber optic cameras. Even the smart TV/computer monitors had cameras and microphones built in. But would they? And, why would they? It was a disturbing thing to ponder late at night, with three screens staring at her from the wall by the door to her office in the lab. The very idea of it all felt like a weight. Carrying it around with her cup of coffee wasn't getting her anywhere.

So, Rosie sat down at her desk in the near darkness of the apartment's south wall, and unplugged the cable that linked her company issued laptop to the Rad-Corp in-house databank system. Then, for almost five minutes, she sipped her coffee tentatively, waiting for some alarm to go off. When that didn't happen, she slipped the SD card into her laptop and opened its only file, a document file comprised of only fourteen words: "I do so solemnly swear to tell the truth and nothing but the truth."

"So," Rosie laughed to herself, thinking of a Jack Nicholson movie, "let's see how well you can handle the truth." Her fingers flew across the keyboard. It was time to for Scheherazade to tell another life-saving story.

Chapter Sixteen

That night at Sherman's once-a-month poker party, just like always, everyone arrived and got buzzed in at one-every-fifteen-minute intervals. Sherman was certain they did it just to make him keep getting up and going to the intercom panel by his apartment's front door. "Shouldn't there be a cell phone app for this?" he wondered.

Benny Lopez always looked tired but never unhappy when he arrived. Sherman watched as Benny began chatting up Sean McKnight as soon as she came in the door. The redhead made everyone call her "Mac", and the name suited her. Dan Stone sauntered in next. The tall gray-haired Miccosukee tribal member always seemed to half glide, half saunter in his black cowboy boots. Somehow, Sherman was fairly certain that his blood pressure dropped at least a couple of points whenever Dan was in the room. There was just something calming about man's bearing.

Either Dave Bartlett, Miami's favorite humor columnist, or Chris Tosh the Miami Heat star, was always last. Tosh smiled mostly with his eyes, but Bartlett always arrived with that damn toothy grin. It was too cheesy, that's what it was, almost like he was up to something—and he probably was. Tonight, Tosh was last—and his bright eyes seemed more mischievous than usual. Kanz could only assume it was because the basketball player hung out with Dave Bartlett too much.

"Smoke 'em if you got 'em," Sherman said. "Food's in the kitchen, help your own damn selves." It was a ritual.

"I brought Mary's famous *tamales*, gentlemen," Benny said, "in case any of you bums want to eat real food."

Chris Tosh, who was halfway back to the poker table with a plastic plateful of nachos, spun on his heel, ducked his head, and re-entered the kitchen. "Where, Benny?" his voice called back out.

"On top of the microwave. Give 'em about 30 seconds, Chris, and they should be perfect."

Everyone already seated rose in unison and returned to the kitchen. Sherman laughed. "You should have shot video of that, Benny. Mary should know the effect her cooking has on folks."

"Oh, she knows!" Benny said as the microwave beeped in the next room. "Even the old ladies on our block want to know how she does it."

"None of us have ever had *tamales* like the ones she makes," Sherman said. "Not anywhere."

"You can say that again," Tosh said, returning to his seat at the table.

Dan Stone came out of the kitchen after the next beep, and bowed his head to Benny respectfully. "This wife of yours," he said with a slow and steady smile, "she is a jewel among women."

"And you butter her up with that cool Indian shit every time you come around the house!" Benny laughed. "Get a woman of your own."

"Didn't you say you had a lady friend once?" Dave Bartlett asked as he pulled his chair out and sat down with his back to the open balcony slider.

"Must have," quipped Tosh, "he has a kid! Speaking of which, where is John tonight?"

"Yup," Dan replied, a faraway look in his eyes. "John's mom was amazing, and for a very brief time, I thought I'd found the woman of my dreams."

"Oh my God, Dave," Mac exclaimed as she arrived from the kitchen, "don't get him started on the 'one that got away' story again. We'll be here all night."

"How long are you in town for, Mac?" Dan asked with a warm smile. "It's good to see you. How's the Ghostwalker?"

"About a week, Dan. John sends his love. He gave me orders to check up on you. How much trouble is Benny getting you into?"

"Hey!" Benny said. "That's not fair!"

"Oh, yes, it is," Dan laughed. "Just when I think we've put every homeless person in Miami into a Space Station pod somewhere, Benny just has to come up with a few more."

Dan and Benny each ran a different Miami non-profit corporation, and they served on each other's boards. Benny's outfit put poor homeless families in temporary and marginally legal housing to keep them safe and build up their job skills, while Dan Stone was the acting president of Personal Space, Inc., an organization which placed homeless individuals in real, albeit, tiny houses that looked like futuristic space pods.

Mac had formed that non-profit with her partner when she inherited her late mother's fortune and didn't want the money. Her partner, John Ghostwalker (an architect with Jacob & Associates in the Brickell district of Miami), had invented the tiny dwellings, which were high tech expansions of the miniature hotel cubicle concept famous at Japanese commuter stations. The two organizations complemented each other perfectly, and the number of homeless people sleeping on the streets or under the foliage in Miami had dropped nearly to zero.

Chris Tosh and Dave Bartlett both volunteered their time and celebrity status, as did Sherman Kanz, so the monthly poker posse had been a natural outcropping of their community activities together. Most were regulars. Mac and John lived aboard two sailboats, depending on whether either or both were in Florida, or on a lake near Lawrence, Kansas where John taught a new Introduction to Sustainable Indigenous Architecture class at Haskell Indian Nations University under the school's

Environmental Sciences department. His job in Miami meant they commuted back and forth quite often.

The traditional seventh seat at the table was usually vacant. It was lovingly reserved for those rare occasions when "everyone's Grandmother" Renee Person asked one of her "children" to drive her in from the nearby Miccosukee Reservation. Grandmother Renee loved all these diverse characters, but that didn't stop her from cleaning their clocks at poker whenever she did decide to partake. But the children around this table didn't mind one bit. The only thing that never changed about poker night was the fact that, hell or high water, Hemingway never left Benny Lopez' side.

So, when Benny and the beagle followed Dan Stone into the kitchen several hours later, no one thought twice.

"Dan?" Benny whispered as the microwave sang its circular song. "Can we talk awhile after? Maybe at my van?"

"Sure," Dan said quietly as his eyebrows rose. "Everything okay?"

"Today?" Benny grinned. "Yes, everything's fine. But we have to talk privately about something that's come up suddenly, a job offer that may not be so okay."

★ ★ ★

It was after midnight, sitting in the white van out in front of the Grand Flamingo, when Benny told Dan what Sherman Kanz had asked of them.

"And that's all the information we have to go on, Benny?"

"Yes, for now, but Sherm was supposed to get another message tonight when he walked Hemingway."

"Looked to me like he'd been mugged when he came in," Dan said smiling, "and Hemingway was psychotic for the rest of the game. That must have been some message."

"Yeah," Benny said, "I don't know who he's talking to, but it's a safe guess that Hem's not very happy about these meetings. And if they are meeting in the park at night, how hard could it be to help this damsel in distress get away and disappear?"

"Trust me," Dan laughed, "Sherman wouldn't have asked us both if it were gonna be easy. I'll think on this. Call me when you know more."

Chapter Seventeen

When all the money migrations around Sherman's poker table came to a halt, and the largest pile was, at best, a highly debatable concept, everyone went home content. That was usually the way of it. Dave Bartlett whined sometimes about being ahead right up until the last four or five inevitable wild card games. These far-fetched hands signaled the final insanity of the monthly gathering. "That's not *real* poker," Dave Bartlett liked to say. But Chris Tosh always acted happy enough so that any observer would assume he'd won as he made his goodnights, even if there was no pile left at his seat at all. Sherman liked Tosh, a lot, but there was something a little suspicious about the man's unnatural, unflagging sense of joy.

Mac gathered up her winnings and deposited it all in the large glass "Grandmother Renee jar" on the coffee table. Usually everyone, even Bartlett, threw something in there before leaving because when everyone's grandmother did show up for poker night, two things were inevitable: (1) Grandmother Renee always took home the biggest pile of loot; and, (2) the kind and gentle Miccosukee woman, known for her deep font of natural wisdom and applicable indigenous lore, somehow never remembered to bring any money to the game with her.

Dan Stone knew Mac had hugging issues, so he always made a point of going in low and scooping her up in his arms so her feet came off the floor. He danced her to the apartment door, watching her face turn red, before kissing her on top on her head and saying "Hug my son John for me—just like that!" Lastly, Benny Lopez winked at Sherman as he gave Hemingway a parting head rub and ushered Dan out the door. When they were gone, Kanz collapsed on the sofa and fished the new SD card out of his cargo shorts pocket. He opened his laptop on the coffee table and his hands were trembling slightly as he inserted the memory card. He knew he should clean up the scratches Hemingway had inflicted on his bare legs while going after the drone, but his curiosity had reached its limits.

Dear Sherman (Can I call you, Sherman?),

I have a few technical issues to solve before being able to pass on the most serious hard data for your story. This involves getting around security cameras and an in-house data base system which cuts employees completely off from the outside world, including the world-wide web and Wi-Fi networks I used to take for granted. After I explain my story tonight, you might think about whether you know anyone who might know how to help me hack a closed system that allows each employee access only to data appropriate to their security clearance. The cable attaching my laptop to the wall appears to be what we used to call HDMI, but, my specialty is micro-engineering design, so a computer is only a tool to me, like a hammer. Outsmarting high tech computers and security protocols is way above my pay grade, and the data I (you) need most is on my boss's computer—or at least I saw his computer access that particular video footage.

For now, I'll focus on explaining how I got where I am, and a bit about life for employees here at "the Cloisters."

★ ★ ★

As he read though the long note, over and over again, Sherman found the life of "Scheherazade" utterly compelling, completely apart from the company where she (he was still convinced this storyteller was, like the original Scheherazade, a woman of great intelligence and imagination) worked and was allegedly living under horrendous security restrictions. Once again, Sherman found himself thinking of Dan Stone and Benny Lopez. They certainly weren't celebrities like Bartlett and Tosh, but they seemed to have, between them, a nearly unlimited network of people-who-know-people-who-know-stuff. Perhaps a hacker wasn't out of the question.

Sherman's potential whistle blower had been honest about her story carrying with it ever more bread crumbs from which he could find out exactly who she was, where she went to grad school, and who had recruited her. But while the reporter in him wanted to rush out and run down every detail, the romantic in him wanted to savor every moment of the mystery.

Her involvement with a grad school research project about bees was a dead giveaway. Anyone might make MIT one of their early guesses for the mystery woman's micro-engineering and design grad school experience, but since the *Miami Herald* had run a series of stories about how the steady drop in honey bee populations was affecting south Florida's citrus and produce industries, he knew that school's documented bionic bee breakthrough for a fact. And Kanz would bet money that, though Scheherazade had not said any such thing, she was most likely the breakthrough's designer.

As he finished the text file of 2,000-some words for a fifth or sixth time, Sherman suddenly understood how thoroughly he had been ensnared. He was, after three non-Arabian nights, a diehard fan of Scheherazade. Had the writer had a Kickstarter or a Patreon site like singer/songwriter/social media wiz, Amanda Palmer, he would have pledged his financial support immediately. He had watched Palmer's TED talk twice, but that intriguing presentation felt trivial now by comparison. The surreal aspects of Scheherazade's compelling life adventure, thus far, were chilling. As was the possibility that becoming involved might prove as dire as she had repeatedly suggested.

But there was no turning back. Had it been his late mother in similar straits, he could not have been any more committed to the rescue effort. Sure, he'd love to land another Pulitzer Prize, but he was enamored beyond reason, and the story had literally become secondary overnight. "Perhaps," he chuckled to himself as he grabbed his Jimmy Buffet Parrothead pillow, "this is why a good reporter isn't supposed to get involved with the subjects in their stories."

"Give it up, Hem," he called to the beagle still curled up staring longingly at the apartment door. "Benny's gone home to Mary, so it's another 30-day diet plan for you, buddy."

Sherman thought he heard a snort as he stretched out on the sofa and pulled the fan merch pillow over his face. "I think I have a perfectly good bed somewhere, Hem. Remind me to go and look for it tomorrow. It can't have gone far."

Chapter Eighteen

When morning finally dawned over Biscayne Bay, Rosie was no nearer to a game plan about Phillip Crowe, but she hoped that breakfast and more coffee would get her moving forward and thinking more clearly. Her SD Card was ready to return to Sherman Kanz, so all she had to do was make it through the day and back to her apartment. She knew that she had to talk—making real grownup sounds—to her boss. And as he was obviously afraid to talk out loud, Rosie decided that her fears and paranoia about how intensely employees were being monitored wasn't so crazy after all.

Breakfast and more coffee seemed to work. Not that she didn't have doubts about her brainstorm, but it felt better to have a questionable plan than to have no plan at all.

"Phillip," Rosie said, sticking her head in his office doorway, "I have a favor to ask you."

"What can I do for you Rosemary?" Phillip Crowe's eyes were only slightly twitchy, but his face looked like it wanted to break into a genuine smile.

"I love that goofy shrimp place by the marina," Rosie said hoping she sounded more casual than she felt, "and I'd like a couple things from the bakery shop that's in the mall near there too. Any interest in having dinner with me some night? I've got some ideas to run by you."

Phillip did smile. There was relief in his eyes, but still signs of tension in his posture. "Sure!" he answered. "I haven't been there in years. Tonight okay?"

"Well, yes, but I didn't fill out a 48-hour outing requisition form yet, so it's probably going to have to be another night."

"No problem about that, Rosemary. I'm sure I can work that out. Seven at the elevator good for you?"

"Wow! Sure, seven is great."

"No, thank *you*. I should get out more than I do."

★ ★ ★

The day went by smoothly enough, although it seemed very slow to Rosie. By lunch time, the whole team knew she had asked the boss out, and more than a few of her workmates gave her a mild jibe or two as the day wore on. Rosie didn't mind that a bit. "There's nothing to see here, no secrets at all. Just a management meeting. Go on about what you were doing please," she said. Everyone she could see did just that. She hoped the same could be said for the unseen watchers.

Her grave error, perhaps fatal error, only occurred to her when she entered her bathroom at a little after 5:45 p.m. to shower.

"Oh shit!" she thought. "I do get distracted." She had counted on the 48 hours it should have taken to arrange a security guard for an outing. Now, if she didn't show up to meet Sherman Kanz at 10:30 p.m., he would assume—because she had told him to assume—that their correspondence had come to a bad end. The next hour was the most hectic in her life, and her normally well-ordered mind went in twenty directions at once.

Rosie tried to stop her hands from shaking as she undid the screws holding her medicine cabinet to the wall studs, but before she had half the screws out, she stopped and hurried out of the bathroom and over to her desk. "A paper clip. I know I have a paper clip somewhere in here. Yes!" she said placing the paper clip between her lips and returning to the medicine cabinet just in time for another "Oh, shit!" moment.

This time Rosie paced from one room to another, looking at every item. "String?" she kept saying to herself. "My kingdom for a piece of string." She looked everywhere to no avail. She didn't even have thread. She checked behind the tropical island picture hanging over her kitchenette sink, but that was hung with wire that was too long, and she had no quick way to cut it. Still frantic, she returned to her medicine cabinet removal project, focused more on finding or creating a piece of string than on the task at hand. When the last remaining screw came out, she had determined that she might be able to tear out the hem of one of her T-shirts, and use that thread, but when the medicine cabinet literally fell out of the wall, so did Rosie's string. She caught the cabinet before it hit the sink and broke its mirror, but not before the door swung open, spilling its contents all over the place. There, in the sink, was an entire roll of string. It was wax coated and slightly minty tasting, but dental floss would work just fine. The mess would have to wait.

She retrieved Podrick, then ran to her desk and quickly disconnected the laptop from the wall cable. Only after doing so did it occur to her that a postscript on toilet paper might have been safer, but she inserted the SD card and added a P.S. to her evening's story for the reporter. She returned the SD card to the baggie, the cable to the laptop, and bent the paperclip into an S-hook on her way back to the bathroom. It was 6:15 p.m., and she was far from being ready to shower and dress for her 7:00 p.m. date with Phillip.

Rosie used one end of the paperclip to poke a hole through both layers of plastic in one corner of the baggie, then used the same end of the wire clip to push one end of her dental floss into the hole on one side of the baggie and out on the other side. She then tied a double knot in the floss, cut the waxy sting to a length of six inches, and tied the other end securely to the S-hook shaped paper clip.

She retrieved the drone controller from it's now full-time home in the pocket of her lab coat and turned it on. Podrick came to life, and she hovered him right in front of her as she electronically asked the drone to open its tiny jaws. After placing the baggie in the pincers, letting them close and get a grip, Rosie set her full attention on getting the drone and its new S-hook shaped tail out the window without snagging it on anything. It snagged on everything. Finally, at 6:35 p.m., Rosie gave it up and went out to her book shelf for her makeshift bathtub step stool of books. This time, she flew Podrick with one hand and used the other hand to ease the S-hook past the window's sill, frame, and wrought iron security bars.

Finally, free, the little drone sped to the park and eased its way into the branchy canopy of trees where she was to meet Sherman Kanz. Rosie's flight plan objective was to snag the hook on a branch tip, release the pincers, and leave the baggie hanging where Kanz could see it. This turned out to be easier than planned, and as the little baggie spun this way and that on its dental floss tether, Rosie flew Podrick home feeling greatly relieved and more than a little bit proud of her own ingenuity.

There'd be no shower. She barely got the medicine cabinet reinstalled, the bathroom cleaned up, and a change of clothes on her body before it was time to meet Phillip Crowe for a night out on the town.

Chapter Nineteen

Rosie knew she must look out-of-sorts to Phillip when she arrived at the elevator in the middle of the lab five minutes late. But those extra five minutes were important. She had written a brief note to her boss on a square of her new least favorite stationary. He would set the tone this night, and the security guard would be a prevailing factor, but if Phillip didn't hiccup the elevator again, she would look for another opportunity to slip him the tiny hastily hand written note. At least he was smiling as she approached.

"Good evening, Rosemary," Phillip said as he swiped his I.D. card and pushed the DOWN elevator button. "You look lovely. Are you hungry?"

"Thank you, Phillip, yes I am, and excited about eating at Bubba Gump's again. I know it's silly, but it's a fun place, and something about it just makes me feel good."

"Nothing silly about it. *Forrest Gump* was great movie, and being reminded of that is fun. I understand one of the new ladies in our cafeteria used to work there."

The elevator door opened, and a young man Rosie didn't recognize nodded and said "Good evening, folks. Can I give you a lift?"

"Thank you, Joseph," Phillip said as he ushered Rosie into the elevator. "I'm glad you could get free tonight." Turning back to Rosie, he said, "Joseph Allen joined the Rad-Corp security team recently. Like me, Joseph served in the 101st Airborne. Two tours in the desert, and then he goes and gets wounded by a piece of a tool shed when a tornado hit Fort Campbell a few years ago."

Rosie looked at the rigid young man, but couldn't think of anything to say in response except: "Thank you for your service. I guess, well, shrapnel is shrapnel pretty much everywhere."

Both men laughed, and the mood in the elevator altered so abruptly that Rosie felt dizzy. "That's a fact, Ma'am," Joseph said with a grin. "I hadn't thought about it that way, but that's sure enough a fact. You said the lady was quick, Gunny. You weren't kidding."

"No, Joe," Phillip said, smiling, "I don't kid around about smart ladies and officers. It's not healthy."

Everybody was grinning as the elevator descended, but Rosie's smile was frozen on. The experience of seeing and hearing genuine laughter come out of Phillip Crowe was like a bad case of culture shock or of dealing with pigs flying. She had assumed he *could* laugh, just never imagined that he actually *did*.

"Can we walk up through the Park?" Rosie asked as they signed out and passed through the ground floor mini-lobby and into the commercial kiosk mall under the building.

"Walk?" both men said in unison.

That's when Rosie noticed the black Mercedes Sprinter parked out on Biscayne Boulevard "Surely we don't need a van on a beautiful evening like this? The restaurant can't be more than a half mile away, can it?"

"Well, no, but..." Joseph looked at Phillip, obviously not wanting to be the one to explain protocol to Rosie.

"You know, Joe," Phillip said, "why not? Tell Terry we'll call if we want a ride back later."

The young security guard trotted over to the black van, spoke to the driver, and joined them as they crossed the street and entered Bayfront Park.

"How do you like working here so far, Joseph?" Rosie said as they strolled east toward the shoreline.

"It's been good so far, Ma'am," He said. "I mean, it sure beats guarding oil wells. I feel like I'm making a difference here, keeping people safe, I mean, instead of, well, stuff."

"Indeed," Rosie said as the young man's face reddened slightly. "My dad used to say: 'What we do for people counts. What we do to acquire shit, not so much.' Is that what you mean?"

Joseph smiled. "Exactly! My dad would have gotten along well with your dad."

So, the boy thinks he's keeping us safe, Rosie thought. She was pretty sure her last escort would have shot her without hesitation had she shown the slightest intention to violate his ideas about protocol. Before she thought to check herself, as they turned north onto the shoreline sidewalk, Rosie glanced over at the grove of trees where she had flown Podrick less than a half hour before, only to see a homeless man shuffle out pulling up the fly of his baggy pants. Stumbling, she gasped, and two sets of hands caught her arms and kept her from falling.

"Are you alright, Rosemary?" Phillip asked as he looked back with suspicion.

"Oh, well, yes I'm fine thanks to you guys. I just get distracted and don't watch where I'm going. What are those black birds with the crooked necks anyway?" she said, pointing to the top of a nearby light post. "I see them sit like that, wings up and out like they're going to take off, but they don't."

Her mind whirled. Of course, people were apt to walk into those trees. And, in the darkness, anyone looking up would see her yellow-glowing baggie hanging in plain sight. It could already be gone.

"I believe they're called cormorants, Ma'am," said Joseph as he carefully released her arm. "A diving duck, I think, but they sure look strange sitting like that."

"Okay, Joe—can I call you Joe?" The young man nodded agreeably. "Good. Joe, my dad used to sing a little ditty, an old blues song, about if the river was filled with whiskey, and he was a diving duck. The gist was, he'd stay drunk all the time. Now, about your dad, did he ever teach you anything about women-of-a-certain-age not being particularly keen on being called 'Ma'am?'"

"No, Ma'am, er, well, no..." He was blushing again.

"It's Rosie," she said, turning to Phillip Crowe. "They won't fire him for calling me by my name, will they?"

"Not out here," Phillip laughed. He seemed genuinely reluctant to return her arm. "Back at the Cloisters, though, I suspect that he's diving in another kind of river."

"Well, good, then that's settled," Rosie said, gently pulling her arm free and using both hands to brush away non-existent wrinkles on the front of her skirt. But I'd still like to know what those strange poser birds are doing."

"I expect they're drying their wings, Rosemary," Phillip said with a grin, but one look at her suddenly stern face, and he amended himself promptly. "I mean, Rosie."

"You see, Joe," she laughed, "despite what they might try to tell you, sometimes you can teach an old Gunny new tricks!"

★ ★ ★

They were still chatting amicably when they passed the amphitheater in Bayfront Park and crossed the street just west of the Bayside Marketplace mall.

"Night and day," Phillip said with a Vanna White sweep of his arm towards giant mall building. When I came here as a kid, it didn't look anything like this."

They passed the mall entrance and from there they could see Bubba Gump's to the northeast.

"A table for three please, for Crowe," Phillip said to the *maître d'* when they enter the shack-ish looking restaurant.

"Wait," Joe said, holding up one hand to the young lady, "would you guys mind if I ate in the bar? There's a game on tonight, and I'll keep an eye on your table, but to tell the truth, I can't imagine any interruption you couldn't handle better than I could, Gunny."

"I appreciate the vote of confidence, Joseph. Enjoy."

It felt like a set-up to Rosie, but under the circumstances, it was a godsend. "I guess that table's for two," she said touching the young and enthusiastic maître d's sleeve. "I love your blouse."

"Why, thank you!" The girl's greenish blue eyes glowed as she led them to their table.

Chapter Twenty

Hemingway wasn't thrilled at how long it had taken his human to get around to their second daily outing, but he had to admit that their time in the park had been especially long and quite rewarding. Now, after a side trip and a stop at his favorite human gathering place, he was comfortably stretched out on the cool, shady concrete, enjoying the frequent attentions of the various young humans nearby, and drinking fresh icy water from a plastic bowl smelling suspiciously like the snacks his alternate human, Benny sometimes brought for him. *Perhaps my human comes here to make up for his obvious slights in that regard.* As if on cue, down came the familiar hand with yet another French fry.

Sherman lounged in a blue canvas backed director's chair, eating a burger with fries, churros, and a Cuban-doctored caramel macchiato. He'd always liked the little kiosk mall under the mysterious building two doors north of his apartment. Now, though, he had a specific reason to reconsider its strangeness more closely. He and Hemingway had walked all the way around the block, confirming what he had already thought he knew: there was no front entrance. Every building this size in Miami had a front entrance, sometimes at street level, sometimes up a set of stairs like his apartment building. Sure, there'd always be an alternative entrance for the furniture haulers and the physically challenged, but this building had only the latter, squarely centered in the middle of this busy kiosk mall.

He watched the two heavy and unmarked metal doors now, picturing the building's residents filing out and boarding the black Mercedes vans he'd often seen parked out front. Yes, the smart money (and in this case that had to be him because he was the *only* money) was on this being the castle where the noble damsel Rosemary "Scheherazade" Weathers (not to mention her faithful squire Podrick the drone) was allegedly being held against her will. Sherman saw that a security camera built into the base of the light fixture mounted over those doors was panning slowly back and forth across the south half of the kiosk mall. Most likely, there was a microphone too. As he pondered about how wide-angled the camera might be, one of the metal doors swung open.

"Can we walk up through the Park?" asked a beautiful woman with silver blonde hair, an almost melodic voice, a bright flower print dress, and, as of this morning's research, a very familiar face. Rosemary Weathers walked out into the mall area with two men, one young, and the other roughly Sherman's own age. That's when he heard the distinctive rumbling purr of a German diesel engine, and looked up to see a black van at the curb.

"Walk?" both men responded to his damsel at very nearly at the same time.

"Surely we don't need a van on a beautiful evening like this? The restaurant can't be more than a half mile away, can it?"

"Well, no, but..." the younger man said, looking to the older man for support.

"You know, Joseph," the older man said, "why not? Tell Terry we'll call if we want a ride back later."

The young man ran out to the black van, spoke to the driver, and joined the other two as they crossed the street into Bayfront Park.

The reporter very nearly got up to follow the trio, but checked himself when he remembered the camera. Instead, he looked away, took a last bite of his angus burger, handed Hemingway another fry, and went to work on the honey-glazed churros.

"Patience, Hem," he whispered, handing down another French fry. "That's the ticket. We don't want to draw attention to ourselves, but damn, that's our damsel—and she's even better looking than her grad school pictures! You don't think she's going to escape by herself do you? Where's the fun in that?"

Hemingway carefully placed the latest treat on the concrete under his human's chair and wandered east toward a familiar scent on the breeze coming in from that direction. It was agitating, and made him edgy without knowing why. He woofed softly, wanting to follow, but saw nothing suspicious to go after. Reluctantly he returned to his human's side, retrieved his French fry, and gobbled it down with a sense that he'd just missed something important.

Sherman threw away his trash and walked out to the south, away from the secret doors in the kiosk mall. He turned east at the sidewalk, strolled up to the corner of the building, stood in its shadow, and watched across Biscayne Boulevard as Rosemary and her companions turned north on the bayside walkway at the far edge of the park. He saw her look back toward the trees, watched the ragged man exit there, and saw Rosemary stumble.

The urge to follow, to watch over her, perhaps to spirit her away right out from under their noses was romantic, but stupid. Instead, he turned south and headed home. She was trusting him to do his part, he must trust her to do hers. Still there was something wrong. Not only had she reacted negatively to seeing the homeless man, but she was heading toward the Biscayne Bay Marina for an undetermined period of time, and the older man, at least, wasn't planning on a return until late.

"She's a smart woman, Hem," he said as they stopped in front of the stairway to his building, "and she must have been aware that this outing had the potential to disrupt our meeting. So, Dr. Watson-Hemingway, what would we do under those circumstances?"

Hemingway refused to take the bait. Instead, as long as his human was being indecisive, he urged him toward the park. Dense as the man was sometimes, perhaps he'd still take the cue.

"Exactly, Hem! She'd go out earlier, just in case."

So, the hunters headed across Biscayne Boulevard together, as close to being on the same page as they were ever apt to get. When they ducked into the dark grove, and Sherman looked up and around, there was the baggie, hanging from a Wild Tamarind branch, with an SD card and a yellow capacitor inside.

Sherman took his SD card out of his shorts pocket, swapped it out with the new one, and hung the paper clip on a nearby branch, a little less conspicuous from below, but easy enough to see from above. He was grinning while Hemingway seemed to be sniffing around for just the right spot.

The beagle, however, had put two and two together. Someone in the shady human hang-out under the French fry building smelled like those things his human kept finding here under these trees. No, that wasn't it exactly. Yes, the strange items smelled like one of the humans who had been under the building when he was snacking today! Now that he knew what he was smelling for, it was just a matter of time before he found it. Hemingway marked the spot to commemorate his keen perception and led his human home.

Chapter Twenty-One

Bubba Gump's was loud, the salad was fresh, and the shrimp wasn't rubbery. The movie quiz went better than she thought it might, but then Phillip liked the movie too. Rosie, despite all the unknowns about her dinner companion, felt freer than she had in years. She had slipped Phillip her note as soon as the maître d' seated them by "accidently" grabbing his napkin and returning it with the tissue note inside. He had very casually read it while placing the napkin on his lap, and with equal ease and certainty had balled it up and destroyed it with the tiny Mason-jar-encased votive candle on their table.

"Here," he said with a smile, answering the question scribbled on her smoking note and setting a cigarette lighter sized device on the table between them. "I think we can talk like adults here. Joseph is a good man, and I trust him. And this gadget is supposed to signal us should an active listening/recording device show up within a hundred feet of us. If that green light turns red, talk about the weather, or anything safe."

"Thank you, Phillip," Rosie said as she watched the tiny green light blink slowly. She hoped the little mp3 player-shaped device wasn't *actually* recording her. "That's important to me—for many reasons. First, men generally don't notice me, so your interest is both flattering and surprising. But secondly, as you must know far better than I do, the Rad-Corp environment hardly fosters acquaintances, let alone deep friendships. At this point, Phillip, I can't imagine how a healthy relationship would survive. Am I missing something about the fraternity of universal purpose I feel in that place?"

Crowe laughed again, but with a hint of sadness.

"Ah, Rosie," he said, "though you can hardly know the half of it, you don't miss a thing. Your heart sees what your eyes cannot. I have been here far longer than you, and to say that you have upset my rickety apple cart is the understatement of the decade!"

"But, Phil..."

"Please, Rosie," Crowe said raising his palm to her as he interrupted her interruption, "We may not have much time," he glanced at the small blinking device with a pointed lift of his eyebrow, "and I can anticipate many of your questions, but can only answer a fraction of them. Can you trust me to do the best I can in whatever time we have?"

Rosie nodded assent, but it wasn't easy.

"Thank you," he said with that new smile which clearly belonged to a very different Phillip Crowe. "The 'fraternity,' as you so aptly call it, is indeed as deadly as you might have figured out. When I began sensing that the frat boys had taken up very serious concerns about you, it felt like I was watching two locomotive engines hurtling towards each other on the same track. I took the only action I could think of to warn you off: I tried to scare you straight."

Rosie's eyebrows rose indignantly. "It worked," she said softly.

"Only the 'scared' part, I'm afraid," Phillip went on. "Had you adopted the 'straight' part, their intensity about my continuing *oversight* of your every move should have backed down to its more normal levels of paranoia. Instead, that intensity has risen significantly. At this point, as you have so carefully suggested, we are both in peril."

"I am so sorry, Phillip..."

"You are to blame only for your own peril. I volunteered for mine—and quite happily I might add. In the Army, my job included keeping my team members alive. This outfit makes the Army look like day care, but here is my best guess as to things you can do. Practice deep breathing. Every day. If you know yoga or meditation practices..."

Rosie's mind tried jumping ahead (because Phillip's tangent about breathing made no sense), but there was nowhere to jump to. Crowe must have recognized her confusion by her facial expression and body language, because he stopped talking mid-sentence, something about suggesting she inhale slowly, then count backwards during a three-count exhale.

"Okay," he said, "my bad. You're not a raw boot camp recruit. I owe you some back story. I'm sorry, but Rad-Corp has some means of tracking its employee whereabouts and vital signs, even in their apartments. I don't believe they have cameras, or they wouldn't need me to investigate, but they seem to know that you spend a great deal of time in your bathroom, and that on these occasions, your pulse rate and body temperature apparently rise with some consistency."

Again, Rosie's face must have said more than enough.

"Wait," Phillip said, holding up his hand again and looking uncomfortable, almost embarrassed, "I realize that there are numerous, ah, quite normal, reasons why this might be the case for any of us, but you are their rainmaker right now, and the cold front coming from the west might bring rain. The evenings are supposed to cool off dramatically over the next few days."

It took Rosie a beat to follow Phillip's eyes and left hand to the device and its blinking red light. It disappeared beneath the table, presumably into his pocket, before she realized he was hoping for a response.

"I hadn't heard that," she managed. "But it should still be fine to walk home tonight, shouldn't it?"

"Oh yes, we shouldn't much change until tomorrow, they said."

The conversation ebbed and flowed throughout the meal, just as Rosie hoped it might under the circumstances of a boss and an employee out for a dinner meeting. And when Phillip Crowe finished a description of his personal fitness routine, Rosie suddenly felt inspired.

"I hate working out, well, maybe just sweating, in front of others," she admitted.

"No wonder I never see you on the roof," Phillip said pleasantly.

"Oh, it's far worse than that," Rosie went on. "My apartment came with some grand piece of exercise machinery right in front of my windows, you know? But even twenty stories up, I'd rather die than work out in front of a window."

Phillip grinned warmly, and played along. "So, you don't work out at all?"

"Oh, of course I do. At my age it would be nearly suicidal to ignore my health. I work out in my bathroom."

"Then your bathroom is larger than mine," Phillip responded with what sounded like sincere doubt.

"Isometrics, they call it," Rosie said with a grin. "My dad said the Navy was big on isometrics, especially aboard smaller ships." She pressed the palm of one hand against the palm of the other. "You can resist yourself for thirty or forty second reps, or push against a wall, or try lifting a fixed object. The real benefit is I can do it one step away from the shower, or even in the shower. That way, you never even feel sweaty!"

"Remarkable!" Phillip said with a smile suggesting he meant more than the ingenuity of her fabrication.

When they rose to leave, Rosie noticed a dark-haired and straight-backed man up near the far end of the bar from young Joseph lay a small stack of bills next to his untouched drink and shuffle towards the side door without looking back. She supposed he thought himself a smooth operator, but saw him twice more before they arrived at the metal doors beneath the Cloisters. Neither Phillip nor Joe gave any hint they'd seen the man, but even this shadow in the night could not ruin her walk in the park.

Chapter Twenty-Two

Reading the latest SD card, Sherman Kanz stared at his laptop in genuine shock. The drone technology being developed on the 20th floor of what Rosemary Weathers called "the Cloisters" was beyond terrifying, but there were over twenty other floors of top secret *something* being created at Rad-Corp as well. That thought hardly inspired confidence. Ms. Weathers was right, though. Without real evidence, her story was not a news story, only horrifying hearsay.

Benny Lopez and Dan Stone were working on finding him a computer hacker, and despite his doubts, they had assured Sherman that he should trust them. It was hard to imagine cracking the encryption for a company like Rad-Corp. Surely they must use every means possible to protect their nearly inaccessible in-house data base. He'd interviewed a Bitcoin expert once who talked about something called "block chain" encryption, a security method that was as close to un-hackable as humanly possible. Nobody Sherman knew at the *Miami Herald*, no one he had ever interviewed, and not even rumors suggested a glimmer of hope of his finding a person capable enough to crack the "un-hackable." And yet Dan and Benny had looked at each other and laughed, urging him to be patient while they made some calls. *Right.*

Despite the intensity of Rosemary's written story, he found himself more than a little distracted by the idea that she was on a dinner date with two hardcore Rad-Corp ex-military types.

"Now what do you suppose that's about, Hem? Our Scheherazade is making friends, perhaps? But are they safe friends? Hell, Hem, I don't know if we're safe friends."

Hemingway ignored all that drivel and pondered the wisdom of a mid-day walk in the early evening. Sure, staying out later was great and all, but it was now long past their last-call outing, he was sleepy, and his human was obviously grossly distracted. The beagle walked to the door, sat down, and stared back into the living room. Enough was enough.

"Okay, Hem, I get it. I know I threw off our schedule today, but what if she doesn't check back in the park tonight? We can't go out there and bring back the SD card we just hung up in that tree. Hell, I have no idea how I'd tell. I should have marked the baggie or something."

His human's tone of voice was pathetically helpless tonight, but Hemingway knew that enabling him wouldn't do him any good in the end. So, he just stood by the door as Sherman gathered up the leash and that sweaty old ball cap.

"Oh, shit, Hem!" the reporter said as he snapped on the leash and opened the door. "The laptop! Wait a second."

After slamming the door back in the disgusted beagle's face, Sherman ran to his bedroom, came out with his backpack, and stuffed the laptop computer inside. "Here we go!"

No fool, Hemingway paused this time before exiting to the hallway. When he was sure that his human was actually going to leave this time, he followed along, shaking his head in frustration.

It was late enough when they entered the quiet grove in Bayfront Park that there wasn't a soul in sight. It wasn't the first time he'd brought Hemingway out this late, but this time Sherman was genuinely glad for the privacy. When he held up his cellphone in flashlight mode, it seemed like the plastic bag hung pretty much where he'd put it, but who pays that much attention to anything? He had to check. When he fired up the laptop, the illumination from the screen seemed like ballroom lights in the small clearing, so he hurriedly inserted the SD card and opened the lone file. It was not his note to Rosemary, so he slammed the lid, stuck the computer back in the backpack, and tugged Hemingway back toward Biscayne Boulevard

"Throwing a party in there?" asked a clean-cut young Hispanic man.

Hemingway woofed suspiciously, but hung back. Sherman stumbled directly into the man, dropping his cellphone in the process.

"Ah, sorry officer," the startled reporter stammered. "I was trying to find Hemingway's evening litter, but either he didn't go, or that task will have to wait until his morning walk. We're both up past our bedtimes."

"You're the reporter from the *Herald,*" the cop said, scooping up the cellphone and handing it back to Sherman. "I see you guys here a lot when I draw nightshift. Hey, boy!" he said, reaching a hand out towards the beagle. "It's Okay, I didn't mean to scare you."

Hemingway woofed at the affront to his courage, but sniffed the hand anyway, just in case. He was rewarded with a dog biscuit, and wagged his tail so as not to seem petty by returning insult for insult. He was bigger than that kind of passive aggressiveness, and this human obviously meant no harm.

"All the dogs love me," said the young officer. "If only it was that easy with the ladies! You guys have a good night, and don't worry, I won't include the missing *mierda de perro* in my report."

"*Gracias!*" Sherman said with a laugh. Now, if he could only get home before his shaky knees gave out.

★ ★ ★

Sherman Kanz's alarm radio went off way too early the next morning, and he cursed at no one in particular. Rosemary's note had been short and sweet: "Unexpected change of plans. Tomorrow night should be good." The message machine light when he and Hemingway had returned home last night signaled a message just as short, but far more cryptic from Dan Stone: "Gotcha covered. Bench behind the Cadillac. 9:00 a.m."

"What the hell, Hem?" he said, pulling on clean cotton sweat pants and heading for the bathroom. "Miami Beach at 9:00 a.m. on a Saturday? Really? Dan's gonna pay for this, well, unless it's *really* good news."

Hemingway picked his leash up off the living room floor where his human had carelessly dropped it the night before and dragged it over to the front door. Just because he'd been a shelter dog, that was no reason to saddle him with a drama queen. But if he didn't watch out for the poor pathetic man, who would?

Sherman drove across the Intracoastal Waterway causeway, parked on 39th Street, just outside Carrabba's restaurant, hooked up Hemingway's lease, and walked east toward the Boardwalk entrance. Each wooden bench along the historic Miami Beach Boardwalk had been cleverly divided into three seating possibilities. These were pointedly demonstrated by the presence of two vertical boards which divided the bench into thirds. These mini-walls served to keep hips from touching those of one's neighbor's, while effectively ruining a homeless person's chances of finding a comfortable seaside sleeping berth.

Just north of the Boardwalk access, behind a historic Art Deco hotel called the Cadillac, Sherman found Dan gingerly sipping a tall cup from the nearby Starbucks franchise. In the middle cavity of the divided bench, sat a similar cup, still emitting steam in the cool ocean breeze.

"For you, Sherman," Dan said with a stately nod. "Take a load off."

Sherman excused himself as he stepped in front of a young Hasidic rabbinical student who sat on the opposite end of the bench from Dan Stone, retrieved the coffee cup, and squeezed himself in between the two very dissimilar men. Stone—a tall, tan, and chiseled Miccosukee man—had served in the Army in Vietnam, and even in his early sixties, he looked formidable. The pale and somewhat scrawny Hasidic lad, with his wire-rim glasses bent over an ancient looking book, wore side locks dangling over his cheeks. Traditional white strings flowing out from under his tidy black vest looked, well, rabbinical. It was, after all, *Shabbat Shalom*, the Jewish Sabbath. That didn't seem to put off Hemingway, who sniffed the young man's knee-high leather boots and curled up contentedly, letting his chin observe a day of rest on his new friend's toe.

"Shouldn't we... "Sherman whispered to Dan, rolling his eyes to suggest that a more private place might be appropriate.

"What?" Dan said. "Ask him to leave? Hell, he's got as much right to sit here on this bench as we Gentiles do!"

Sherman blanched as several Hasidic families passing by on their way to Temple stared at him pointedly. "Hey, no, I mean..."

"I thought you said he was a *mensch*, Dan," said the young Jewish student, leaning across toward Dan, eye-to-eye with Sherman, just to cause a little further discomfort for the embarrassed reporter.

"Well," Dan laughed, "there are human beings and there are human beings—it's like Forrest Gump's box of chocolates, you never know what you're going to get! Sherman Kanz, I'd like you to meet my friend, Seth Lowenstein. Seth, this enlightened human being is the *Miami Herald's* star reporter, Sherman Kanz."

Kanz laughed in beet-red embarrassment, and shook the extended hand. "Glad to meet you, Seth. It's a rather unusual sideline for a rabbinical student, I'd imagine, but I take it you're my computer hacker?"

"At your disposal," Seth said with a broad grin, "and don't let the costume fool you. I have a gift for fitting in. Along those very lines, I have already checked out your secret red doors, taken a few discrete photos, and have a tailor friend in Baltimore making us a couple of our own silver Rad-Corp security blazers as we speak. I have a plan, and this is going to be fun."

"You have a strange idea about fun," Sherman said. "But I shouldn't be surprised if you're friends with Dan and Benny."

"I can't imagine what you mean," Dan said. "Seth was a Navy SEAL, and is now a private investigator and security consultant in Baltimore. We met him through Mac and John. Mac's originally from Baltimore, and Seth helped them out of a bind a year or so back."

"Not without help from you, Dan," Seth said. "Sherman, if you've never seen Dan polish up his boots and strut his stuff in a tailored chauffer's uniform, you've never lived."

Just by the way Dan was shaking his head, Sherman knew he was going to love that story. By the time they broke up their boardwalk meeting, Sherman hurt from laughing. As he walked Hemingway back to his car, he kept checking his pocket and the tiny gadget Seth had given him. He hoped it was light enough for Rosie's drone to carry the heavier baggie back to her without incident, and beyond that primary task, Sherman *really* hoped that the gizmo would work.

Chapter Twenty-Three

Rosie Weather's bathroom work-out studio and drone hanger was the epitome of calm when she flew Podrick back to the park after her dinner with Phillip Crowe. "This breathing stuff really works," she thought as she watched the heart monitoring arm band she had bought back in college, but never worn since. As she breathed in through her nose and let the air out slowly through relaxed lips, Rosie noted that Sherman had left his baggie where he hung the last one, which meant there was little danger that she was just picking up the one she put out that morning. Rosie brought the drone back without incident, without undo rises in her pulse rate, and tucked it away behind the medicine cabinet. Morning would come too soon.

★ ★ ★

When morning did come, Rosie stumbled through her shower and dressing without so much as a sniff through the bathroom window. She wondered at herself as she joined several of her team members on the elevator ride up to breakfast. She felt different. She was different.

"How was your date?" asked Linda Ulrich, her innocent smile not quite as innocent as usual.

Barry Cole snickered. "Hardly the romantic type, I'd guess."

"People can surprise you, Barry," Peter Bloom said thoughtfully. "Around here nothing is quite what it seems."

Rosie realized early that Peter was different. He lived in his own space, in his own head, in a manner unlike anyone else on her team. The tall light-haired man had an air about him. Not like wealth, exactly, but certainly an attitude of knowing he was set apart, and being okay with it. Peter had a knack for making seemingly benign comments that brought conversation to a dead standstill—for reasons Rosie could never quite put a finger on.

"It was nice," Rosie said to fill the dead air. "We had a great walk in the park both ways, and you girls keep your eyes out for a new security guard named 'Joe.' He's too young for me, but I'm just sayin'..."

Everyone was laughing as the elevator opened into the cafeteria, and the chatter carried through the serving line. Apparently, Rosie's group lunches had a loosening effect, because not only did the four of them gravitate to a larger round table for breakfast, but within ten minutes, her whole team had pulled up chairs—Patty Jenkins, Lou Garcia, even Phillip Crowe and Joe Allen. Rosie just watched. She never said a word. But, as the morning meal progressed, she explored the new feelings in herself. In a way, chagrinned as it made her feel, it felt almost like she was only now beginning to see her team for who they were, as individuals and as a group. She and her team shared a common experience, an experience none of them dared speak about. And yet each one of them was unique as well.

It seemed so obvious now that Lou Garcia was far smarter than he let on. He was always the last to volunteer information, especially anything insightful about himself. He always seemed content with any assignment, and carried through regardless of any complications that might arise. Here, for the first time in her tenure at Rad-Corp, Rosie watched him smile. It was a beautiful smile. What was Lou's recruitment interview like? What had he thought he was signing on for? Patty Jenkins smiled a lot, but it was the "Am I pleasing you now?" smile of someone who could have been abused, someone who walked on ice, desperate not to rock the boat. "Why haven't I noticed that before now?" Rosie asked herself. "Because," she thought, "I am awake now—or at least I'm waking up from the Rad-Corp dream." She made up her mind, then and there, that her overall game plan must change radically.

★ ★ ★

After work, with no thought about supper, Rosie hammered away at the computer keyboard in her apartment. Sherman's note was short and sweet. He loved the name "Rosemary Weathers" (it had "a ring to it"), his friends thought they knew a hacker, they were working up a plan to rescue her, and he loved her blue and yellow flower print dress. Well, the reporter was paying attention, she had to give him that. Tonight, her story had to beat the others by miles. Just when she'd thought it was unnecessary to continue her Scheherazade impersonation (she and Sherman-the-researcher were now on a first name basis), Rosie knew she must weave one more snare, and a sizable one at that.

As she typed, Rosie couldn't help thinking about the "watcher" in her ceiling. It had to be in her ceiling. How else could they keep track of what room an employee was in, and monitor vital signs? Not precise vital signs, maybe, but at least their heat signature. FLIR technology, though not her area of interest, had been around since the '70s, and if a Forward Looking Infra-Red device was sensitive enough, it would show body temperature rising, a sure sign that pulse and blood pressure were doing the same. Satellite FLIR could watch body signature battles inside buildings around the world, but somehow she thought a 27-story building might confound even the best satellite when it came to picking out individual heat signatures stacked 27 deep on top of one another. It had to be in the individual ceilings.

Rosie finished typing, reread quickly, took several deep breathes, and went to Podrick's hanger. Her walks in the park, her dinner out, and her breakfast and workday with her team had flipped a switch in her brain. She was free. The minute she had made the decision to get out, or at least get information out, she knew she had retaken control of her own life. But not until today did she realize that decision, and not some future rescue, had truly made her free. "Why not take two walks tonight?" she thought, just because she could.

Rosie flew Podrick just above the treetops, freer than she'd felt in years, grinning like a child. She need not worry about her vital signs, because she was no longer afraid. She watched the picketers at the Grand Flamingo packing it in for the night. They seemed buoyed by something that made their demeanor seem lighter. She saw the Filling Empty Houses, Inc., crew filing out to the white van, and watched them pause as their leader veered away towards a hefty black king-cab pick-up truck parked just down the block. The white van's driver walked directly up to the other driver who wore a black straw cowboy hat that shielded his face from Rosie's view. A conversation ensued. The black truck said "Personal Space, Inc." on its doors in bold white lettering. It was hooked up to a trailer that reminded Rosie of a canoe trip she'd taken down the Delaware River when she was attending NYU. The canoes were hauled back up river stacked four high on both sides of a trailer like the one below her, but these weren't canoes. She wasn't sure what they were.

Maybe ten feet long, four-foot high and wide, the high-tech units looked like space shuttles without the wings. Zooming in Podrick's camera, Rosie saw "Space Station, Inc." on each of the strange pods, as well as a "Personal Space, Inc." sticker thanking ten corporate and individual donors for providing a safe and suitable dwelling for a homeless person. The discussion between the two drivers was punctuated with hand gestures, and then the man in the pick-up truck pointed over at the Miami River Walk. The man from the white van walked across the street and stood on the sidewalk by the bay.

Rosie zoomed back out enough to see them both, and watched as the man in the pick-up fiddled with his wrist watch and seemed to shout something to his friend across the street. That good-natured looking Latino man walked back towards the tail end of the black pickup, looked both ways, opened a door to one of the pods, climbed in, and pulled the door closed behind him. Seconds later, he crawled back out and resumed his discussion with the pick-up's driver. The two men shook hands, the Latino man returned to the white van, and both vehicles drove off into the growing dusk. Rosie had no idea what to make of this street performance.

"Life on the outside is strange," she whispered as she flew Podrick along the shoreline back towards Bayfront Park. She directed the drone along the shoreline all the way up to the Bayside Mall and Marina. There, she hovered over the boats docked row-upon-row, dock-upon-dock beneath her. Rosie had never been on a sailboat, but there was something romantic about the idea of sailing, something empowering about learning to use the world's winds to fly free across the water. As she panned Podrick's camera above a string of tall-masted sloops and double-masted ketches, a fiery redhead caught her eye. There below her, a young lady sat in a swiveling cockpit chair, with her legs stretched up on the sailboat's safety lines, hands working a laptop computer in the fading light. That was a life of freedom.

The drone controller display suggested that Podrick needed to think about a recharge, especially as he had work to do long after dark, so Rosie reluctantly flew him home, all while picturing herself aboard a sailboat with her legs up like that red-headed woman. And why not?

Chapter Twenty-Four

"Why not?" Dan Stone asked as he scratched his forehead where the old straw cowboy hat always left a red line on his skin. "It's as close as I can think to making a person actually disappear."

"I'm with you there," said Benny Lopez as he nodded his head slowly. "But the timing will be crucial. How close to the building can you park without being seen on the camera Sherman showed us?"

"Well that's the beauty of my plan, we've already got an install planned for the office complex right behind to the west. I'll be coming and going for a week, and nobody will think anything of seeing this rig parked there. Besides, Seth says Sherman's balloons and his tunnel will completely block the cameras when the big moment arrives."

"That sounds more promising," Benny said. "How far of a walk would that be from the Rad-Corp doors to your trailer, and how long do you think it would take her to get there supposing Seth finds a way to get the doors open for her?"

"Less than fifty yards, I'd say, like over there on the Riverwalk," Dan said, pointing out the cab window and across the street. "Let's time it. Stand over by that Palm tree, and when I say go, just walk to the back of my truck, casually look around, climb into one of the stations, and I'll stop my watch when I hear the door close."

"Okay, sounds easy enough. Let's give it a go." Benny walked across the street and across the River Walk, and then stood by the Palm tree as instructed. When Dan shouted "go," he headed back, crossed Biscayne Boulevard Way without incident, and paused between the black truck's tailgate and the double rack of Space Station pods. After looking around, waving to his puzzled work crew who stood staring at him from the white van behind the trailer, he opened a pod door, climbed in, and shut the door firmly behind him.

When Benny popped out seconds later and walked back to Dan's window, he said: "Have I told you lately how awesome those things are? Who'd of thought that John and Mac would change the face of homelessness for so many people? How did I do?"

"About ninety seconds, Benny," Dan said with a smile, "and if it's as crowded at the kiosk mall as we hope, who'd ever notice?"

"Well, that all depends on our decoys. Has Sherman agreed to that yet?"

"I don't think Seth has mentioned that part of the plan to Sherman yet," Dan said with a wide grin. "But he's so psyched about saving this lady, he'll do it. He won't like it, but he'll do it."

"Yeah, you're right, Dan. Are we fuckin' crazy or what?"

Dan extended his hand to his friend and said: "Crazy as it gets. See you at Sherman's."

Ben shook his head all the way back to his van, and both trucks pulled away from the curb and drove away.

★ ★ ★

An hour later, a half block away, and a dozen stories up, Sherman Kanz was tidying up the final draft of his latest Grand Flamingo Hotel story. He was dumbfounded by the impact his series was having on Miami. The city council was actually scheduled to meet in a special session, and his friend John Ghostwalker was flying in from Kansas to consult with the city on behalf of Jacobs & Associates, the

Miami based architectural firm he worked for. Was someone seriously going to find a way to save the old hotel? It seemed like a fairy tale bound for a dismal ending. Still, why not? Sometimes, a reminder of our past isn't a bad thing.

Hemingway was still sitting by the door, and he wasn't happy. Not at all. He liked to think of himself as a very tolerant individual, and he was generally quick to forgive human foibles, certainly when it came to his own flawed human. But Benny? He had come to expect more from that one. It was an outrage, really, Benny and Dan had swept in all aflutter like he didn't exist, chatted up his human, and then swept out like they had nothing better to do than ignore him completely. Forgiving though he was, Hemingway would not soon forget this breach of propriety.

"Get over it, Hem," Sherman said from his coffee table desk. "They've got lives too, you know. It can't always be about you."

The story was near enough to finished, so Sherman switched to the SD card and filled Rosemary Weathers in on some of Seth's rescue plan so far. Sherman knew that Seth was holding some back on the whole scheme, leaving out crucial bits, but he'd cough it up when he was ready. He just hoped his damsel would survive her magical disappearance. What he knew about Seth's plan so far was pretty damn clever. Dan's trailer rig was as common a sight around Miami as the city busses that used to boast a picture of his own smiling face. Those were the days.

When Sherman's cell phone rang, he was jerked out of his *Glory Days* reverie. He considered ignoring the call as too close to a normal person's bedtime, but a normal person's bedtime was his evening deadline for the morning paper. Besides, he was hoping for a call back from an owner in the Bradford Group, the hotel and resort conglomerate that was putting up the mega resort and spa on the land where the little Grand Flamingo sat awaiting its fate on the southeast corner of the otherwise barren block. When he looked, he saw that it was indeed the call he'd been hoping to get in time for his deadline.

"Good news twice in one night, Hem!" he said as he pushed the button to accept the call. "Kanz here. How are you Mr. Drake?"

Sherman chatted up the executive, asked his questions, and was suddenly surprised again. "Who came up to see you?" Sherman asked. "Dave Bartlett and Chris Tosh came to Orlando to meet with you guys? Who sent them after you? Really? Somebody named Seth, I see."

For the rest of the conversation, scribbling away in his notebook, Sherman just said "Really?" and "I see" a lot, and finally ended the call with: "Well, thanks for the exclusive." He had about twenty minutes in which to rewrite and send in his copy to the paper before he had to meet Podrick the flying mystery squire in the park. He went at it with a will while Hemingway continued to pout by the door. The Bradford Group had decided to change their corporate mind and save the old Grand Flamingo Hotel!

An hour and a half later, and a dozen flights up from the street, Sherman Kanz had exchanged his SD card and Seth's computer hack gadget with Rosemary Weathers' amazing little drone. Now, back from Bayfront Park, he sat on his couch saying "shit!" over and over to no one in particular. Sure, he threw in a "Oh, hell no!" occasionally, but that was more of a futile afterthought. He had now read Rosemary's long SD card message several times, each time in hopes that it would somehow auto-correct between readings. It never did. Everyone had their share of "oh shit moments," he knew, but this one not only approached the edge of the proverbial shit ceiling fan blades, it leapt out into space.

Rosemary Weathers, an otherwise brilliant and sensible human being, had thanked him for his earlier news and compliment, joked about his "stalking" her the night before, and then told him—in no uncertain terms—that she would be needing rescue for as many as eight additional people. The crazy woman was determined to at least give them each the option when the time came.

"Shit!"

Hemingway was mostly over his snit, and genuinely concerned about his deeply disturbed human. He rested his chin on the reporter's knee, hoping to calm the poor man.

"Oh, hell no!" was all Hemingway got for his trouble.

Chapter Twenty-Five

Rosemary was liking herself, and it felt good. She'd taken a couple of Psych classes at NYU, breezed through, and never given the content a second thought. They were prerequisites, time-wasting courses every university piles on in order to support the fiscal bottom line. She'd even read a book by Michael A. Singer called *The Untethered Soul: The Journey Beyond Yourself.* At the time, busy with grad school, she had accepted the suggestion that she read it because it came from a professor who seemed particularly supportive. But she could remember vividly now that the suggestion she read about her psyche had felt like an assignment, a gentle condemnation of her life, her personality. Professor Hastings had handed her a yellow Post-it note with the title and the author's name on it and said: "Rosemary Weathers, you have not found yourself yet, but you will."

"I am here now," she whispered as she sat down and plugged the SD card into her apartment laptop computer. "I think I've discovered something of my true self at last, Dr. H. Thank you for planting that seed."

Sherman Kanz's note was short and to the point: "Good luck! You'll need it. (I really like this guy, Lowenstein, but I can't understand half of what he says about computers.)"

Seth Lowenstein's discourse was long and complicated. Rosie read it through twice before trying to attach the new gadget to her computer's wall connection cable. Much of his instruction read like a very basic computer class she had taken in high school where her teacher tried to explain two concepts. The first was binary language, the use of zeros and ones as "off" and "on." The second had to do with the logic of computer programming language; which, if Rosie remembered correctly, boiled down to a series of "if" and "then" pathway markers. *If this thing happens, then go do this thing* seemed to summarize all computer programs, and after telling her how to install his device between the wall cable and her computer, the rest of Seth's instructions to her were no different.

After a long-winded synopsis of his objectives— (1) discovering how much of the building's data was accessible through the various individual wall interfaces; (2) figuring out what computers were in the line between her apartment, her office, her boss's office, and the central data base; and, (3) what type of encryptions defined who saw what—Seth got to Rosie's secondary assignment.

"Turn on your computer at midnight. A small window should open up on your screen," Seth's instructions said. "It should resemble a download window with a horizontal progress bar that, in this case, records the device's progress in analyzing the fiber optic cable coming from the wall. And just like a download window, it reads from zero to one hundred percent. If the green bar reaches the right end of this scale in the first five or ten minutes, then turn your bathroom light on and off once. If the green progress bar reaches the right side within an hour, then turn your bathroom light on, leave it for ten minutes, and then turn it off."

Rosie watched the green bar with great intensity, but when it was still just a tiny sliver at ten minutes after midnight, she breathed a sigh of relief. Lowenstein's notes had assured her that the slower it progressed, the more live optic fibers there were in her branch of the cable. The rest of her progress checks were simpler, and more spread out, so Seth had suggested that she spend the intervening time between chores in bed, or wherever she usually spent the time between midnight and breakfast. He reminded her (unnecessarily) that if they were checking her apartment, the infra-red scan was showing the security desk where she was at all times, so the less out-of-the-ordinary her movements were, the better.

"Go to the bathroom or the kitchen each time you get up, passing your desk both going and coming back, but don't use the light unless it's for a signal to me. And if there's a task to be accomplished at the computer just do it as you walk back to your bedroom. Think about what you saw going by, the instruction you're going to carry out on your way back to the bedroom, and try not to stop anywhere but in the bathroom or the kitchen. On the way back to your bedroom, just slow down as you pass your desk and tap, or click, or flip as you go by."

Rosie thought of it as a ballet recital or a stage director's instruction. She hadn't performed anything since elementary school, but the butterflies were just as intense as when she'd played the part of a daffodil breaking ground in Mrs. Becker's fourth grade Spring play, *Life is a Garden*. This time, though, she knew about calming breaths. Everything went well during the two- and four-hour checks, and each time she had responded as directed. Seth Lowenstein's "self-destruct" sequence had not been triggered. No one from security had broken down her door, so the last instruction before breakfast was all that remained.

"Use a pencil, a pen, or even the tine of a fork to press (once) on the tiny concave button on the side of my mini-me-hacker. You've probably seen these switches on watches, and once you push it, your computer should use the power cord and the electric cables in the wall as an antenna so it can talk to mine. Before you leave for breakfast, wave to me out your bathroom window. You'll know me by my fabulous hardhat!"

Rosie was tired and exhilarated all at once. She held her breath as she used a ball point pen to press in the button. The little antenna icon on Seth's pop-up window began flashing, and a line of type ran across the bottom of her screen like those news flash items that ran along below the news shows on TV. She laughed out loud as she read along: "Good morning Rosemary! You're not alone anymore. Come wave hello!"

She'd already piled the books up in her bathtub, so she went in, climbed up, and looked out at the building across to the north. There on the south face of the office building, a window washing scaffold hung just over the roof's edge. Two men in yellow hard hats scurried back and forth on the roof tending to rope and cable lines in the blooming sunlight, but out on the scaffold platform itself, a smaller man sat cross-legged with his back to her. It had to be Seth Lowenstein. The pink hard hat and the casual queen's wave above his right shoulder without turning to expose his face or his laptop to anyone in the Rad-Corp building was a dead giveaway.

Rosie stuck her arm out through the grillwork and waved back, even though she knew Seth couldn't see her. But before heading for breakfast, she grabbed the binoculars hanging on the back of the bathroom door. The men in the yellow hard hats looked strangely familiar, and sure enough, the shorter one was the Latino man who drove the white van that she'd often seen parked at the old hotel. She couldn't see the taller man's face, but his movements felt profoundly familiar. Maybe he was the man in the straw cowboy hat who drove the black pick-up truck, but she'd never seen that guy on his feet.

It didn't matter. She was hungry, it was time for breakfast, and Sherman Kanz had come through for her. By the time she broke for lunch, she might know more about how much access Seth had managed to get via her laptop, and for now, she was overjoyed at the prospect. Little Rosemary Weathers was in the driver's seat of her own life, for the first time in her life, and even from the Rad-Corp Cloisters Prison, she loved the way that felt.

Chapter Twenty-Six

It wasn't poker night. It wasn't even night. But at 10:00 a.m., Sherman's poker table showed a full house. All seven seats were occupied, and the host was feeling a bit overwhelmed. The rescue team, under Seth's brief watch, had grown. Sherman was honored, but worried about his friends.

"Really?" he said again. "Do you realize what these guys are capable of doing to anyone who gets in their way? I mean, if half of what this lady says is true, we could all die from robotic killer bee stings."

"So now you want to back out, *gimoozaabi*?" Dan said with a smile. "I don't think you do, and neither do we. You and your mystery woman are stuck with us. We know too much to turn back—or at least we think we do."

"Well, no, of course not," Sherman said quickly, "but I just, well, I appreciate it, that's all."

"Is it really apt to be dangerous?" Dave Bartlett asked. "Not that I mind helping a good cause, but it seems more than a little far-fetched, like 'Evil-Corp' from that Cable TV show, *Mr. Robot*. Or am I the only guy wearing rose-colored glasses about something this obscene sounding?"

"Not what I would usually choose to be doing with my free time," remarked John Ghostwalker." The young architect had just taken a cab in from Miami International and his blond pony-tail flipped as he turned toward Seth Lowenstein who was, by choice, the odd-man-out, sitting on the sofa with his laptop open on the coffee table, right on top of Sherman's closed one. "but when Seth said it was fishy, then I was betting it was fishy even before Abraham Jacobs told me there was no copy of the building's blueprint on file with the city or the county."

"He ought to know," Mac laughed. "Didn't you tell me Abe studies the blueprints of every big job he doesn't win the bid on?"

John nodded to his lady love. "Every last one."

"Well," Chris Tosh said, "I don't mind admitting that I have some pre-game jitters here, but I'm sure not backing down if Dave Bartlett is crazy enough to do this." He tapped Bartlett affectionately on the back of his head, eliciting that toothy grin that used to be seen nearly everywhere a newspaper could be purchased.

"I hate to enhance anybody's jitters," Seth said as he picked up his laptop, carried it to the poker table, and set it in the center, "but the encryption on the Rad-Corp main frame does resemble block-chain technology from a distance, at least. It may be what's sometimes called a 'private' instance, but that's not what sorts out who sees what. Something in Rosemary's computer screens out certain specific accessing capabilities, but we're intruding just outside of that, so everything her boss's computer sees is live in the fiber optic cable. I don't know whose computer is next in line yet, but Phillip Crowe's laptop seems atypical, very unlike Rosemary's. His level of access appears unusually high, almost like he has second-floor administrative privileges. I might even get past his restrictions eventually, but for now—hopefully--what he's tied into will be all you need, Sherman."

While Seth explained what they had gleaned, hoped to glean, and probably couldn't glean from the repeater array he had installed on the roof of the building just north of Rad-Corp, Sherman sat in awe. He'd heard Seth Lowenstein stories around the poker table and knew the man had remarkable skills, but neither he, Dave Bartlett, nor Chris Tosh had met the ex-Navy SEAL before. Watching him at work was a life lesson in the chasm between a group of well-meaning do-gooders and a viable squad with a seasoned sergeant to lead them. Maybe they had a chance after all.

Then Seth motioned for those behind the laptop screen to move where they could see, and as he double-clicked a video file called "DCC-13" he began singing softly in a very convincing Bob Dylan impersonation:

Come gather 'round people, wherever you roam, and admit that the waters around you have grown, and accept it that soon you'll be drenched to the bone. If your time to you is worth savin', then you better start swimmin' or you'll sink like a stone, for the times they are a-changin'.

No one around the table moved. Some held their breath. The video Rosemary had described played out as Seth ended his haunting one-verse soundtrack. Even before the Hispanic workers dropped lifelessly to the ground, tears were forming in every eye around Sherman's poker table. There is no silence quite like stunned silence, and for a moment or two after the video clip ended, no one spoke.

"They are alive," Seth said finally. "Else those Rad-Corp bastards would have taken back the money they handed out instead of throwing down the rest."

"Small comfort," Dan Stone said sternly.

"Right," Chris Tosh said. "They could put any kind of poison or germ culture in those robot bees."

"And I'm sure they will," Sherman said, "if the price is right. But who the hell are they? I mean, I've been assuming they are being funded by our own government, but I can't find any evidence of their corporate structure in any of the public references. Beyond the Rad-Corp brand being associated with drone technology and the military industrial complex, it's a dead end. I can track companies like Halliburton and Monsanto, even subsidiaries like Kellogg, Brown & Root and Blackwater, at least up to a point, but this brand just seems to hang in mid-air. I can track some of their products around the globe, but there's nothing out there about the producers themselves."

"Are there really any major American corporations anymore?" Mac asked. "I mean, watching my late father's dirty dealings, it seems like every really big corporation is multi-national. That used to mean a company sold its goods or services world-wide, but now it seems to mean that no one is really sure who owns controlling interest, where, or if, they pay taxes, or what foreign country they do their banking in. Something I read suggested that many have their corporate offices in Dubai."

"I wish we had a local politician who gave a shit," Dave Bartlett said, "but who could we approach with something like this? Sherman, do you have the news editor's blessing on this story? I had to watch that my humor columns didn't upset big money when I was there, and a disabled writer friend got canned from the *Detroit Free Press* for rightly pointing out some of Jerry Lewis's manipulative and less-than-honest use of disabled children in order to manipulate the emotions of telethon viewers, so I can't imagine the *Miami Herald* just running with this story, regardless of how much evidence we provide. These guys give the term 'scary people' a whole new level of meaning."

"Well, I haven't approached her yet," Sherman admitted. "You all know how crazy it sounded. Now with this, and especially if we can get Rosemary out alive, I'd like to think she'd listen. But you're right, Dave, we could use someone trustworthy who's way above our pay grade."

"I may know someone," Seth said thoughtfully. "But we have to decide how and when to approach him. If he's willing to risk his career on this, maybe your editor would be more willing to step up to her editor and suggest some old school journalistic integrity."

"He who holds the coins, holds the loins," Dan said.

"Miccosukee wisdom?" Benny asked.

"Doubt it," Dan said with a grin. "More likely John Wayne. I say we give Seth's contact a chance, but it's your neck you're risking, Seth. How sure are you about this guy, and what exactly does he do?"

"He's a Congressman," Seth said, "and a Muslim. And yes, I trust him."

"Oh, shit," Sherman muttered. "This just gets better and better."

Chapter Twenty-Seven

While Seth was out of town, everyone else had what he'd called "voluntary assignments." Even Rosie had a job. She recognized Seth's level of intelligence and was profoundly glad for his help, but she missed her clandestine meetings with Sherman Kanz. Their nighttime rendezvous had become a comforting, even amusing, part of her life. Seth Lowenstein had given her nearly instantaneous access to the outside, but only through his laptop computer. Seth was an unknown. Even Sherman didn't seem all that familiar with the man. Rosie had become much more aware of freedom and restriction lately, and the difference felt profound. Seth was all business. He saw the challenge, and he took charge. She realized how much less enthusiasm she had for allowing others to be in charge of her life now and couldn't help thinking that maybe she had what it takes to be a take-charge person too. Saving her wasn't necessarily the others' priority in life, but it had to be her own.

Still, Rosie began Seth's assignment without really understanding how it could possibly work. Seth's source code selections were drag & paste, and his detailed instructions about where to paste each line of code was a bit daunting. But one-by-one, Rosie followed the directions, located the appropriate programming code line at the locations Seth had specified, and inserted the additional lines of code he had sent her. What those lines of code were each for, she had no idea.

Each morning she pasted one or two lines before breakfast, and each night she did as many as she could before she had to sleep. "I call them 'Trojan Tunnel Ponies,'" Seth had written, "and you are putting them where they can hopefully build a tunnel system in and around the Rad-Corp databank servers. These tunnels are the shortcuts we will need for a hasty enough snatch and grab so that you and your people can get out more easily, with enough evidence and enough system confusion all at the same time." As she drifted off to sleep at night, Rosie pictured Seth's ponies galloping free inside the Rad-Corp network.

★ ★ ★

The rest of Seth's assignments to Sherman's rescue team volunteers were delivered in person. Chris Tosh's task was next. After chatting for a few minutes, asking seemingly innocuous questions, Seth found the perfect job for the basketball superstar. One comment Chris made was the kicker.

"If I hadn't made it in the NBA?" he said in answer to Seth's question. "I think I'd have tried out for the fire department. Those guys are real stars. Of course, I'd have coached a kids' basketball team on my days off!"

"I was wondering whether any of you might be willing, let alone perfect, to try this mission," Seth laughed, "but you are the man! Sherman, John, and I have been desperately hunting for something which may not exist outside the Rad-Corp building. But if it does, and you can get it for us, Chris, we may actually have a shot at pulling this off without anybody getting hurt or worse. Here's what we need you to do..."

★ ★ ★

Lowenstein's next meeting was with John Ghostwalker and his red-headed life partner Sean "Mac" McKnight. This chat was a little bumpier.

"You want us to what?" Mac asked, her red hair flipping as she gave Seth a genuine double-take.

"Oh, come on," Seth said. "You know it would be fun."

"I must not have heard you right, Seth," she said. "That, or you're crazier than I thought."

"I think we heard him just fine, my lady love," John Ghostwalker said. "But aren't you just a little curious why he'd ask us to destroy a sailboat. I certainly am."

"Oh, no!" Seth said. "I didn't say 'destroy it.' You just need to buy it and set it on fire. Here, look."

"Well," Mac huffed as she took the ragged page from a recent *Boat Trader*, "it's certainly all cleared up now. Are you getting any of this, John?"

"Yes," her partner smiled, "I think I'm at least on the right track. This Rena 744 sailboat listed here is like the one in the article Sherman wrote about the Grand Flamingo Hotel. The original belonged to the owner of the hotel, and it used to be parked where that mega yacht is docked over by the Miami River Walk. Don't tell Sherman I only skimmed his article, but I think the original boat caught on fire there at its dock. Something about an alcohol stove."

"Bingo!" Seth said. "Don't you love the poetic symmetry? We're saving lives and we're creating historical theater."

"Okay, Seth," John said, shaking his head, "now you lost me again."

"Doesn't matter, John," Seth said. "You two buy this piece of history before someone else does. We'll all pitch in if need be. Then study up on John Alden, its designer. We're going set it ablaze, and all of Miami is going to help us restore it."

★ ★ ★

Next, Seth met Dave Bartlett for coffee at a Starbucks near the humor writer's home. He had read the man's syndicated columns in the *Baltimore Sun*, had enjoyed several of his books through the years, and had even attended a Rock Bottom Remainders concert when the writer's band played Baltimore on their 2010 Wordstock Tour. Seth hung a wooden plaque on his office wall with a quote taken from Bartlett's column about the list of things he's learned by age 50: *"If someone is nice to you, but mean to the waiter, then they're not a nice person."* He might have been a bit star-struck, and just maybe Seth came on a bit too strong for a first time one-on-one.

"We're putting the band back together!" Seth sort of blurted out as they sat down with their coffees.

"That's great," Dave Bartlett replied calmly. "I'm sorry, though, I didn't know you had a band."

Dave didn't know exactly what to make of Seth Lowenstein, but within the first two minutes, the humor columns were writing themselves in his head. Sure, Dave was retired, but sarcasm is a life-long addiction. Seth was a bundle of enthusiasm and energy—two of the things that Dave's retirement seemed to be leaking like helium from an old party balloon. It was hard not to dislike the guy right off, but then Dave had always looked up to Will Rogers who famously said: *"I joked about every prominent man of my time, but I never met a man I didn't like."* Regardless, Seth Lowenstein was pushing the limits.

"Not my band," Seth said, only mildly exasperated. "Your band, the Rock Bottom Remainders! My God, Dave, it's perfect. And don't tell me that you don't know that Kathi would have been all over this rescue. You're going to organize a concert in her honor, and dammit, don't give me that "we're all old now" shit, or I swear I'll call Keith Richards right now!" He waved his cellphone for emphasis.

Dave Bartlett just shook his head and smiled that smile Sherman always belittled. It was not just his best smile; it was his only smile. That boy-next-door smile had always worked well for him, and so he worked it, just like Jennifer Aniston worked her girl-next-door persona. It was profoundly comfortable too, in a '65 Mustang bucket seats kind of way. It suited him. Yes, his brother's late wife, Kathi, had created the classic rock band made up entirely of writers, but they were all older now, and hell, Stephen King had been run over by truck. Amy Tan, Scott Turrow, Roy Blount, Jr., they all had busy careers. Even so, would they come? Could the Rock Bottom Remainders come out of retirement—again. Hell, yes! But, the humorist couldn't help wondering whether Lowenstein was bluffing. Was it even remotely possible that the wiry little man really had Keith Richards on speed dial?

★ ★ ★

Sherman Kanz's marching orders came next. His beagle, Hemingway, settled his chin on Seth's foot the minute the human sank down on the sofa. He was disappointed that sneakers had replaced the aromatic leather knee boots from their Miami Boardwalk introduction, but humans were very odd and unpredictable about the wide variety of stuff they decorated their bodies with. This human could be forgiven because, for reasons Hemingway couldn't explain, the man made him feel safe and secure. His human, however, was less than pleased by the other's arrival.

"Clowns?" Sherman said. "You're putting me in charge of clowns?"

"You know people," Seth said, "and your big assignment is the articles you're going to write, but somebody's got to send in the clowns."

"If there was ever a job for Dave Bartlett," Sherman began.

"Oh, stop it," Seth laughed. "He's got an assignment already, and besides, he's going to be here at the band stand, and you're going to be here by the Rad-Corp entrance doors." Seth pointed to the situation mock-up he'd built on Sherman's poker table. There were cereal and cracker boxes for buildings, strips of newspaper for the streets, and a green rubber dish drain for Bayfront Park.

"The clowns are totally wasted unless you make absolutely sure that they are right here, at exactly the right moment. This assignment is of strategic importance, Sherman. Do you really think Dave Bartlett is a better man for this than job you are?"

"Jesus, Mary, and Joseph, Seth," Sherman sighed, "You and Dave must be related. You both have the crazy bullshit gene."

★ ★ ★

Unlike Sherman Kanz, Benny Lopez had been involved back when Mac's late father had tried to destroy John Ghostwalker's Sky Mall at the New World Center in Miami Beach just over a year ago. He'd watched Seth out-finagle the Baltimore mobster sent to Miami to straighten out Mac and reacquire the money her mom had skimmed off her dad's dirty mob deals. Benny knew an operator when he met one. Thank God Seth was one of the good guys. Yes, his assignment was as obscure as it was absurd, but when somebody like Seth Lowenstein asks you to put together a volunteer painting crew (something he obviously knows you already have), you ask what color paint he wants.

"I think robin's egg, no wait, sky blue," Seth laughed. "Yes, sky blue would be perfect!"

Benny knew a number of ex-Navy SEALs. His cousin, Emilio, had served proudly. But Benny had never watched an ex-Navy SEAL clap with such delightful abandon. He knew that there must be other gay Navy SEALs, but it was hard to imagine any who were as comfortable with who they were as Seth Lowenstein. "That," Benny thought, "demonstrates a whole other level of courage."

★ ★ ★

Dan Stone's assignment began with a journey back to the home of his favorite person in the world. It was her loving attention, in great part, that pulled the alcohol-addicted and Agent Orange-poisoned Vietnam vet out of his deep and longstanding depression. Dan's return to humanity began with John Ghostwalker, a blond-haired abandoned baby boy, adopted by the Miccosukee tribe, who turned out to be the son Dan never knew he had. But if it were not for Grandmother Renee, the great transformation in both of their lives might never have come. He and John were still amazed that the elderly woman had secretly done DNA testing and figured it all out, but Grandmother Renee was a force of nature, and her love knew no bounds.

"Seth Lowenstein sent me to you, Grandmother," Dan Stone said as he kissed Grandmother Renee on the head and lowered himself into the rocking chair next to her. "But first, how are you?"

"I am well, child. And always glad to see one of my children. Is Seth here in Florida again?" Grandmother Renee's cottage sat on Miccosukee Reservation land in the Everglades west of Miami. She had no living kin as far as anyone on the rez was aware, but she was everyone's grandmother just the same. When folks gathered for official affairs, the tribe's casino served well enough, but when matters were personal and important, folk gathered in her tiny living room.

"He was, but I just dropped him off at the airport. He'll be back in a couple of days, and he said he'd see you then."

"If Seth is here again," she said with a slight shake of her head, "something serious needs fixing, doesn't it?" Grandmother Renee's easy chair sat facing the old TV set, and she smiled at the Milky Way Bar Dan had discreetly placed on the lamp table beside her.

"Well, yes," Dan said. "And this assignment he's asked you and me to take on has to be a secret between just us for now. The whole poker group is working together on a rather bizarre rescue, but you know Seth. He's all about the little details, and this particular detail he wants kept within as small a group of folks as possible. To tell you the truth, it even scares me, but we have to trust someone. Seth told me you would know best who to ask."

"Then it must be important," Grandmother Renee said firmly. "What are we supposed to do?"

"Seth thinks that if the rescue comes off OK, the folks who get out will need to hide somewhere safe, away from downtown Miami. And I reckon there will be some very smart children—somewhere between 8 and 200--who are going to need a grandmother." The heels of Dan's cowboy boots dug into the round woven throw rug, and he rocked the old chair with determination.

"That sounds easy enough, Daniel," Grandmother Renee said. "This isn't my first rodeo, you know."

"No, it's not, Grandmother, but you've not seen this particular bull before—and it's as big and mean as they come."

"In that case," she winked, "we shall ride, boldly ride!"

Chapter Twenty-Eight

In a window seat, on a plane to Minnesota, Seth faced the only enemy he was afraid of. He loved strategic planning. He performed best when the conditions and the odds were worst. But the waiting was an enemy that could not be vanquished, only endured. He'd gone over the plan, briefed his team, and gathered enough evidence to either convince the Congressman to help, or to convince someone up the command chain to make them both disappear. He trusted that when he had last spoken to the young politician, there was a depth of integrity in the man. But it was historically documented that a few years in Washington had a way of corroding away a well-intended politician's early character traits. What remained of that young, earnest, progressive Democrat who successfully had run for a seat in United States House of Representatives? Only time would tell.

Regardless of what style of barbeque a person might favor, one joint in Minnesota's fifth Congressional District claimed that they could serve it up. Shorty's Ribs was a local legend. It sat proudly on one of the shabbiest street corners in Minneapolis. When Seth arrived, Shorty met him at the door, unlocked it, and ushered him in.

"I shoulda figured it was you," he said as he relocked the front door and pointed Seth to the back room. "Even as a punk-ass kid, you always liked that cloak and dagger shit. He's back there, and you both better be outta here before my lunch crowd starts arrivin'. I ain't lockin' out my regulars for the likes of you two thugs!"

"Message received, Shorty," Seth said as he hugged the old man. "Loud and clear." He knew perfectly well that Shorty would defend their privacy with his life, customers be damned.

The back room at Shorty's hadn't changed since Seth was the little kid Shorty Johnson had befriended. Back then, Seth was often the only white face for five blocks in any direction. His neighborhood, the next one over, wasn't much better off, but any job was easier to get with white skin. And Seth's dad wanted his sister and him to understand what that meant. "Until there is freedom and justice for all," his old man said often, "there is no freedom or justice." Seth always thought his dad made that up until the first time the old men invited him into the back room at Shorty's where it was hand-painted on the old tongue and groove pine wall boards.

Seth's father had walked his family to Shorty's every weekend, and every weekend Shorty asked Izzy Lowenstein the same question: "Izzy? You gonna try some of my barbeque kosher pork ribs today?" Seth's dad always laughed, shook Shorty's hand with gusto, and said: "Shorty, if God ever came in here and smelled your ribs, he'd convert to Christianity!" No sooner would the Lowenstein family be settled in at their table, then Shorty's late wife, Maybelle, would bring in a platter of beef brisket, a bowl of greens (cooked with ox tail instead of pig's knuckles), and a big basket of French fries.

Seth was smiling at the smells and the memories when he walked in off the restaurant floor and saw that the old message was still on the wall, right behind the distinguished gentleman from Minnesota.

"A clandestine meeting at Shorty's is nothing new for us," said the man at the old table, pointing to the food between them. "Sit down and dig in."

"How are you, Kicks?" Seth said as he sat. His boyhood friend got that nickname after buying a high-dollar pair of sneakers with his first real paycheck. They were stolen within the week.

"I'm good, Seth," the tall man said. "I can actually afford a new pair now, but I've learned enough about life not to flaunt that anymore. Hell of a thing."

"Most of the important lessons are like that," Seth said, taking up a barbeque chicken wing. "I've got to show you something bad, and I wanted to do it in person. If it's not our government behind this, then it's just a really bad thing, and I hope you'll know how to deal with it. If it is our people behind this, you won't thank me for involving you, but hell, I don't have anywhere else to go with this. If you say 'no' and walk away, no harm, no foul. You feel me?"

"Yeah, I hear you, Seth. As long as they don't make me take you out, I'm good. Let's see what you've got."

The lunch crowd at Shorty's Ribs came and went, but nobody bothered the two old friends in the back room. Seth went through his PowerPoint presentation step-by-step. He presented everything he'd learned so far about Rad-Corp, every snapshot he'd stolen off the security camera feeds, and the names and backgrounds of dozens of employees who, as far as the outside world could tell, had simply fallen off the grid.

"All of their stories are the same. No immediate family, no significant others, and very high technical and/or military skills. The only thing they do once they begin work at Rad-Corp is whatever they're told to do. Well, that and killer bees," Seth added, looking to see if he was having any impact, and whether there was any sign his friend already knew."

"Killer bees?"

"Yes," Seth said. "Apparently, they're the next big thing in drone technology and crowd control. Watch this." He played the final video for the Representative of Minnesota's 5th Congressional District and watched as his boyhood friend sank back into his chair, the light in his eyes nearly draining away.

Long after the video ended, they sat looking at each other in silence.

"Not exactly why I went to law school, or why you joined the Navy, eh, Seth?"

"Not exactly."

"How are you involved here, Seth? If I'm going to stick my neck out, I have to know."

"I've agreed to help a reporter rescue one of the engineers. She wants to put a stop to it all. She thought her technology was going to be used to help people until her boss showed off that video."

"A reporter? A real one?"

"A Pulitzer Prize winning reporter."

"Really?"

"Yeah, really."

"And you have a plan?"

"Don't I always?"

"Can I have a copy of that presentation?"

Seth handed over an SD card and got to his feet. "It think I'd rather storm Rad-Corp in my skivvies than take that to Washington."

"You and me both. I thought I had it bad when they bussed me all over the Middle East as the good Muslim boy who swore his congressional oath of office on a Koran. Only Allah knows what I'll get for this."

"Be strong, my brother. God is great," Seth said as he embraced his old friend. "They can only kill us once."

"Sure, Seth, but inside the beltway, sometimes that looks like your best possible outcome. How much time can you give me?"

"My guys have got to move soon," Seth answered. "Rad-Corp was already suspicious of the lady before I started smuggling data off her computer. A week or two, maybe?"

"I'll see what I can do. You watch your back."

"I will, Kicks. You too."

In a window seat, on the plane back to Miami, Seth wondered if he'd done the right thing. "Kicks" had never been easy to read. What was left of the boy he'd shot hoops with, not to mention the progressive Democrat who had decided to run for a seat in the United States House of Representatives? Only time would tell.

Chapter Twenty-Nine

Benny was sure the assignment Seth gave him was going to be interesting. When his wife Mary came back from her stroll around the various vendors in the kiosk mall (arranged neatly among the huge concrete stilts under the Rad-Corp building), things went from interesting to strange. The question she had innocently asked a number of the vendors seemed simple and straight-forward: "Who leases out the spaces here?" Leasing spots for kiosks and food trucks was big business in Miami, and leasing agencies were usually easy to find—just follow the long lines of folks wanting a space to peddle their wares. But this situation was clearly different, the kind of different no one wanted to talk about.

"People got very uncomfortable when I asked anything about the logistics of leasing a space," Mary said after she walked back down Biscayne Boulevard and around the corner to where Benny's white van was parked in front of the old Grand Flamingo Hotel. She handed Benny the fruit smoothie and other goodies she'd purchased. "At first I thought they were put off thinking I might want one of their spots, but they act more afraid, like illegal immigrants, but they all have Miami permits on display. Here, I'll write down a couple I memorized. Maybe we can check back with public records at the city. Shouldn't there be a location or at least an area associated with those permits?"

"I have no idea, Mary," Benny said. "It can't hurt to ask somebody how it works, but maybe not the city. Getting folks kicked out of there would only make things worse for us. What about that lady in Little Havana with the trailer kitchenette thing? We see her all over the place, at festivals, construction sites, and street fairs. Haven't you talked to her a few times?"

"Louisa, yes! That's a great idea, Benny. Let's go track her down."

When they finally spotted Louisa's food truck, they stopped to learn what they could. Fortunately, Louisa remembered Mary, and Benny watched from the van as the women chatted as hungry customers came and went. On the drive home Mary filled him in. As it turned out, the kiosk mall under Rad-Corp was the best kept secret in Miami.

"The kiosk mall started after the building was renovated in the '90s," Mary said, "Louisa told me that a pushcart pretzel guy named 'Bronx Billy' used to work the Bayfront Park. As long as he never set up anywhere, nobody official bothered him. He was something of a food vendor legend, but he was getting too old to push his heavy cart all day. So, according to Louisa, when the construction crews cleared out, he wheeled over under Rad-Corp, knocked on the doors there, and asked the guards inside if he could stay there out of the sun with his cart. They said 'sure,' even bought pretzels and canned drinks from him." Mary smiled.

"Just like that?" Benny said, laughing as he slurped the last of his smoothie.

"Just like that," Mary said. "Pretty soon old Billy was selling hot dogs too, and as more black vans brought more employees to work there, he started renting spaces to other venders he knew. He sold his cart and retired after five very good years, and now everybody manages their own space, and keeps very quiet about it until they want to retire. If a family member doesn't want to pay you monthly for your spot, there's an auction. If you're lucky enough to get to participate in one of those, the winning bids go for over a million dollars—most of it paid out monthly, of course."

"Mother of God," Benny said. "Miami never ceases to amaze me. The things people do to make a living. Who would've guessed?"

"So what are you going to do?" Mary asked as they pulled up in front of their apartment building.

"Just what old Bronx Billy did. I'm gonna act like I own the place, and just start painting all that gray concrete a fabulous sky blue. I may even throw in some clouds just for fun. Hey! What about trees? Those huge stilt columns could be tree trunks!"

★ ★ ★

Benny's office was an old janitor's closet off the loading dock of a major Miami mattress company. His desk and shelving units were scrap lumber laid out across hundreds of stacked up paint cans. The donated paint came from all over North and South America, and the printing on those cans might be in any one of four languages. The office and adjacent loading bay were donated to Filling Empty Houses, Inc. by Benny's friend, Ted Connors. Ted's alter ego, "the Sultan of Snooze," was a well-recognized fixture on Miami's various media outlets, and he served with Benny on several non-profit boards. The workers on Benny's mattress restoration, building fix-up, and paint crews were all local volunteers, and whenever he gathered them for a meeting to announce a new community project, he was always astounded at the turnout.

"Thanks for coming," he said as over 200 people crowded into the loading bay workshop. "This project is different than anything we've ever done before. It has nothing to do with putting folks in houses, so if you can't find the time, that's cool. No one's going to call you out. This is a paint project, a tricky one, and we'll be working in shifts, like always, but we're going to be rigging drop cloths up in the air instead of on the floor. You'll be pairing up for this, and taking turns working the paint rollers and holding the ladder. We're painting the walls and ceiling of that kiosk mall where we sometimes get lunch around the corner from the Grand Flamingo Hotel. And we're going to be painting while the folks below are open and serving customers, so neatness and polite consideration count more than usual."

His faithful flock looked at one another and laughed. Nobody was ever allowed to be messy or rude on one of Benny's jobs, even if there wasn't a civilian within a block.

"I know, I know," Benny laughed along, "what's new about that? Well, there are two new things you need to know before you sign on. First, this is more unauthorized than usual, so keep quiet about it. Anybody asks you about anything, call me immediately. I'll handle it. Second, this is a mandatory hard hats and jump suits worksite—no exceptions. Yes, I know," Benny said over the murmurs of displeasure, "they're hot and heavy, but we'll be in the shade all day, so suck it up! Shift one is 7:00 a.m. to 2:00 p.m., and shift two ends at 9:00 p.m. If you can only work part of a shift, that's cool. There's plenty of work for everybody. We can't park on Biscayne Boulevard, so we'll form up around the corner at the old hotel. Shift one meets there tomorrow morning. If you need a ride, meet me here a half hour before. Any questions?"

When the queries were all asked and answered, and everyone but the morning mattress restoration crew had drifted out, Ted Conners followed Benny into the office and parked himself on the paint can bench by the door.

"What the hell are you up to now?" asked the Sultan of Snooze.

"The adventure of a lifetime," Benny answered. "What else would I be doing?"

"I'm just grasping at straws here, but I'm guessing whatever it is you're up to, Benny, won't be run by our fellow board members at Filling Empty Houses, Inc."

"I think it's called plausible deniability, Ted," Benny said with a smile. "And if you want to claim any of it later, this line of questioning probably ought to end here."

"Where's the fun in that?" Ted laughed. "Is this you turning tagger, or did somebody put you up to it?"

"Seth Lowenstein gave me the assignment."

"Oh, hell, this should be good. Tell me everything."

When Benny's story about a rescue wound down, Ted Conners was nodding his head in a conspiratorial way. "It makes sense that someone would want out of there. That's a spooky place, Benny. I've been in there several times. My guys don't like to do deliveries and pickups there at all." Ted worked his hands together and looked at the ground.

"Really? You've been inside? Seth's gonna want to talk to you ASAP. Is that okay?"

"Sure. Imagine working at a factory and living in dormitory room attached to the factory. In this case there are a couple dozen factories, workshops, labs, you know, high tech stuff work on every floor I expect. I've seen three or four of them. When we take a mattress up the elevator, we have to carry it through the shop space to get to the employee's dorm room. And they cover everything in the workshops with tarps so we can't really see anything. A couple of guards stick to us like glue until the old mattress is down the elevator and out the door. We never see anybody but the guards, and sometimes the person who ordered the mattress. Do you know what they do there, Benny?"

"Bad shit, Ted. Very bad shit."

"And you're really going to rescue one of their employees?"

"We're going to try," Benny said. "And, to be totally honest, it could be a few more employees than just the one. She wants to offer her team the chance to run too."

"Then she's crazier than you guys are."

"Yeah, Ted, the vote's pretty much unanimous on that."

"Well," Ted said as he rose from the precarious bench of buckets and headed out the door and back toward his warehouse and showroom, "send Seth over and I'll tell him what I saw there."

Chapter Thirty

NBA star, Chris Tosh had his people call ahead. When he arrived at Miami Fire Station #12, the shift crew crowed around him and Captain Jay O'Connor headed up the welcoming committee himself, pumping Tosh's hand with great enthusiasm. The firehouse was only a few blocks southwest of the American Airlines Arena where the Miami Heat played basketball, and a few blocks northwest of the Rad-Corp building. It was Chris' job to make friends. He was genuinely good at that. After an official tour, and a Q&A that went both ways over lunch, he and the firehouse crew played a pick-up game of basketball for nearly an hour. When he asked if he could come back and hang sometime, they offered him room, board, and his own fire truck.

A couple of days later, Chris walked in unannounced in the middle of a maintenance day. When he saw that everyone was busy with assigned tasks, he grabbed up a sponge and joined in with a team washing one of the fire trucks.

"You don't have to do that!" the captain said quickly.

"You said I could hang out and learn what it means to be a fire fighter," Tosh said, gesturing around the fire station with his soapy sponge, "so let's call this Lesson One."

Everybody laughed, and for the next couple of hours, Chris tried his hand at every task, and picked their brains along the way.

"So, if a call comes in," he said, "like right now, who does what?"

They took enthusiastic turns talking him through the process, explaining who cleared away the various gear, who suited up first, and how long it generally took for each vehicle called for to roll out.

"No kidding?" Chris said. "You can suit up and go that fast?"

While the men and women assured him they could, the captain slipped into the office and whispered in dispatcher's ear. Seconds later, alarms sounded and instructions came through the P.A. speakers overhead. Before Tosh could even acclimate to the startling noise, everybody was suddenly somewhere else, the huge doors were rolling upwards, and by twos and threes, suited-up squad members jumped into and onto the various vehicles. By the time Chris had spun around twice to take it all in, the first truck was headed toward the street with it lights and sirens going full bore. Within a few minutes from the initial alarm sound, the final vehicle had pulled away, and Tosh stood alone in the middle of the station's empty bays.

"Not bad," the captain said walking up behind him with a stopwatch. "They were showing off for you, but that's about their average time. I'm proud of this house for good reason."

"I can see that," Chris said. "I didn't recognize that address. How bad is the fire?"

"It's a vacant lot," the captain laughed, "and unless some homeless guy's hauled a fire barrel in there for him and his buddies since I drove by this morning, there's nothing there to burn."

"So it's a drill, and they don't know until they get there?"

"The sharp ones would have figured it out before they got their gear on," the captain answered. "They're all supposed to know our turf like the back of their hand, especially the engine and ambulance drivers, but it takes the newbies awhile longer to learn the hood."

"Well I'm impressed," Chris said.

"Seconds count," the captain said shaking his head, "and everybody in this house knows what it feels like when our best wasn't fast enough to save some fellow Miamian's life."

"Oh shit," Chris said, his eyes wide, "I never thought about living with that every day. You guys really do rock. And thank you." He shook the captain's hand with all the enthusiasm he had been given on his first visit.

On his next visit, by way of thanks, Chris invited the captain to join him for a Cuban coffee at his favorite nearby hideaway.

"I'd like to walk on a day like this, Captain Jay," Tosh said, "but we might be approached by Heat fans. Would that be too distracting?"

"No," the captain said, "but I've got a better idea. Hey, Carson! Have you got a spare uniform in your locker?"

"Of course," answered the tall young firefighter.

"Well, loan it to Chris so we can sneak out for walk. Your cap too."

"Yes sir!"

Moments later, the two men strolled down to Biscayne Boulevard, turned south, and headed for the kiosk mall.

"Okay," the captain said, "what's really on your mind?"

"It's that obvious?"

"I'm a coach too, in my own profession, and I've seen a lot of young men and women with something on their minds."

"Well, you're spot on, and I do want to ask you for help, but it's an awkward situation, dangerous maybe, and could get you in trouble if something goes wrong. I won't mind if you say no, but if you tell anyone, at least one lady's life will be in more danger."

Chris ordered two Cuban coffees and led the captain to a table where they could just see the metal Rad-Corp doors.

"Don't be obvious about looking," he said, "but how much do you know about those doors and this building?"

The captain laughed and said: "I knew that someday something bad was going to happen here, and somebody was going to ask me questions about this place, but I damn-sure never thought it would be Chris Tosh. I was waiting for more guys in black suits."

"More guys? Guys in black suits already talked to you?"

"Whenever this building was put up, and the time came for our normal new structure inspection tour and emergency protocol mapping, these governmental-looking guys pulled up to the firehouse in a black van, marched me into my own office, and fed me a bunch of top-secret gobble-dee-gook about everything being handled in-house, so inspections could not happen and our services 'would not be required.' Why are you interested in that place?"

Chris wasn't sure what to say, but deep in his heart he trusted Captain Jay. "There's a really smart lady works in there, Captain, and she wants out, except they're not keen on letting folks go once they hire them. My friends and I, well, we sort of agreed to help her. It's a long story I probably shouldn't share at this point, but we thought you might have a code or something to get us in."

"Normally, I would. These friends of yours, would I have heard of them too, or are you the only celebrity hero?"

"Some of them, yeah, you'd have heard of them," Chris said sheepishly. "It all sounds crazy, I know, but I really did grow up thinking you guys were heroes, and it just made sense that you'd know how to get in. There are no architectural drawings on file anywhere, and nobody seems to know, or want to talk about, why that is."

"Well, considering the guys who came in my stationhouse to put me off, that's little wonder, is it?"

"No it's not." Tosh looked up and met the captain's eyes.

"So, what are you going to do, Chris?"

"Whatever I can to help. Fortunately for that lady and her friends, I'm the beauty, not the brains, behind this rescue."

"She has friends who want out too?" the captain said.

"That's what they tell me," Chris said with a shrug. "I hope Seth's as good as they say he is."

"And Seth would be the leader of your merry band of superheroes?"

"Yeah," Chris said. "He's an ex-Navy SEAL."

"I was a firefighter on an aircraft carrier, Chris. I'm Navy to the core, so you bring this Seth by to see me. If I think he's any good, my team will plan a training drill, and we'll get you in those doors. But if this rescue goes south, you're paying to replace the doors when we're done using the jaws-of-life on them. Fair enough?"

Chris practically bounced to his feet. "Yes! Thank you, Captain! Now we have a shot."

They wandered out to Biscayne Bay the long way, avoiding the roving security camera, and neither said much on the way back to the station house.

Chapter Thirty-One

Mac and John bought the decrepit Alden classic sailing ship for less than what Grandmother Renee might call "a song." John had watched in awe as Mac handled complicated social interactions in the past, but her horse trading skills suggested this purchase wasn't her first go 'round with an experienced huckster. After laughing at the well-dressed broker several times, and walking away several more, it became clear to everyone that the salesperson was putty in her hands. Every time he tried to stand firm, Mac asked a dozen new questions about missing hardware, teak accent pieces, and rotten sailcloth.

"If I wanted a well-cared for Rena-77," Mac said, about to walk off a fourth time, "trust me, I can afford it. But we want a project boat to rebuild together, and everything about this piece-of-shit boat fits that bill—except what you think an experienced sailor would pay for it. Perhaps a survey would convince you that I know what I'm looking at?"

John had studied the concepts of land survey while getting his Masters in Architectural Design at Georgia Tech, but he didn't have a clue what the word meant in the world of sailboats. But by the look in the broker's eyes as they headed back toward the car, he certainly did. And he wanted no part of it.

"No, no, that won't be necessary," the broker called after them. "I surrender. The truth is, the boss told me to sell it or sink it. Sinking it costs time and money."

"How about this?" Mac said. "You convince your boss to donate the boat—with a good set of spare sails off some other boat or boats in your inventory—to Personal Space, Inc., a non-profit corporation helping the homeless here in Miami, and he can grab a hefty tax write-off for any amount he wants. Just tell him I said the deal is contingent on your getting ten percent of the tax write-off as a bonus for hooking him up."

The broker shook his head in awe, turned to John, and said: "No wonder you don't say anything." The salesman was chuckling as he walked back toward the office.

"What's a survey?" John asked when the broker disappeared.

"It's like having a home inspection before the bank will loan you money," Mac laughed. "The surveyor finds and officially documents every flaw, including some that would land a shady boat broker in hot water."

"So they're just going to give us the boat Seth sent us here to buy?"

"You do pay attention sometimes," Mac said as she kissed John on the cheek. "Yes they are—and some passible sails, I hope."

John looked back at the boat, his brows lowering and his forehead forming wrinkles of disbelief. "We're going to sail this wreck? I don't know anything beyond what you've taught me, and that's mostly about how to live on a sailboat and how to scrape the barnacles off the hull, but from what I think I see here, we'll be lucky if this boat even floats. I mean, Mac, I can see through the cracks in between the bottom boards. If I step closer, I suspect I could look in through this side and out through the far side. That can't be good."

"Well, as a matter of fact, those cracks are a good thing, and tomorrow you're going to learn why."

"Fiberglass!" John said, lighting up at his clever insight. "The fiberglass epoxy resin flows in between hull boards and the glass fiber sheets stick to the hull better, right?"

"Oh, John," Mac said shaking her head sadly. "You mean well, but sometimes you can be a hazard to yourself and to others. No one in their right mind would glass over a classic wooden hull like this. Don't you remember what Seth said about restoring this amazing ketch?"

"Okay, wait!" John said, holding up his hand. "A minute ago it was 'a piece of shit,' and now it's an amazing and classic catch? How is that possible?"

"Tonight over supper, I will teach you the difference between a sloop, a ketch, and a catch, but for the moment, perhaps the broker was right," Mac smiled as she pointed towards the returning salesman. "It's probably better if you don't talk."

Mac signed all the papers, handed John the title with a wicked little grin just for him, and told the delighted salesman that they'd be back in the morning to prep it for launch.

★ ★ ★

The next morning, after filling his rental car with items on his honey-do-list from Mac, John arrived at the brokerage marina to find that Seth and Mac had a team of a dozen workers drinking coffee and eating pastries while they outlined the day's objectives. Benny had texted him that, for some of the workers he'd sent over, this boat project would be the first real paycheck they had ever earned using the skills they'd learned through volunteering for Filling Empty Houses, Inc. That felt good. And the entire board at John and Mac's pet non-profit project, Personal Space, Inc., had voted enthusiastically for the idea of refurbishing the old sailboat's hull and then donating the old yacht to the Grand Flamingo Hotel restoration project. Everyone was delighted that Sherman Kanz's articles in the *Miami Herald* had spurred public support and ultimately led to the new resort management's change of heart. Of course, Seth and Mac hadn't told the board members anything about their plan to set the boat on fire. That was "highly classified, need-to-know information," at least according to Seth.

John nodded good morning, and set his first arm-load of boat fixing supplies on the plywood and saw-horse work table next to the dilapidated sailboat. The old boat seemed, from a distance, to float a foot above the ground, but it was held upright by a series of support braces. As he headed back to the car for another load, John heard a voice coming up behind him.

"Hello, Mr. Ghostwalker," said the young Latino boy who ran up beside him. "I'm Hector Nuneo, and Miss Mac said I was your assistant gooper. What is a gooper anyway?"

"Hi, Hector," John said as he laughed and stuck out his hand. "Call me John. Mac said something about me being a gooper yesterday, but while I don't have any idea what that means either, I'm pretty sure it's going to be hot and messy. Are you up for that?"

"You bet! Will this boat really float?"

John laughed again. "I asked the same question yesterday, Hector, and Mac assured me that if I didn't screw up the gooping, it would be floating by tonight."

"So, wow, our job must be important! I hope we don't screw up."

"Me too," John said, handing Hector an armload of papery disposable coveralls from the car's backseat.

Between the two of them, they nearly covered the empty areas on the plywood table with palm sanders, sandpaper, extension cords, several whisk brooms, a hand-held vacuum, putty knives, hammers, and wide-faced chisel-like tools. Then came cans of primer, paint, putty, linseed oil, turpentine, and pine tar. The last load contained a variety of paint brushes, a few empty plastic pails, and large balls of what looked like narrow cotton bandaging from a World War I museum.

"Sanders, chinkers, and goopers!" Mac yelled out. "Front and center, and suit up!"

"I guess that's us," Hector said, looking up at John who grinned back.

They each donned a set of coveralls. John helped Hector roll up the sleeves and the pant legs so the boy's hands and feet were useable. All around the make-shift table, the three teams were climbing into white coveralls, while Seth began to demonstrate how to mix gray primer into a ball of white putty for the chinking squad. Mac poured linseed oil, pine tar and turpentine into a plastic bucket, next to which sat two paint brushes that John thought looked more like the lovechild of an old-fashioned shaving cream brush and a petite cotton floor mop.

"I'm guessing that's our goop," John said, elbowing the boy.

"Stinks," Hector said, wrinkling up his nose.

"Get used to it, gentlemen," Mac laughed, "because you're going to smell like this for days. Before I start with the sanding team, you gooper guys will each have a bucket of goop and a goop brush, with which you'll swab every inch of the inside of that hull. Put it on thick, and if it gets between the hull planks, that's a good thing."

John and Hector grabbed their mop brushes while Mac started pouring her goop mix into a second plastic pail.

"There's a lot of dust in there," Mac went on, "but fortunately no paint to remove, so your biggest challenge will be access. And Hector, you saved the day. I thought John would be my only tunnel rat, and there are several places he just won't fit. So, that would have meant I would have had to crawl around through the tight spots. I'm so glad you're here to save me. I'll see to it you get a bonus."

"You mean more money, Miss Mac?"

"Yes, sir, I do. Thank you from the bottom of my heart!"

Hector beamed like the hero of the hour, and John gave him a high five as they each took a pail and headed up the ladder leaning against the old boat.

On the outside, Mac and her fellow sanders broke into two squads, and both started at the bow and worked their way aft, one squad to port, and the other to starboard. Close behind them, Seth's team split into four workers per side, each with a different task. The leaders, under his steady guidance, fed the twisted cotton into the chink, or gap, between the first and the second hull boards, playing it out of a plastic bucket they kicked along the ground as they moved aft following the sanding team at a much slower pace.

The person behind them used the strange steel chisels to force the line of cloth further into the crack, careful to stop at the mark on the tool Seth had pointed out to them. "Push past that," he explained, "and you'll just pop the cloth through into the boat."

The third person on each side followed along with a ball of the gray primer-putty mix and used a putty knife to cover the cotton cloth filler. Behind those workers, the last squad member used a putty knife to smooth it all out evenly, so that the hull would look good when painted.

By the time Mary's friend, Louisa, showed up with her food truck and catered lunch, Mac's dusty looking sanding team had finished, created their own balls of primer-infused putty, and were following Seth's teams who had by that time, filled the first two chinks on each side of the sailing yacht. Seth's crews had filled half the third chink on both sides, and Mac's group was close behind on the fourth, when Louisa called out that lunch of grilled chicken, black beans, and rice was ready. Everyone gathered around the plywood table, filled a plate, and found a spot in the shade.

They all looked hot and tired, but no one looked as bedraggled as the goopers. John's and Hector's coveralls were no longer white. Along with a liberal amount of the fragrant goop, they were soaked through with sweat. Neither John nor Hector was surprised that no one seemed to be willing to sit too close to the gooper brigade, but they had come to enjoy one another's company. John was a natural listener and Hector was an idea machine who loved having a grown-up willing to listen to his grand designs.

By mid-afternoon, when the goopers emerged, climbed wearily down the ladder, and set aside their buckets, everyone was working quietly. Even in the late fall and early winter, Miami temperatures can hit the high 80s and low 90s. Everyone was hot and sweaty. For a moment, they all stood transfixed as John and Hector struggled out of their coveralls, placed their valuables on the table, and pulled off their shoes and socks. But when the two sweaty goopers began racing each other down the nearest dock toward the bay, the spell was broken. The rest followed, as fast as their weary arms and legs allowed. The weary workforce ran to the sea like a desperate community of lemmings.

When work resumed, the nearby Mangrove trees were draped with wet clothing. Disposable coveralls hid only damp undergarments, and the mood had elevated significantly. More than a few remarked that they should have thought of the idea much sooner. By 6:00 p.m. when pizza arrived, everyone was painting with either a white hull paint, or an emerald green copper-infused bottom paint that ran from the boat's keel to just above what would be its waterline. Mac had explained that as salt water moved across this special bottom paint, it reacted with the tiny copper particles. This reaction severely inhibited the tiny creatures which John had come to hate—barnacles—from attaching themselves to the hull.

Everyone was so thrilled with the way the old hull looked with its new paint job, they pressed on, paint brush in one hand, and pizza slice in the other. By 7:00 p.m., it was done, an hour earlier than Seth and Mac had estimated.

The brokerage's fork lift driver returned at 9:00 p.m. as promised, and with dock and ramp lights blazing, he set the boat gently in the bay.

"There!" Mac said to John, "I told you she'd float!"

"Yes, you did," he laughed, "and now, I believe you taught me, is when someone wastes a perfectly good bottle of champagne."

"You're learning so much, my love," Mac laughed, but fear not, I brought plenty for everyone. Seth! I think the honor goes to you for this craziness."

Mac opened a nearby cooler, pulled out one of several bottles with lots of crinkled gold foil around the neck, and handed it to Seth. He was beaming like a proud father.

"Thank you, Mac, and everyone else. You've done so many cool things today, and over the next week or so, you'll see what your efforts mean to a lot of different people. But, and there's always a but, I still need you. Please keep helping Benny with his paint project if you can. We're on a deadline over there. Okay, enough. Time for the magic words. I christen you this day '*The Phoenix*,' in honor of second chances and new beginnings for all who might need to rise up from the ashes and claim them!"

The bottle broke, the small crowd cheered, and there were plastic champagne glasses for everyone—even Hector, though its contents were heavily cut with Sprite.

Chapter Thirty-Two

Rosie didn't fly Podrick every night. At least she swore that she wouldn't. But Podrick gave her a different taste of freedom than anything she'd experienced in years. "I was good," she told herself when she woke up from dreams about two men staring across a table at each other and of herself sailing away on a beautiful sailboat. "I didn't fly last night." As her memory of the dreams faded, and she wondered who or what the two men stood for, she recalled the flashing vision of a man standing under tree branches, looking up at her. "That must be Sherman," she thought. "He seems very focused on that old hotel lately." Rosie read Phillip's copy of the *Miami Herald* at lunch sometimes as Phillip sat eating quietly across the cafeteria table.

"If I took a quick flight before I go to breakfast, that wouldn't be breaking my promise." She reasoned this out while stretching, getting out of bed, and heading for the bathroom. Rosie stared at the pile of books now on the lid of the toilet tank. "It would only take a couple of minutes to set up and go."

The romantic Free Bird side of her newly evolving self-image longed for the freedom outside soaring always brought with it. On the other hand, the intelligent woman-of-a-certain-age knew that the Wild Tamarind pods were mostly gone from tree and ground. With each passing day, Podrick would have less synchronicity with the neighborhood when she flew him. He would stand out because the wind was no longer carrying pods up and over Biscayne Boulevard throughout the day. She had no urgent task, no assignment to spy out something important—just a longing for the little grove of trees, a sense of loss now that Sherman's infrequent greetings came like texts on Seth's pop-up window on her laptop, and an inexplicable curiosity about the redheaded woman and her beautiful white-and-blue sailboat.

It occurred to Rosie that perhaps the redhead's sailboat was an itch she could scratch without needlessly exposing her drone to unwanted notice. She lifted the books into the tub, grabbed the binoculars from the back of the bathroom door, and climbed up on her perch. She focused in on the distant marina, and sure enough, not only could she see the sloop with the dark blue sail bag on its boom, she could see the redhead and a tall male companion with a long blond ponytail on the deck. They were casting off the lines, and, with the redhead at the wheel, the couple backed the beautiful boat out of its slip, turned the bow north, and motored out of sight behind the Bayside Marketplace building. Something about seeing the boat leave felt sad. As she got ready for breakfast, Rosie hoped it would return.

Rosie's day wore on. There were two things that she could not ignore. First, her team had both gelled and blossomed. The banter was more frequent and more friendly. As a byproduct, they had clearly adopted her. Rosie couldn't make a specific list of the reasons why she knew this, but she just knew it to be true. The second thing that was irrefutable to her was that Phillip was trying to bond with his department members too. He was less distracted, more interactive, and most definitely keeping a closer eye on everything. She had given more than a little thought to what felt like a shift in his level of interest in her.

Quite naturally, she chided herself for wondering why his attentiveness suddenly felt less like that of a man pursuing a woman, and more like a big brother watching out for a sibling. "What am I now," Rosie thought, "back in junior high school, wondering if a boy likes me? But if one date has that effect on a possible suitor, well, I shouldn't wonder why I'm single—except that I usually don't get asked on a first date at all. This is just too silly, and I'm wasting time on nothing." Rosie forced herself to pay attention to the reports on her desk, and nearly fell backwards in her office chair when Seth's pop-up window appeared.

"Hello Rosemary!" the scrolling text said. "Our Trojan Tunnel Ponies are working! I can do this on almost any Rad-Corp computer now, individually or all at once. You did good!"

As the window disappeared, Rosie couldn't help glancing at the wall behind her, the wall separating her office from her apartment. Intellectually she knew there were no cameras mounted there, but the glance to be sure was instinctual. When she turned back to her desk, the pop-up popped up again.

"OBTW, we can see through all the security cameras now too. You rock! You can talk safely in your apartment. Traced all the mics. Get ready."

Rosie typed "When?" as fast as she could, but Seth was gone.

Without looking up, she saw movement coming her way. What must her face have looked like? How would she explain her behavior? As the shadow reached her office door, Rosie switched files on her screen.

"Are you okay?" Phillip said as he stopped at her desk and leaned toward her screen. "Bad news?"

"More order mix-ups," Rosie blurted too quickly as she looked up. "We just got crossed wires and the mistakes seem to have compounded in the back and forth correspondence. Nothing fatal."

"Does it have something to do we our being late paying them? I was told we'd fixed that."

"I don't think so," Rosie said, "at least nobody's referenced that. Just a run of parts errors. Something could have been shelved right next to the ones we needed and the order-filler got confused, or maybe something got put back in the wrong bin, and then grabbed for our order. Who knows?"

Phillip watched quietly as Rosie filled out the order form on her screen. She was afraid to look up. For over a week she'd been orchestrating minor parts switches that no one was likely to recognize, but which would set back the A-4 Stinger drones chances of success. She saw this as an important parting shot, regardless of how her rescue worked out. She might go down, but she'd go down fighting.

"You are the little engine that could," Phillip said as he turned for the door. They don't stand a chance."

Rosie grinned at Phillip's back. "At least I'd like to think so," she said under her breath.

At lunch, around the same round table that her team seemed to have claimed as their own, Rosie threw out a suggestion before Phillip arrived: "Anybody interested in game night? I used to play spades and a little poker, but I'm a quick learner if you have games you guys like."

"Sure!" Barry Cole, laughed. "I haven't played cards in forever!"

"Where?" Linda Ulrich asked. "The rec floor?"

"I was thinking my apartment, maybe?" Rosie said. "But it would have to be BYOC."

"I don't share my chocolate with just anyone," Peter Bloom said grinning.

"I think she meant chips, like poker chips," Patty Jenkins added. "What will we use for chips?"

"Parts!" Lou Garcia said. "Mother boards, ten bucks, servos are five bucks, big capacitors are a buck, and those little yellow ones can be a quarter."

"Not a bad idea, Lou," Peter said, patting him on the shoulder, "but I don't think Rosemary's 'C' stood for any of those things. Think a bit more practically. Could any of us sit everybody at the table in our apartments? My real guess is the 'C' is for chair."

Rosie's pointer finger was on her nose when their faces turned her way, and everybody laughed. "But," she added, "let's keep this party just amongst us. Any objections?"

After a full second's pause, her team nodded in unison. The idea of inviting Phillip Crowe hadn't occurred to them until Rosie made this request, but when it did, the response was universal.

Chapter Thirty-Three

When the tribal officials of the Miccosukee Nation meet to manage the affairs of the people, there are fine guest rooms, grand conference tables, and comfortable leather executive chairs at the tribe's hotel and casino at the intersection of Chrome Avenue and the Tamiami Trail just west of Miami.

On this day, however, the most prestigious leaders of the Miccosukee tribal council sat shoulder-to-shoulder on the floor, looking up expectantly at an old woman in an ancient cozy chair. On the lamp table next to the cozy chair, there was a disheveled stack of Milky Way bars that looked ready to topple towards the tall member in an adjacent rocking chair. His name was Dan Stone, and he was not an official tribal leader. He had tried, repeatedly, to give away his seat to any of the council members, but there had been no takers. So, he rocked carefully, one eye sliding frequently toward the teetering tower of Milky Way bars.

"It is simply not possible, Grandmother," said the heavy-set man squeezed into a corner of the small living room where the tall lampstand just behind him held a shiny silk lampshade over his head like the conductor helmet ominously suspended in old black & white pictures of "Sparky," Florida's infamous antique electric chair. "Reservations at the casino hotel have been booked well in advance, and the revenue involved is significant."

He spoke in a way Dan Stone thought a man might speak if he were actually strapped into Sparky, desperately hoping the governor of Florida would be calling any second to avert his impending doom.

"Then you must unbook them," Grandmother Renee said calmly. "Either that, or you must be willing to give these refugees sanctuary in your own homes."

"For how long?" asked a man on the floor near what had been called an entertainment center in the '70s. The TV volume was muted, but Oprah Winfrey gesticulated enthusiastically just above the man's head.

Over the past hour, Dan had marveled at the various visual, mystical, and metaphorical ironies throughout the small room. These were his official council members, some older and some younger than himself. Two had served in Vietnam when he did, two had served in the various desert wars, and all were successful in business affairs. Well, he thought looking at old Joe "Walking Fish" Lamont, that one's retired, but he did well enough too. Joe was the only one who might actually be close to Grandmother Renee's age, and his placid silence had said more than all the uneasy questions of the rest.

"We do not know how many," Grandmother Renee said, "perhaps only a few, but potentially many more. May I tell you a story?"

This change of direction took most of the men by surprise, but Dan noticed a sly smile turn at the corner of Joe Lamont's mouth. No one in the tribe would refuse the offer of an elder's story—especially if the offering came from Grandmother Renee.

While everyone nodded respectful assent, Dan continued to glance at old Joe. Nearly every child in the tribe had known from birth that Joe Walking Fish would come for them one night. And not one of them forgot the dark and rainy evening when old Joe Walking Fish had shown up at their house. Their parents had always told them that his summons would call them from their beds one stormy night: "It is time. You must rise and meet the fish who walks." Dan remembered that his parents had been trying not to laugh as Joe urged him out the door and into the pouring rain; but still, the ten-year-old boy could not help feeling a little anxious.

Surely all the children, when it was their turn, had asked the same question ten-year-old Dan Stone had asked: "It's a trick, right? Fish can't really walk can they?"

"Very seldom," the mysterious old man had answered, "but when they do, a child should be there to see it. That is what my grandfather said."

Dan had missed her opening words while he reminisced, but when he returned his attention to the cozy chair, Grandmother Renee was clearly setting the leaders up with a tale about what they could only believe was their own history, a story she had told most of them when they were young.

"And these human beings were an earnest, trusting, and skilled people. So, when the fathers promised them a rich land in which they could live, and create, and bless Mother Earth with their gifts and talents, they began a long journey south."

Faces darkened around the circle on the living room floor, and their questions about the outsiders were forgotten. These men were on all-too-familiar ground now, and all but Joe Lamont leaned in, telling the story to themselves as Grandmother Renee spoke it to them.

Joe winked at Dan mischievously, just as he had done on that night fifty years before when they sat together in the mud near an Everglades feeder canal singing a simple chant he had never heard before. Dan nearly laughed out loud as he recalled the first odd catfish hobbling through the mud into the rain-sparkled circle from Joe's flashlight. Others followed, walking toward them as if their fins were turning into legs. If that weren't magical enough, the full moon broke through the clouds and the rain let up as Joe Walking Fish herded his soaking student home from Miccosukee night school in the Everglades.

"But the promised land was nothing like the human beings had been led to believe," Grandmother was saying, shaking her head sadly. "They had been betrayed."

"Many times!" one of the younger men burst out. The others looked at him reprovingly, but nodded their heads in agreement.

"No," Grandmother Renee said to the enthusiastic speaker, "I do not speak of our betrayals by the European fathers. These human beings were not betrayed by foreign conquerors, but by their own people. They were tricked into slavery by promises of a Miami lifestyle they cannot enjoy. In their story, you and I have the opportunity and the honor to be the trickster who frees them from their bondage. It is a job for warriors perhaps, rather than merchants and old folks, but we are all they have, and so we must suffice."

The tide, when it shifted, did so suddenly. The men on the floor spoke urgently amongst themselves, offering suggestions and scenarios, almost as if the rescue had been their idea all along. Across the circle, Joe Lamont eased himself to his feet, gingerly crossed through the conference of warriors around him, and whispered to Grandmother Renee and Dan: "I brought some beer and put it in the fridge. Can I get you one while I'm up?"

"Thank you, Joseph," Grandmother Renee replied. "I believe I've earned one."

"Yes, you have, my dear heart. Yes, you have."

Chapter Thirty-Four

Sherman Kanz had been spending so much time at his computer, Hemingway was getting concerned. Sure, they went out for the requisite walks, but even then, he was certain that his human was still writing in his head. Why did humans feel the need to write things down? And worse, with his human at least, why did he read what he wrote over and over again? Worrying about his human's mental state never got him anywhere, so Hemingway lowered his head and went back to sleep.

"It's not time yet," Sherman said, glancing over the computer screen at his little beagle. He'd produced a piece on the Grand Flamingo Hotel every day for weeks. At first, no one seemed to pay any attention. Then, little by little, the people of Miami began to drive by the site to see it for themselves. Facebook and Twitter pictures of the old building and its small but relentless band of picketers trended, then went viral.

The Bradford Group had just announced that their newly-revised project, The Deco Nuevo Resort and Spa, was to be another John Ghostwalker co-operative design, centered in the northwest corner of the block they now owned, with arms of rooms reaching out along both the north and west sides of the block. The tropical waterpark filling the block's center would be replete with every imaginable swimming option, from a hidden adult pool with grotto hot tubs around it to a kid-friendly pirate pool to the mandatory water slide. The southeast corner of the block where the Grand Flamingo stood was to be a period-style history park called Miami: The Dawn of Deco. Besides a full restoration of the Grand Flamingo hotel in bright Deco pastels, it would actually accept guests, with the proviso that they brought, bought, or rented early '50s attire and dressed for dinner, as was the rule back in those days. All hotel staff would wear period uniforms, the menu and the drinks would be retro, and professional impersonators would roam the grounds, mingling with guests. The young actor who would be playing a 1950 Jackie Gleason was doing in-character interviews on every local television channel, and rumors ran wild around Miami and L.A. that Kevin Spacey would be doing the occasional cameo appearance as Bogart, Sinatra, or a dozen other period celebrities.

The centerpiece of the museum park exhibits would be a complete and accurate replica of *The Phoenix,* a 45-foot-long, two-masted, John G. Alden-designed sailing yacht that had carried V.I.P. guests out for grand moonlight parties in the bay. Allegedly, Ernest Hemingway had been allowed to take the classic ketch out for a shake-down cruise in the open Atlantic. Rumors also suggest that the hotel's owner never allowed his prize out through the jetty again. Sadly a few years later, according to the *Miami Herald*, a careless chef failed to properly shut down the galley's alcohol stove, and the classic yacht burned to its waterline in the middle of the night.

Sherman had enjoyed writing the series, both the research and the composition, but he was feeling guilty. At Seth's urging, he had inserted several carefully concocted rumors into his articles. At least that's what Seth called them, and Seth was, conveniently, the unnamed source Sherman could be called upon to protect. Just as Seth had predicted, these new rumors became self-fulfilling overnight. As soon as he'd suggested that there were calls for a Save the Grand Flamingo victory celebration in Bayfront Park, the city of Miami moved quickly to schedule and organize just such an event. And when he quoted public sentiment (the public being his band of co-conspirators) about restoring an old John Alden look-alike Rena-77, both the *Miami Herald* and the city offices of Miami were swamped with calls from willing volunteers.

Sure, the end was a noble one, Sherman reasoned, but this was an uncomfortable aspect of the media's power that had been used too often for nefarious reasons. And the power he was wielding was actually fun. That's the part that made him feel guilty.

"It just growed, Hem," Sherman said as he organized the Rad-Corp article presentation for his editor. "And it's so complicated now, I'm not sure I can keep track of it all."

"Oh my god," Hemingway thought. "Not that damn poem again." It was bad enough that his human dragged him to nearly every public speaking engagement. Oh, sure, he didn't mind the attention he got from the school kids, but couldn't his human freshen up the act once in a while?

Sherman sat back on the sofa, locked his fingers together behind his head, and began to recite a poem by Rachael Richmond called "It Just Growed and Growed." He read or recited this work whenever he was called upon to address prospective writers. In classrooms he would carry a hairbrush up and down the rows of students, setting it on this desk and then that, examining it from various angles, then take it up and move on again, using the brush for a dozen different unlikely purposes as he went.

i set myself a challenge
to write about the first thing i saw
when i opened my eyes....

it was a hairbrush.

that hairbrush became
a catalyst, a tool,
to carry my imagination
to the full.

then the poem took over,

it started to write
itself, unled,
it just bled words
onto the screen
words i'd never seen
before.

and it just growed and growed,
it flowed, at great speed
to form a read
of sorts.

it twisted and turned,
burned,
became its own thing
its own entity
i was just an on-looker
hooked on
to its gruesome content.

but i was content
to let it live its own life
and run away with itself.

and when it was done
i found it had been one
of those fun things
i will do again,
and again.

"That's just the way it is, Hem," Sherman said leaning back into his work. "Whether it's a poem, a novel, or a newspaper story. The words take on a life of their own." At his school appearances, he usually followed this oration with an exercise requiring that the students pretend the *Miami Herald* had hired them to write a 75-word news blurb about a handsome reporter giving a speech at a local school. He gave them ten to twenty minutes, depending on their age, and then read several of the better ones out loud.

Tomorrow was the day his next batch of words would bleed to form a read of sorts. Perhaps. Seth said that if the *Herald* wanted to scoop whatever came of this, and he wanted another Pulitzer, it was time to pitch the Rad-Corp story idea to his editor. Sally Roebuck was sharp. She came up through the ranks, had done a lot of serious journalism, but she was corporate now. Sherman had read the data saying that seven super-rich individuals essentially owned or controlled 95% of public media output. Sure, there were board members, hand-picked board members, but those seven power brokers determined what would be news and what would not. The Internet was making inroads, in small ways, but the *Miami Herald* was not a small media outlet.

"Who is Rad-Corp, Hem?" Sherman said running through his Power-Point presentation again. "She's going to ask me that, but does she want to know? And what media outlets do you think the Rad-Corp folks own, and what boards do these people sit on? Hell, what politicians do they own? Do you think Sally will even hear me out?"

Hemingway raised his head and shook it so that his ears flapped back and forth, the universal signal for "Shut up so I can sleep in peace." To emphasize the point, he rolled over and curled up facing the door.

"I know," Sherman said. "I'm getting a little crazy. But I guess it's just one of those gruesome fun things I will do again and again!"

The next morning, when Sherman Kanz walked out of Sally Roebuck's office, the exhausting hour-long meeting boiled down to basically two things. First, he'd never heard "fuck" come out of a woman's mouth so often, in such a relatively short time. Sally had certainly given internet sensation, musician, author, and T.E.D. talker Amanda "Fucking" Palmer a real run for the money. Second, as he shuffled towards the breakroom coffee machine like a shell-shocked infantryman shambling off a suddenly silent field of battle, her final words were burning in his brain to the point that he would not be surprised to find smoke exiting his ears: "Get it right!"

Seth had called it on the nose. Despite the horrifying evidence that clearly shocked his editor, it was his mention of a Congressman who had initiated an investigation that turned the tide. Sally Roebuck knew a hornet's nest when she saw one, and without knowing exactly what power brokers they were up against, having a Congressman involved made the risk of outraging her bosses lower. Sherman hoped like hell that this particular detail of Seth's story would prove to be true. Sherman was glad he hadn't mentioned how, exactly, he had become aware of a rescue attempt, because Sally had called the would-be rescuers a lot of less-than-complimentary names—all of which began with the f-word. In the end, of course, she had clearly warmed to the idea of having the only reporter in the world onsite during the rescue attempt. It might be an effing stupid endeavor, but an exclusive was hard to come by in the new world of the Internet.

Seth's plan was so multi-layered that Sherman could barely keep it all straight, but the part about a Personal Space, Inc. film crew that would just happen to be in the neighborhood was genius. Exclusive footage of the rescue could potentially make a small fortune for the group's two local non-profit organizations and the homeless people they served. Sherman's first newspaper story would go public online within an hour or two of the rescue attempt, and by the time real local news TV crews showed up to replace the third-stringers covering the festival, the rescue, successful or not, might all be over. Personal Space might have the only footage in the world. Since one of the local TV stations was a sister company of the *Miami Herald*, he and Seth had agreed that mentioning this detail to Sally Roebuck wasn't a good idea. Hopefully, because Sally thought the story might be huge but the rescue "effing ridiculous," it wouldn't occur to her to risk her exclusive by talking about it to the brass.

It was hard for Sherman not to recall Robert Burns' poem about a plowing farmer turning up a field mouse nest at moments like this: "The best laid schemes of mice and men go often askew."

Chapter Thirty-Five

Benny Lopez met Seth at Sherman's apartment to brief him on the paint project. Sherman had offered Seth his guest room for the duration, and the arrangement worked well for everyone. They were all used to coming to Sherman's place for poker anyway. Normally, a painting project like the one Benny Lopez and his crew were attempting in the open-air kiosk mall would begin at the ceiling and work down the walls. He had tried to explain that to Seth. Ceiling first, THEN walls. Why risk dripping ceiling paint on newly finished paint?

"Of course," Seth Lowenstein had said, "but we need the central ceiling tarps up on game day Sunday. If there's going to be trouble from the Rad-Corp security people just inside those red doors, we'd rather know sooner than later. This way, by the time you get ready to begin hanging tarps and painting the ceiling by their entry, they will be so used to your presence, they won't even be watching you anymore."

Like all of Seth's organizational aspirations, this sounded logical enough on first blush. Then there was reality. Life, the Universe, and Everything—at least in Benny's experience—seldom took note of his aspirations before doing whatever it chose to do. His wife, Mary, was reading a book by Byron Katie, and she had just read him a fitting question from the text: "How do you know that something was supposed to happen?" Benny had shrugged his shoulders, waiting for Mary to answer her own question: "Because it happened." That, in his opinion, was decidedly cosmic and pretty damn real. But Seth was the obvious mastermind among them, so he agreed to start at the bottom on Friday and work his way upwards.

Thirteen massive concrete and steel-rebar reinforced columns held up the Rad-Corp building. They made the support columns in a parking garage look like underachievers. Along Biscayne Boulevard, and the many other waterfront sections of Miami, stilted buildings were now mandatory by code. No one wanted to admit that the sea levels were rising even faster than Al Gore's scientists had predicted decades before, but they were doing so despite the silence. It was Benny's idea to turn these huge square pillars into trees, and nobody had objected.

On Friday morning, Benny and his first shift crew arrived early, and they began rolling black paint on each of the monolithic stilts. The busy kiosk operators all seemed surprised by the influx of white jump-suited painters in yellow hardhats, but it all looked so officially orchestrated, their only concern was the color.

"Black?" was the universal question, and all of Benny's team members were drilled in how to correspond with the shop keepers and the public.

"We just do what we're told," or some similar response, was given with friendly winks and nods all day. "They say it will be awesome when it's done," or "I just got a peek at the design artwork, and you won't believe how cool it will look," were comments dropped here and there throughout that first morning. These tid-bits fed the rumor mill and created anticipation.

From time-to-time, a Rad-Corp security guard would step out for a cigarette, or several would pop out for a look-see or a snack, but none of them seemed concerned. Instead, there was a buzz of excitement that grew throughout the morning.

"Do you think it's for the Grand Flamingo celebration?" Benny heard one vendor ask a security guard who was buying a cup of Cuban coffee.

"Well," the young man said, "I guess we'll all find out together."

Benny breathed a sigh of relief. It appeared that his adventure was just so much more Miami weirdness and additional entertainment for the security teams who, otherwise, did and saw the same things day after day. The celebration and concert in Bayfront park was set for Sunday, and Seth was insistent that they *not* finish ahead of schedule, since Sunday evening would be the big rescue event.

★ ★ ★

At 2:00 p.m. Friday afternoon, when the second shift appeared, most of the first shift roller and cut-in crew workers hung around for the show. They had painted all the columns black, as instructed, and concluded their work with a drunken black circular pattern on the floor at the base of each support. These floor paintings were all unique, and gave the illusion that paint had run off the columns and pooled in a different pattern around the base of each square post. Benny was still amazed about his good fortune, finding this particular second shift team. All but one of the anxious paid volunteers was unknown to him just days ago. They were all young Miami artists, friends of his youngest regular crew member.

The second shift "tagger crew" arrived exactly on time, and Benny thanked Life, the Universe, and Everything for the remarkable team of young artists who had morphed almost out of nowhere. Thanks to Hector Nuneo, the young man who had helped John Ghostwalker goop the inner hull of the old sailboat, the talented troupe had shown up at Benny's office on the Monday before.

"Do you trust me, Benny?" Hector had asked, walking into Benny's office trailing a dozen wildly unique young people carrying spray cans and paint brushes.

"Yes," Benny had grinned, "within reason."

"Good!" the boy had beamed. "In that case, please allow my friends to use your office for the next thirty minutes.

You and I will supervise from out there," he said, pointing to the bay where old mattresses were being refurbished. "Deal?"

Benny's office, aside from a chair, hundreds of paint cans, and a lot of 1" X 12" shelving boards, was just taped and unpainted drywall. "I should probably ask the Sultan of Sleep first, but what could they hurt?" Benny laughed. "We can always paint over it. Come on, Hector, we'll raid the snack machines and get them some cold drinks."

When they returned with refreshments, everything that had been along the walls in the small office was stacked to the ceiling on and around Benny's makeshift desk. There was now a working corridor just shy of two feet wide around the walls. With their noses and mouths covered with colorful bandanas, a dozen kids were wildly waving spray cans and paint brushes in the tight space they had created. The scene was a mesmerizing ballet of color, and Benny Lopez stood slack-jawed in the doorway and watched as his walls grew into a tropical forest, replete with palm trees, bougainvillea, banyan, and dozens of exotic orchids. The kids were done in under twenty minutes, and they neatly rebuilt the surrounding wall shelves without so much as a smudge in their vibrant mural-scape.

"Holy cow," Benny had said, handing out sodas and snack bags. "You guys are hired for second shift, Friday through Sunday—and thank you! I love it!"

"This is Spray Ray Colors," Hector said to Benny as he ushered the tagger crews' leader forward. "Ray, this is my friend, Benny Lopez."

Everybody on all Benny's regular crews had seen his office by Friday, and none of the first shifters wanted to miss seeing the kids turn the massive columns into trees that afternoon. No one, including the kiosk operators and Rad-Corp guards, was disappointed by the show.

Spray Ray Colors and his tagger crew of also-known-as artists walked once around the kiosk mall, checking out the black base coat they had requested.

"Excellent work!" Spray Ray said to the first shifters. "A work of fine art always begins with a base coat, and this one is perfect—perhaps a bit too perfect, as you will soon see."

Spray Ray was definitely a showman. His street busker skills were obvious, as one kiosk operator after another left their stalls and push carts for a better view.

"The most beautiful tree in Florida, the most wondrous to behold, is the mighty Banyan," Spray Ray said with a series of hand signals to his crew. They surrounded a nearby column adjacent to the sidewalk along Biscayne Boulevard and began their dance with spray cans and brushes. "If you've seen an ancient Banyan tree, then perhaps you understand the peril. Like all great art, the Banyan tree will draw you in."

As he spoke, his crew simultaneously created four slender tree trunks, one in the very center of each column's face. Spray Ray walked through the gathering crowd, adding a touch here and there to each of the four paintings. Though skinny, seemingly the *least* mighty of trees, the detail was exquisite. Benny didn't know much about Florida trees, but it looked like a scrawny Scrub Oak tree to him.

"The Banyan, this Banyan, is really just a *Ficus carica*, a fig tree on steroids," Spray Ray went on as several of his taggers disappeared through the crowd, only to return with ladders.

"Like many trees," he said winking at Benny, "the Banyan begins its life as a seed, blown away by the very breath of Mother Earth. But, unlike many other trees, if its tiny seeds fall to earth, they will perish."

A ladder now stood on each side of the column, with one artist on top and another halfway up. The spindly Scrub Oak trunk grew withered branches with deep-veined bark, sprinkled here and there with both fuzzy green moss and dangling gray Spanish moss. Passersby on the sidewalk along Biscayne Boulevard began stopping to watch and listen.

"On the other hand," Spray Ray said as he worked his way through the pressing crowd, "if the Banyan seed flies true, it will land on the branch of some other variety of tree, and lodge itself in the bark." He gestured toward the old oak branches which ended halfway up the black pillar. "And yes, it's true that our little oak tree here has had a hard life and seen better days, but its greatest service to the Great Mother has just begun. The mighty Banyan is an epiphyte, a plant which must begin its life on a host plant like our humble Scrub Oak."

The next magical hour or two went by so fast that kiosk shop keepers forgot their wares. Approaching customers soon forgot why they'd come, and jockeyed for any view they could find. People walking south on the sidewalk often had to walk out into the street to get around the awe-struck audience of passersby. Benny was pretty sure that the entire Rad-Corp guardhouse had emptied as he watched silver-jacketed security personnel straining for a glance at the flurry of dancing colors that seemed to coalesce into a dozen descending vines on each side of the column. Some grew writhing down the oak's trunk, while others evolved from the outer reaches of the oak's limbs and down into the elliptical mass of black paint at the pillar's base.

This way and that, the dropping vines twisted and turned before the audience's eyes, taking root somewhere on the floor. Even 3-D glasses at the movie theater never gave a better sense of depth perception than these young people seemed to throw up so dramatically.

"You might see now why this great tree is often called a 'strangler.'" Spray Ray said with a wicked grin. "The Banyan will not only draw you into its depths, but should you lose your way in its maze of trunks, you may find yourself trapped forever like our ill-fated oak."

There was complete silence. In ones and twos, Spray Ray and his team disappeared through the crowd, ladders and all, and set up in smaller teams around two nearby columns. But the crowd didn't notice that. There before them, from floor to ceiling, stood the multi-stilted base and lower limbs of a Banyan tree so expansive and cavernous that they all felt as if they could wander into the blackness amongst the many trunks, and perhaps even find the old ruined oak at its core.

Seth Lowenstein walked up beside a stunned Benny Lopez, laid a gentle hand on his shoulder, and said: "Not at all what I expected, Benny, but damn! You done good."

Chapter Thirty-Six

Dave Bartlett's assignment wasn't nearly as colorful and entertaining as Benny's, but his performance art would come on Sunday afternoon—if he could persuade his fellow writers and musicians to come to Miami. He did some due diligence before he hit the phone-a-friend routine, visiting city hall, the parks department, and the musical gear rental company owned by Miami's own Carlos Santana. His cleverest ploy—at least in his own estimation—was checking with their publicists and publishers first, certain he'd get some back-up support from those who owned a piece of his friends' book sales action. Dave even booked rooms at the nearby Marriott Marque and checked on flight times for each member of the Rock Bottom Remainders.

He was about to call Stephen King when he thought of one more thing. Dave had recently given a graduation speech at the University of Miami where he met Howie Wales, the director of purchasing for the college bookstore. Howie seemed quite enthused about their general fiction selection at the campus store, even said there was a "featured locals" shelf boasting luminaries like himself and Carl Hiaasen. Dave grabbed up the phone.

"Hi Howie! It's Dave Bartlett. We met last spring after the graduation ceremony. Have you got a couple of minutes?"

"Wow, cool! Yeah, hi Dave. What's up?"

"I was wondering if you might be interested in an authors' roundtable event sponsored by the University of Miami bookstore, maybe as an event at the Grand Flamingo celebration in Bayfront Park. I'm working on getting the Rock Bottom Remainders together for a concert there."

"All of them?" Howie asked. "Even King and Turrow? Amy Tan, really? What an event that would be for readers in Miami. We stayed at the Mohonk Mountain House for our honeymoon, up in New York State, and Stephen King was doing a signing there. The line ran down two flights of stairs, across the lobby, out the lobby door, and down the driveway. Sandy and I took hour-long turns in line, and even near the end, he was pleasant and gracious."

"Well, I hope they'll come," Dave laughed, "but, an authors' event and signing would help me sell them on a trip to Miami. And, for the record, I tried to be pleasant and gracious like Stephen King once," Dave said with a sigh, "and I suppose if I had his personal grace training staff, it might have gone better. The officers called to the scene were very gracious."

He waited as Howie laughed and said: "Right!"

"If you don't have enough student muscle available, Howie, just let me know and we'll send over some volunteers. There's a map online at the city website showing where you'll be setting up in Bayfront Park. Does the university have cabana tents for events like this? It could get hot out there."

"Just wait until I call the Alumni Association and get them involved. There will be tents, trucks, and staff volunteers to spare!"

One after another, he called the old gang. One by one, they gave in to his boyish charms. Dave wasn't sure any of them believed him, but he even threw in a whispered tidbit about how they were actually acting as a distraction for a local rescue team who was going after a kidnapped lady. Even if they didn't believe the story, he thought they'd give him credit for creative imagination. Writers are like that.

At last Dave Bartlett could focus on what was *really* important, the show's set list.

★ ★ ★

Friday night, back at Sherman's apartment, Seth was furiously honing a new Rad-Corp computer hack when he got a call after midnight from an unknown number in Washington, DC.

"Hello?"

"Seth, it's me, Kicks. I'm a United States Congressman using a damn burner phone like a thug, just in case. I've been discreetly asking around about Rad-Corp like a newbie who'd never heard of them. Well, I hardly have. I'll tell you what, I sure don't like any of the looks I get when I say that name out loud."

"I would imagine so, Kicks," Seth said. "Catch anything useful?"

"The guys who pretend not to know anything are the scariest. A fifth-grader could tell you they were lying out their asses. But the other guys—actually, just two—hinted that I shouldn't be so publicly curious, but then sort of gave me a wink and a nod, adding that 'the FBI's on it.'"

"Did you think they were playing you or reassuring you?"

"It's a great way to put me off the scent, telling me that the big dogs are on down the trail ahead, but if there really is an active FBI investigation going on, you and your playmates might step into two shit storms at once."

"Did you show those last guys the video?"

"No I didn't. It just didn't seem like they wanted to know anything. But I did make an appointment for a breakfast meeting in Virginia today. A fellow classmate in law school is an agent with the FBI. We were in a study group together, and I pegged her for a straight shooter. If she shows any interest at all, I'll show her the video and see how she reacts. I gotta go, my driver's outside the bodega, probably reporting in on how long I take to buy a cup of coffee."

"Okay, thanks Kicks!" Seth said, grateful that his life wasn't under a microscope like that of his old friend. "Let me know what you find out. Good luck."

After hanging up, Seth returned to his computer code. He was creating a subliminal computer game and had hoped that the Rad-Corp employees would have already been playing it unknowingly, but the programming turned out to be harder than he thought. Graphics and animation were never his strong suit, let alone animation and graphics you couldn't see, but necessity is the mother of any number of things, invention being only the most well-known. Seth's eyes were shot by the time he was ready to test his program again, so he padded out of Sherman Kanz's guestroom with his laptop, nearly tripping over Hemingway. The little beagle woofed at having been startled, but followed his new housemate to the living room.

"Sherman!" Seth called as he plopped down on the reporter's sofa and shook his knee cap. "Wakey, wakey!"

"What the hell!" Kanz groused. "Are you crazy? What time is it?"

"Time to test my latest creation."

"Can't it wait 'till the sun rises, at least?"

"No. Sit up and watch this," Seth said, opening the laptop, pointing it at Kanz, and clicking on one of the desktop icons. "What do you see?"

Sherman blinked his eyes, then rubbed them, then squinted. "Is this a trick question? It looks like the same old Shelby GT Mustang you've had on there since you came. Are there new desktop icons or something?"

"Okay," Seth said. "What about now?"

A window popped up with a light blue sky above a meadow covered with wildflowers. Sherman described it.

"Great! Now this?"

A new window popped up, a dark and cloudy nightscape with the faintest hint of building outlines here and there. Sherman said as much, but added a disclaimer: "Except it's fuzzy somehow, a little like on TV in the old days when you needed to adjust your antenna. Like static snow maybe?"

"Great!" Seth said, sitting back where Sherman's legs had been. "This will have to do. If a Rad-Corp employee is using an all-black desktop, some static is the best I can manage. Here, Sherman, push this key."

"What did I just do?" Kanz said after pressing the indicated spot.

"You sent a morally questionable computer hack into the Rad-Corp system. From now until Sunday night, it will run non-stop on every live computer monitor and TV screen in the building."

"How morally bankrupt is 'morally questionable?'" Sherman asked.

"I guess that depends on what you think about the practice of subliminal advertising. We're playing with their minds, Sherman, trying to sort the sheep from the goats as it were."

Chapter Thirty-Seven

Rosie Weathers got up early on Saturday morning, long before sunrise, to fly Podrick—perhaps for the last time. Pop-up computer notes from both Sherman and Seth suggested that Sunday was to be the day of the great escape. She had many undecided issues floating around in her mind, but liberating Podrick wasn't an undecided question. The controller that seemed to live on her desk? Well, she could always build one, but why go to all that trouble? By her reckoning, however this thing played out, her Rad-Corp salary and retirement accounts weren't likely to be something she would have access to out in the real world, so absconding with a drone controller unit seemed like a reasonable tit-for-tat.

The most difficult choice hovering just beyond Rosie's grasp was about how much control she should retain over her own bid for freedom. The dreadful information she knew was largely passed on, along with myriad data from Rad-Corp's computers and security cameras. Seth's Trojan Tunnel Ponies had been wildly successful. Sherman said he had two or three weeks' worth of newspaper follow-up articles either outlined or in near final draft condition. The Monday morning *Miami Herald* would break the story—of Rad-Corp's underbelly, and (hopefully) a whistle-blower's escape. The public would know, and the government either would or wouldn't sort it out. But what happened to Rosie and her team was ultimately her responsibility.

Rosie believed that their safe extraction was exactly what Sherman, Seth, and the others intended. What she didn't believe was that the universal law of unintended consequences would be suspended this weekend in honor of her personal preferences.

"Rosie girl," her father often said, "the wheels never fall off the bus at the most convenient time."

Like most of his working class aphorisms, this one was a no-brainer in Rosie's experience, so as she pulled Podrick out of his hidden hanger and revved him up, she refined her to-do list for the day. She flew over Bayfront Park just as the sun peeked over the watery horizon, turned north along the shoreline, and came at last to the marina, hoping that the redhead's sailboat had returned. Unfortunately, the slip was still empty, so she banked Podrick west toward the nearby shopping mall building. Just on the periphery of the drone's camera range, she spotted the familiar blue-and-white fiberglass hulled sloop approaching from the north. It was not alone.

The redhead stood at the wheel motoring toward her slip, but behind her, attached by a long orange tow rope, she saw the dilapidated remains of what had surely been a classic beauty in its heyday. The tall and strangely familiar blond man stood at the wheel of the second boat with the breeze blowing his ponytail shoreward. He was clearly combating that same force with his rudder, pulling the wheel hard to port so that his old wooden craft would glide toward the slip just east of the redhead's berth.

Rosie swooped for a closer look at the old wreck, an idea blossoming in her mind. As the lady skipper gunned her boat's throttle, the young man's old boat looked like a water skier swinging out to the left, and at the last second before crashing, the redhead reversed the little sloop's engine, stopping almost instantly. They both lifted their ends of the tow rope so that the older boat glided into the adjacent slip as the orange rope cleared the end of the wooden finger dock between them. Both skippers hurried to avert that boat's impending impact, and in seconds, both water-craft were safely secured. The watery ballet was mesmerizing, and Rosie found herself grinning as enthusiastically as the couple on the dock below.

Yes, from this distance, there was something vaguely familiar about the blond man, but she couldn't put her finger on it. As Rosie flew Podrick home, her new plan settled into a comfortable firmness in her mind. Rosie appreciated what Sherman, Seth, and the others were doing for her, and she hoped it worked, but she simply would not count on that.

"Faith is a good thing, Rosie girl," was another of her father's favorites, "but blind faith isn't faith at all. It's only foolishness dressed up as faith."

After putting Podrick away, she settled at her apartment desk, fired up her laptop computer, and left a message for Phillip on the Rad-Corp inner-office mail system.

★ ★ ★

That same Saturday morning, Chris Tosh and Captain Jay O'Connor visited all twelve Miami fire stations. Even without announcing their intensions, after the first three stops, each subsequent fire station had more crew and family members present by the time they arrived. Chis loved his fans, accepted the good wishes with real gratitude, shook a lot of hands, and signed many autographs by the time he reached what could only be called a block party at station #12.

"You knew this would happen, didn't you," he whispered to the captain as they eased through the jubilant crowd that stretched along Northwest 46th Street from the middle school to the firehouse.

"Yes, I did," Jay laughed. "Did I mention that besides being the captain at Station #12, I'm also the department's morale officer this year?"

"That never came up, now that you mention it," Tosh quipped, "but I'm glad to help out."

"Thanks, Chris. These crews and their families deserve it, and they obviously appreciate it."

When they finally left the party at Station #12, it was long past lunchtime. The captain's pick-up truck bed was filled with every spare yellow fire suit and visored hardhat the city of Miami owned.

"It was a good day, Captain Jay!" Chris said as he peeked back at their load.

"I rather thought so too," the captain grinned.

★ ★ ★

John Ghostwalker had begun his life as a Miccosukee tribal member in the middle of the Florida Everglades, right here at the entrance to the Miccosukee Museum Village. The little blond baby boy had been abandoned in a cardboard box, just yards from the Tamiami Trail canal and the many alligators who swam in it every day. Teenaged Miccosukee Museum Village staff members had discovered him when they arrived for their summer job, and the rest was history.

It was Grandmother Renee who had eventually figured out that the tribe's resident alcoholic Vietnam war vet, Dan Stone, was the boy's father. But in the twenty-some years since, there had been no clues as to the whereabouts of John Ghostwalker's mother. She was the only woman Dan Stone had ever loved, and whom he had lost in what seemed like an instant. After their first and only night of intimacy, the nurse he had fallen so deeply in love with simply vanished. This trait, she had clearly passed on to her son, who often seemed to appear in, or disappear from, a crowded room without anyone taking notice of his approach or his egress. Grandmother Renee liked to call this gift "the Ghostwalker gene."

But earlier on this Saturday morning, twenty-some years later, Dan Stone, Joe "Walking Fish" Lamont, and Grandmother Renee pulled into the same entrance gates where John Ghostwalker and his cardboard box had been abandoned shortly after his birth.

Grandmother Renee led them to the Native regalia storeroom where both show and festival costumes were stored alongside handmade Miccosukee garments made available for sale to museum village visitors.

"Remember," she reminded them, "these disguises are all for adults, so—wait for it—don't sweat the small stuff. I crack myself up! Anything that is a poncho or pullover is good. The more colorful, the less they look like Rad-Corp employees, the better.

Dan and old Joe grinned and shook their heads, dug in, and began setting aside the articles of Native clothing that matched Grandmother Renee's criteria. Their minds must have been running along in the same track because every few minutes they'd glance at each other and chuckle softly. The subliminal humor came to a head when Grandmother Renee spoke up suddenly: "Hey, Victor! Do you think any of us have ever played dress-up with real white people instead of white dolls before?"

The movie reference would likely be lost on most Americans, but all three Native adults laughed so hard they had to sit down and rest for a spell.

★ ★ ★

Benny Lopez' paint crews had created their own Saturday problems by working too fast on Friday. In order to be at precisely the right spot by late Sunday afternoon, Benny knew he was going to have to slow them down. "Where else in modern America," he thought, "do you have to ask your workers to slow down?"

He always felt good when he placed a homeless family under a safe roof, but he felt better still when he saw that the job skills and the work ethic he taught them remained when their emergency was over. He was proud of these people who refused to give up, who refused to be stereotyped by the rich and the powerful. They were what America was supposed to be about.

Still, he had too much time to kill, and too many helpers with which to kill it. When he told Seth about his problem, Seth solved it. All day long, through both first and second shift, runners came and went from Bayfront park, borrowing helpers to set up vendor tents, rig stage lighting, clean up litter, and set up parking cones and miscellaneous signage, most of which ended up being created by his taggers.

In the end, Benny decided, this unusual Saturday was a very interesting and emotionally fulfilling day. Something about the elaborate public art project spoke to his heart, and the festivities across the street only elevated the positives feelings he was experiencing.

★ ★ ★

The clowns were turning out to be problematic. Sherman Kanz had assumed that every city had party clowns and Shriners. So far, he'd left phone messages all over town, but nobody was calling back. He even left phone messages at the Ringling Brothers and the Barnum & Bailey Circus offices in both Sarasota and Orlando. Nothing.

"Maybe they've all been bought out by *Cirque de Soleil*," he said to Hemingway. "Think about it, Hem, if all the clowns have gone over to the dark side, who are we going to send in tomorrow afternoon?"

Finally, late Saturday afternoon, dejected and bemused, Sherman and Hemingway took a cab to the nearest Party City store and rented a few clown costumes—including one for his beagle with a frilly little collar and a colorful hat held in place by a rubber band.

Hemingway was not amused.

Chapter Thirty-Eight

Saturday night was the I.M.P. team's poker party at Rosie's apartment, and everyone brought his or her favorite chair. The caterer had sent party goodies over from the Bayfront Mall and a guard had piled all the foil containers, miscellaneous bags, and bottled beverages outside her door that afternoon. Rosie had spared no expense from her imaginary Rad-Corp income and retirement account. She had ceased seeing it as belonging to her long ago, so spending Rad-Corp's money on her team was a satisfying pound of flesh.

Lou Garcia and Linda Ulrich had raided the electronics inventory and borrowed enough micro-parts to divvy out as poker chips.

"We all start out with just under $25,000," Lou said, "and if you run out, you have to serve food and drinks for thirty minutes before you can beg your way back into the game."

"Be careful with the ones still in the baggies," Linda added. "They're really expensive, and I signed them out."

Rosie's tiny round dining table, even with the little insert usually stored on the underside, was barely big enough for her whole team, but no one minded. Aside from the company-sponsored sports nights and excursion trips, no one had ever suggested team fraternization of this sort. In fact, Peter Bloom said what everyone was feeling.

"Isn't this against some rule? It feels like we're doing something illegal."

There was an uncomfortable pause—not unusual after Peter spoke—but then came nervous giggles followed by genuine laughter.

"Rebels!" Patty Jenkins said with enthusiasm. "Here's to the leader of our guerilla band!" She held up her can of lite beer, and everyone joined the salute.

"Well, thank you," Rosie blushed. "I hope you feel the same way once I've taken all your electronic poker chips!"

The evening could not have begun more perfectly. Rosie had assumed it might take considerable time to even remotely bring up the sense of restriction at Rad-Corp—a subject never voiced in all her years here—and yet there it was, right out of the blocks. She let the conversation rise and fall, took her turns dealing, and tried to keep up on all the various games called and wild cards selected, but her mind was always listening for the perfect moment to interject the first of her surprises. Strangely, each time someone expressed a hint of dissatisfaction or isolation (the subjects she was hoping for), she couldn't get a word in fast enough before someone else chimed in along the same lines.

At the first real pause in the game chatter, Peter dropped another observation bomb.

"I think the boss wants to tell us something."

The young man was smiling at her, like he was reading her mind, and Rosie watched as every other face at the small table joined in and focused in on her own.

"Yes, well," Rosie faltered under the intense scrutiny of all those eyes, "there is something. It's rather important, at least to me, that you all know *exactly* what Rad-Corp has planned for our drones. First, am I the only one who actually does know?"

Now the scrutiny was all directed toward her. Rosie searched every face at the table, hoping to catch a subtle clue about whom to be wary of in her potential followers. She saw no clues, and the several assumptions put forth were similar to her own early naiveté about doing good in the world.

"That's what I thought," she said, feeling the profound silence between her words. "But Phillip shared an A3 test program video with me. He said he wasn't supposed to, but wanted me to know how proud he was of our team. I haven't slept well since, but I think each of you deserve to make up your own mind about how you feel about the fruits of your labors. I may be unusually paranoid now, but I suspect that by showing you the video, I may be literally trusting you with my life, and endangering yours. If you don't want to see it, that's okay. You can leave now, and I'll never mention it again."

Now the silence was thundering. Every face seemed to be encased in it. Years of working in wrongness, while trying to pretend nothing was wrong had to be hard on any human's psyche, but voluntarily looking at proof that your reality was a house of cards was not an easy thing to digest.

Not surprisingly, Peter Bloom spoke up first. "I've always suspected," he said, "and hated myself for being too afraid to try and find out. I'm in."

"I'm always afraid," Linda said, "and this is why. But I want to know."

"Me too," said Patty Jenkins.

Lou Garcia got up and begun walking back and forth in front of the kitchenette. "Shit! I knew there was a catch. This job, this fucking top secret Project I.M.P., was just too perfect to be true. Oh shit, oh shit, oh shit!"

"Come on, Lou," Peter said softly, "we're in this together. Let's watch it together."

"Okay," Lou said, pausing, "but then we say 'oh shit' together, right?"

"I promise," Rosie said, stepping over to her desk, opening her laptop, and linking it to the three monitors on the wall. "Despite what you see and think about this, please remember that this video is *not* on my laptop," she said with a wicked grin on her face, "and that I certainly would *never* have anything inappropriately purloined in this apartment."

The team's nervous smiles and glances stopped when the video began. Soon the silent energy in the room became silently electric, a pulse increasing in frequency as the video played out. Tears ran openly down several cheeks, and Lou was mouthing "oh shit!" like a silent repetitive prayer. When the clip ended, they all teetered toward the chairs they'd brought and sank into them with looks of hysteria in their eyes. Rosie was closing the lid of her laptop when someone, obviously in her lab office, knocked loudly on the door beside her apartment desk.

Her heart stopped, even as she staggered backwards from the shock. A sound Rosie had never heard before erupted up out of her throat, but when she tried to say "Who's there?" nothing but a squeak came out.

"You all right in there?" came a strong male voice. "Rosemary Weathers, please open the door!"

Rosie was frozen, so immobile that she couldn't turn her head to look at her team behind her. Her eyes felt glued to the door.

"Here," Peter whispered in her ear, "take a breath. Let me help you to your seat so you can be dealing cards. I'll get the door."

He turned her and got her seated, placed the deck of playing cards in her hands, shut off the monitors and the laptop computer, and walked back to the door.

"I told you all that the word would get out," Peter said loudly as he opened the door and faced the silver jacketed security guard. "Hi," he said, "did you come to play? Come in, though we're out of chairs."

Peter stepped aside and the guard's eyes fixed on Rosemary, then the table covered with electronics parts, and then on each of the faces around the table.

"Hi Joseph," Rosie managed when she recognized Phillip's Army friend. "Can I deal you in? We've got lots of snacks."

"Ah, no thank you, Ma'am," he replied. "There was some concern about the, ah," his eyes flicked toward the ceiling, "noise, and we were concerned. But I can see that everything's fine here. Enjoy your weekend."

Joseph Allen slapped Peter's shoulder, said "thanks," and walked out, through Rosie's office to the lab. Peter stood watching until Joseph stepped into the elevator. Then Peter closed the apartment door and turned back toward the table.

"Okay, Lou," he whispered, "let's not get crazy, but I think now's the time."

They all whispered "oh shit!" over and over in unison until the mantra began turning into giggles.

When everyone had recovered, Peter turned to Rosie. "How did they know? We weren't making any noise. Besides, there can't be microphones, or we'd have been hauled off. You, especially."

"You're right, Peter," Rosie nodded at his obvious deductive reasoning skills. "There's some kind of medical or maybe temperature scanners in our ceilings," she said. "They can tell if there's a sudden rise in our body temperature or blood pressure signatures. Phillip warned me that the brass was concerned about me, even suggested I practice relaxation breathing."

"No shit," Lou laughed. "He really does have a crush on you!"

"I'm not sure about that," Rosie replied, "but he did seem genuinely concerned about me drawing too much attention."

"So, naturally, you threw a poker party," Peter said, being Peter.

"Well, yes I did, but I had to. We're out of time, and I had to talk to you all at once."

"Out of time for what?" Linda asked. "What's going on?"

There were all those eyes focused on her again, but Rosie sucked it up and forged on. "I've decided to escape," she said. "And I have some friends on the outside who want to help. I will take any or all of you who want to come. But it might be dangerous, of course. Oh, and it's tomorrow afternoon."

"Oh shit!" Lou said, and the whispered group mantra began again.

Chapter Thirty-Nine

Early Sunday morning, well before dawn, a private-looking plane with a pilot and seven passengers lifted off at a remote runway in Virginia. Instead of the expected rows of seating, two Spartan bench seats faced each other across the passenger compartment. Even without the personal body armor, the deadly weaponry, and the black uniforms, something about the occupants' steady posture and dedicated silence would have tipped most observers off that six of these seven individuals were not people you wanted to jack around with. You might take a run at the seventh guy in the finely-tailored suit, on a good night and in a public place, but never in surroundings like these. No, these people were on a mission, and no one in his or her right mind would even consider getting in the way. Six hours after take-off, the silence was finally broken.

"We're landing in ten," the pilot shouted back to the profoundly quiet group. "It's a grass strip, so it might get bumpy."

The dark man in the suit glanced around at the others, but none of them so much as shifted a hand at the pilot's announcement. Not one of them had made eye contact with anyone else since boarding.

"Any landing you walk away from," the passenger in the expensive suit said softly to himself, trying to mimic the rounded forward posture of the others, "is a good landing." Maybe that posture was how they were trained not to snap their spines in situations like this. The plane would land near the edge of the Everglades in Homestead, he'd been told, and he couldn't help thinking about snakes, alligators, and all the plane-crashes-upside-down-in-the-swamp TV news videos he'd seen through the years.

★ ★ ★

When Rosie's nervous team left the Rad-Corp building early on Sunday morning, with Phillip Crowe and Joseph Allen in close attendance, she was thrilled with nearly everyone's ability to act calmly in a highly stressful situation. The exception was Lou Garcia. He looked like he might throw up. Given her performance the night before when Joe had knocked on her apartment door, she had no inclination to judge. Everyone casually glanced at the crew of workers busy on ladders, drilling holes here and there in the ceiling of the kiosk mall, and inserting shiny silver eye-bolts. They all stopped in their tracks, though, when they saw the closest concrete support column.

"They've been working on these Banyan tree trunk paintings for a few days now," Joseph said. "We sneak out and watch them, especially in the afternoons when the taggers come."

As Rosie's team walked around the column, dumbstruck with awe, she spotted one of the men from Sherman and Seth's gang, the Latino man who drove the white van with "Filling Empty Houses, Inc." on its doors. Rosie watched him turn away and pull out a cell phone.

"I'll treat for coffee," she said, glancing away quickly, "and we can drink it while we tour the festivities in the park."

"I can get that, Rosemary," Phillip said, stepping closer.

"Ah, but then I'd feel bad asking you to pay for brunch!"

Phillip's eyebrows rose, everyone laughed, and the tension relaxed. Even Lou's shoulders dropped and his steps smoothed as he turned toward the Cuban coffee stand. As they took their turns, they chatted with each other about the painted trees, the coming festivities in

Bayfront Park, and the things they were hoping to buy at the waterfront mall. Peter Bloom wore his newly issued Rad-Corp excursion debit card on a lime green lanyard around his neck.

Rosie's instructions Saturday night had stressed three conversational items: excitement about the late afternoon happenings in the park, the desire to shop at the mall before and after brunch, and the loudness of Peter Bloom's Hawaiian shirt. The bright yellow oversized apparel had taken several good jibes already as they rode the elevator to ground level.

Her team was doing great, and she was proud of them.

★ ★ ★

"She what?" Seth barked into his cellphone. "Benny, tell me you're kidding."

"Sorry, Seth, they're all right here in front of me, drinking Cuban coffee and talking about a walk in the park and shopping."

"That wasn't part of the plan!"

"Maybe not your plan, Seth," Benny laughed, "but it looks like our damsel in distress has made up a plan of her own."

"She's smart, Benny. Maybe...," Seth pondered, "maybe she figured that if she arrived back at the right time, the doors opening for her would help us."

"Did you actually tell her we had that covered, with two back-up plans?" Benny asked.

"Well, no, but...oh shit! It will be fine. Just keep to the schedule, Benny."

"You got it, boss!"

★ ★ ★

There is nothing so lonely as a single clown, in over-large shoes and a red nose, whose only companion is mad as hell. Sherman Kanz's sometimes faithful dog Hemingway had almost quit trying to shake the dreadful clown hat abomination off his head—but not quite. After yet another angry shake that set his long ears spinning outwards like helicopter blades, the look he gave his ridiculously dressed human was withering. How long had he lived with this human? Did the man not know what a color wheel was? Sure, dressing up was beneath him on general principle, but these colors? Hemingway was justifiably mortified.

Sherman dutifully trolled Bayfront Park for possible clown volunteers; hell, he'd gladly pay them whatever it was real clowns got paid, but he needed help. There were three dozen helium balloons clipped to the back of his wide red clown belt, but he'd forgotten about them. They trailed along above and behind him like a confused rainbow coalition of drunken, erratic clouds. He wasn't quite dragging the woebegone beagle, but it was a close thing. Sherman spotted his third potential clown recruit, a colorfully dressed young woman who was merrily skipping along the sidewalk behind the amphitheater where workers were setting up lights and amplifiers for the all-day string of local bands who would play before the main event, Miami's own Dave Bartlett and his Rock Bottom Remainders. Somehow, it just wasn't fair. Why did Bartlett have all the fun?

Sherman wasn't at his circus-clown best when he approached the dancing flowerchild. It was hot out, he was sweating, and his beagle was fighting the leash. He saw the young lady's earbuds, so he tapped her lightly on the shoulder. He was sort of expecting a '60s Joni Mitchell in San Francisco kind of vibe from the girl, so the blood curdling scream, followed by pepper spray caught him off guard. Fortunately, the pepper spray missed a direct hit when he fell backwards over Hemingway, but he thought he felt and smelled it dripping lightly on him from above as he tried to rise, apologize, and explain all at once.

"Phoenix! It's a perv clown! Call the cops!" the girl screamed, taking a step back and trying to get the keychain weapon to fire again.

Sherman recognized the name and looked toward the bandstand. Phoenix Rivera was one of Miami's busiest working drummers, and Sherman had several old vinyl LP jazz records Phoenix's dad had played on in his personal collection. The late Mario *"El Commandante"* Rivera had been a Miami music legend, a Dominican American sax player *extraordinaire*. But, Sherman hadn't ever met the son. He noticed right away that Phoenix was way bigger than his late father, and, at the moment at least, had none of the old man's winning smile.

"Do we have a problem here?" asked the big man, with a drum stick pointed directly at Sherman's eye.

"I sure hope not," Sherman said, making a warding gesture with his hands. "Please let me explain."

★ ★ ★

First thing Sunday morning, Dan Stone and Grandmother Renee drove into Miami from the rez together in Dan's pickup. They were towing a trailer maxed out with eight new Space Station dwelling pods. They were being followed by several shuttle vans emblazoned with "Miccosukee Resort and Casino" and filled with Native drummers and dancers in full regalia.

"This is crazy, isn't it?" Dan asked Grandmother Renee as the strange convoy drove east on the Tamiami Trail towards Little Havana and the Brickell District of Miami.

"Of course," she said, smiling. "Nothing done for the purpose of helping others seems sane by this culture's standards. We are taught to get for ourselves, lest others beat us to our dreams. America has become largely about competition, and if we aren't out to win something for ourselves, this kind of world makes us feel like we don't belong, like we're failing. But we aren't the problem, are we?"

"No, grandmother," Dan said slowly, "I guess we're not. We sort of live in opposite worlds."

"Yes," Grandmother Renee said, "our culture was very different from the western Europeans. But their culture wasn't always so very different long ago, before the Vikings and the Romans taught them the principle of conquer or be conquered. But there is still hope. Just as Crazy Horse predicted, some Europeans are remembering their roots now and looking to us for traditional healing ways they have forgotten. When we can step back and see community, we can feel oneness with Spirit and with the Mother. We can abide. 'Winning' and 'losing' are words without Spirit. But the words 'trying' and 'helping' are blessing words."

"All righty then," Dan laughed, "let's put a blessing on them that they won't soon forget!"

Chapter Forty

The first shift painters were doing well. It was mid-morning Sunday, and Benny was amazed at how easily they'd managed the complicated series of ceiling hooks and suspended plastic tarps. It all seemed overly complicated to the kiosk operators and the Sunday morning coffee and breakfast crowd, but Benny's crew explained that they didn't want to risk dripping paint on anyone while they worked on the great Banyan canopy in the afternoon. This explanation, though only a half-truth, was readily accepted by the curious. As the brunch crowd wandered in, they all stared up at the random blue tarp/white tarp patchwork of drooping dropped ceiling like they were walking into an ancient European cathedral. Benny Lopez saw their point. There was something Da Vincian about Seth's elaborate hanging tarps.

After the tarps were hung, the paint roller and brush wielding began. The painters' ladders poked up strategically through the junction boundaries of the blue tarps and the white tarps in the tapestry, and Benny's crew duplicated on the ceiling the elliptical blackness they'd created on the floor around each great column. But on the ceiling, the size of each black drunken circle was larger by tenfold.

His paint crew worked their way steadily from the streets on all four sides of the building toward the center column of the thirteen. Gasps of wonder burst out each time a ladder was withdrawn and the enchanted onlookers caught a glimpse of the progressing forest canopy. But it wasn't the sky of black paint that inspired the crowd's awe. It was the spaces between.

Each oddly shaped mass of black paint touched those spreading out from the adjacent columns, and the gray concrete ceiling in between the blackness was steadily turning into the kind of brilliant Miami sky that attracted tourists from around the world. Soft white clouds billowed here and there like they were being pushed across the sky ceiling by a sea breeze. There were wheeling swallow-tailed kites, soaring seagulls, and swooping pelicans, all with the profoundest sense of movement in their wings. Individual feathers appeared about to blow free and take flight on their own.

Benny Lopez had done good things with his life, and he'd had a hand in more than a few amazing life transformations, but this mural project struck a powerful chord. It was, he decided as he wandered around with his ladder and his black paint, a metaphor for the of humanity and of the energy that sparks Life, the Universe, and Everything. This work of art was a communal legacy that would speak of hope to every soul curious enough to see it.

★ ★ ★

Seth's eyes were tired as Sunday morning wore on. He knew he should go out for a walk, check on the paint job just up the street from Sherman's apartment, anything but stare at his laptop screen. But he couldn't help it. Ever since 11:00 p.m. Saturday night when he broke into the Rad-Corp TV system, the number of employees and security personnel watching his invisible mind altering propaganda graphics had tripled. He hadn't thought about the possibility that guards on duty wouldn't necessarily be watching only the security computer screens until he was ready for bed. When it dawned on him that, unlike himself, more employees were apt to be watching TV on a weekend than prowling the internet or playing computer games, he set to work expanding his program's audience. And it worked, bigtime.

Throughout the night, he watched the numbers of how many people in the Rad-Corp building were watching a screen, and how long they were doing it. Subliminal advertising was now illegal, but all the statistical data from its years on America's early television stations and movie theater screens, and from the military's propaganda studies, was clear: the more times you didn't see the box of popcorn flash up on your screen, the more apt you were to go wandering off in search of popcorn without even knowing why. Subliminal triggering was a gray area morally, but the science was rock solid.

He assuaged his conscience by reminding himself that unlike advertisers and spies, he wasn't brainwashing the Rad-Corp employees to choose anything any particular way, but rather making it easier for them to make a quick decision in the impending chaos that served their own self-interests. Sure, he had a bias about what separated the sheep from the goats morally, but he didn't concern himself with the riddle of which Rad-Corp employees were which. When the escape opportunity presented itself (and that was nowhere near to being a certainty yet), Seth wanted the sheep and the goats to run in opposite directions.

★ ★ ★

Sunday sunrise aboard Mac's Hake 32RK was a sparkling spectacle of light on the water, but John Ghostwalker missed it as he often did. Mac was the early riser, ever pursuing the proverbial worm. By the time he lumbered to the galley, poured himself a cup of coffee, and climbed up out of the modern sloop's cabin, Mac had turned the finger dock between old boat and new into an organized chaos of unusual supplies.

"Twenty fireproof survival blankets?" John Ghostwalker laughed, looking at the shipping invoice stuck on the stack of silver bundles leaning against a shiny new 55-gallon steel drum. "Really?"

"Yup," Mac said with a wink, "and you have the esteemed privilege of stapling them up in the Rena's cabin!"

"Captain, my captain, I serve at your pleasure, but why do we now own a large pile of bricks?"

"The bricks were an afterthought," she answered. "Have you ever roasted wieners or marshmallows over a fire barrel?"

"Native Americans don't do fire in rusty barrels, so no I haven't," John said.

"Well," Mac said, "that's probably because the barrel gets so hot you can't stand close enough to cook anything. And if you get a long enough sharp stick, the food tends to fall off into the fire because the longer stick multiples any movement you make geometrically."

"You've actually done this barrel cooking? It's really a thing?"

"Sometimes, down at the shore in south Baltimore, kids would gather on weekends. Bonfires were illegal, and you couldn't drag rocks and shit out onto the beach, so we'd borrow a city trash barrel. It sucked when all the beaches and parks switched to those blue plastic barrels."

"The bricks, my love," John said. "I get the barrel part."

'Well," Mac said thoughtfully, "a living pine tree can flash burn at 1400 degrees, and ancient dead wood can flash at a whole lot lower temperature than that. If our fire burns hotter than we hope, the metal barrel will radiate a lot of the heat outward toward the cabin walls. What if our fire blankets aren't enough?"

"You are the genius, my love. The bricks will contain the heat like insulation in a hot water heater. Hopefully our oily rags won't have to burn long enough to generate that much heat, but if we really want to restore this relic, better safe than sorry."

★ ★ ★

As Rosie Weather's Rad-Corp team field trip wended its way through the Sunday morning festival preparations in Bayfront Park, they were hitting all the talking points meant to set up their handlers; but, more thrilling than that, they were obviously enjoying it. Even Lou Garcia was cutting up, doing his famous Cheech Marin impersonation.

"*Hey, I'm just a love machine,*" Lou sang as they passed through the sea of vendor cabana tents, "*and I don't work for nobody but you. Woman, my temperature rise, and then I go for her thighs...*"

Her team was actually singing along as they danced down the sidewalk, and Phillip Crowe and Joe Allen were clearly stunned. Their faces and their shared glances, made it clear to Rosie that they were so far out of their regimented element that they were both at a loss. The inmates were, for once, running the asylum.

Chapter Forty-One

By mid-day on Sunday, Firehouse #12 in downtown Miami looked like a disaster relief volunteer center. Most of the station's crew was on hand--regardless of their roster status, along with wives, children, and even a few grandparents. The shiny green firetrucks stood foursquare outside in the sun, while in their station bays folding mess tables lined the outer walls. Shoulder-to-shoulder volunteers stood behind each table. A continuous line of human beings moved from volunteer-to-volunteer and from table to table on the opposite side, each carrying or wearing a single yellow fireman's coat. It looked like a Halloween event, with each trick-or-treater getting goodies at each position around the open garage bay: from trail-mix bars to M&M's, and from foil-wrapped cheese balls to spring water in plastic bottles, Seth had put a great deal of thought toward provisioning his potential refugees.

For some of the firefighter's kids, dwarfed in the large fire suits, it looked almost like their yellow coats were gliding along the floor on their own because there were neither legs nor feet to be seen below the hovering hem. The coats' pockets had all been emptied, and at each stop the former first aid and safety supply locations were being resupplied with things escaping Rad-Corp employees might need in the aftermath of Seth's impending invasion. Seth was a micro-manager and an over-thinker by nature, and had reminded Chris Tosh and the fire chief several times to be sure each coat contained three of each item. "I doubt that the Miccosukee regalia and the clown costumes from Party City are equipped with the necessary pockets, so if folks end up in hiding for a few hours, I want to make sure there will be enough drink and snacks to go around." Chris Tosh and Captain Jay O'Connor still chuckled from time to time, repeating Seth's motherly reminder to each other.

"That Seth, he's hell on the details," Captain Jay whispered to Chris as he stuffed three water bottles into the coat being proffered by a tyke barely taller than the table. Finally, at the next-to-the-last stop, the little guy was teetering under the heavy load, but the promise of a personally signed Chris Tosh fan jersey at the journey's end had carried him through the thirty-minute ordeal. Nearly submerged beneath the coat's high collar, the boy's eyes were beaming as he struggled out of the yellow tent-sized garment and handed it up to Tosh.

"Yup," Chris replied to the captain, "Seth leaves no stones unturned." He took the offered fire coat, handed it to one of the runners, who would deliver it to a wrapper, and bent over to the kid in front of him. "Get up here little man," he said, lifting the awe-struck boy up onto the table. "You're a good worker. Thanks for helping out! Let's get you sized up."

While Tosh found a jersey for the kid and set about signing it, the next runner hurried the heavily laden coat to a pair of the volunteers sitting around the center of the fire station's truck bay. There, the bulky coats were being carefully folded, and then, while one team member held it firmly in place, the other tied the bulky bundle together with black Velcro straps. Then each team member affixed a shoulder strap. It wasn't much of an exaggeration to say that each Station #12 firefighter charging into harm's way that evening would be carrying another fireman on his back.

***

At the same time an excited Miami firefighter's son was getting his very own Miami Heat jersey signed by Chris Tosh in his father's very own fire station, John Ghostwalker and Mac McKnight were down at the marina several blocks to the east, surveying their morning's efforts.

"Sure is brighter in that cabin with aluminum fire blankets on the walls, floor, and ceiling," John said as he bent over and glanced around down in the old wooden sailboat's main cabin. "Did we forget anything?"

"I don't think so," Mac laughed, "but I'm still smarting from the brick debacle."

"It wasn't a debacle," John said, glancing at the fifty-five-gallon metal drum at the bottom of the cabin steps. "Think of it as more of a belated 'Plan B.'"

"You are a generous victor," Mac laughed. "I was just flummoxed."

"Yes," John laughed, "and determined!"

"I know, I know. I wanted to figure it out by myself, while you knew already."

They had lined the cabin in fireproof blankets, covered a small section of the now silver cabin floor with a layer of bricks, hauled the heavy drum down the steps, and placed it squarely on the section of bricks. Then Rosie begun lining the inner barrel's wall with more bricks tipped up on end. This, she hoped, would direct most of the heat and smoke up and out of the cabin hatchway, creating one of the dramatic diversions Seth was counting on to facilitate Rosemary Weather's extraction at Rad-Corp. But every time the bay waters rolled beneath the hull, Mac's circle of insulating bricks fell over. She stacked them ten different ways, but nothing worked. Even as John tried to offer his alternative approach, she ignored him, insisting instead that he go get a caulk gun and caulk. He only just began an assault on the flaws inherent in that idea, when the look in Mac's eye sent him off to the marina store at a run.

The first row of vertically stacked bricks stood up a bit longer than they previously had, given the gooey caulk on the backs of each brick, but since only two edges of each brick made contact with the rounded drum sides, every third or fourth Biscayne Bay swell toppled Mac's seeming progress. She came a little closer on her third attempt, crisscrossing the bricks and stacking them lengthwise in the barrel rather than on end. She hated losing so much of the inner barrel space. Her new brick design covered half the drum's bottom. And since bricks lying on their long sides still only touched the walls at two points, and those points were now at least three times farther from each other than before, the first fishing boat motoring slowly out of the marina toppled her work for the third time. Mac, looking like a volcano ready to erupt, had climbed out of the cabin, and disappeared down the dock.

Wondering whether she might return with a hundred tiny tubes of Crazy Glue, John set to creating a pyramid of crisscrossed insulating bricks around the *outside* of the barrel.

"If we can't get our insulation to stack inside the barrel," John said to himself as he removed Mac's fallen bricks, "let's see how things stack up on the outside!" As any architectural designer knows, the pyramid is the strongest and most stable design in all of human history.

He had to admit that her caulk helped him set up a more stable circular pyramid of bricks around the drum, but he doubted that the caulk would dry up very much by show time. Still, boat after boat motored by and his architectural creation never shifted. When Mac returned, clearly more ready to listen, he didn't have to say a word.

"Of course!" she laughed, throwing all the oily rags she'd been collecting on the dock into the barrel. "Why didn't I think of that? Let's go for brunch. I'll buy!"

★ ★ ★

As Sunday morning rolled on, and the Rad-Corp mini-excursion approached the band shell, Rosie and her chatty posse noticed that the opening act band was setting up their amps. It was approaching 10:00 a.m. The four young men wearing t-shirts and shorts finished up, and turned to watch a tall and sturdy man make final adjustments to one of the drum kits that would remain on stage all day. When the older musician was satisfied, he motioned for the band's drummer to hand over his badly beaten-up drumsticks. Rosie thought it odd, since the man had a stick bag hanging from his hip, but the younger man complied immediately.

Looking at the ratty sticks with some dismay, the older man fell into a slow and steady sound check of the various drum heads and cymbals, taking cues from another man sitting at the sound mixing board at the rear of the outdoor amphitheater. The hits were routine, to the point of boring, and the youngsters passed back and forth looks that said "lame" to anyone watching. But the seemingly random thumping turned, by the barest of degrees, into a more complicated pattern that got progressively faster. Every fourth backbeat, the right hand drum stick spun 180 degrees, its thick end dropping for a rim shot or a cymbal hit before whirling back into place so fast Rosie only saw a blur. The big man never missed a beat. The speeding percussive pattern tore through toe-tapping riffs, paused briefly at dizzying heights, and leveled out at a pace that created the kind of emotional anxiety of being lifted up into the air by a tornado. As quickly as the percussive storm had come, it blew over, settled back into the original rhythmic thumping, and then stopped.

The kids stood mesmerized as the old hand stood up, dug into his stick bag, and handed the band's young drummer back his battered drumsticks, along with brand new set.

"Try these," he said as he walked toward the sound board technician. "Have a good gig."

When the neophyte percussionist looked at the virgin sticks, his eyebrows rose suddenly. "Phoenix Rivera signatures! These must have cost a fortune. You think he knows Phoenix?" he asked his bandmates.

"You, idiot!" the bass player said, swatting the back of the boy's head. "That *was* Phoenix Rivera. And that guy at the sound board, that's Tito Fuentes, Jr."

Rosie and her team laughed as they moved on, and soon passed out of the park and into the shopping mall's mid-way doors. She had no way of knowing it, but at the west end of the mall, John and Mac, each carrying a Kosher hot dog and a drink, were passing out those doors for a stroll through the park she had just left behind.

Chapter Forty-Two

Inside the long Bayfront Mall concourse, Rosie's team, agreeing to meet up at the café and bakery in 45-minutes, broke up and spread out so fast that Phillip Crowe and Joe Allen sort of froze. They stood staring at each other, while trying to look everywhere else at the same time.

"Shit," Phillip said. "That woman will be the death of me yet. You go that way, I'll go this. Keep track of them as best you can, and call me if you spot a tail."

"Got it, Gunny!" Joe said, moving east, his head swiveling like it might fall off.

Phillip had kept his eye on the store Rosie disappeared into, and he intended to follow her in, until he noticed the mannequins in the glass storefront. It's not that the pastel panties and nearly non-existent bras weren't eye-catching, but they somehow killed his instinctual desire to follow at Rosie's heels.

He watched from the concourse as first one, and then another, of Rosie's team members popped out of one store and into another all up and down the length of the mall. As near as he could tell, their number remained constant overall, though the shopping bags seemed to multiply exponentially.

At 11:00 a.m., like a Swiss Cuckoo clock, all the little people Phillip and Joe were trying desperately to keep track of shuffled out of the appropriate doors and waddled all their bags toward the café and bakery shop. It was only then that either man drew a truly relaxed breath. While the others pushed tables together, set their shopping bags beneath them, and lined up at the counter, the two old Army vets collapsed into chairs like they'd just finished a five mile double-time march with full packs.

When Rosie and her team returned with their food, and Phillip and Joe got up to order theirs, an unusual game of footsies was played briefly under the joined string of café tables. From the lap up, everything looked normal should either of their minders glance back. Hands were occupied with food and chatter flowed liberally between bites.

"They seem unusually excited about that last band that plays tonight, Gunny," Joe said after placing his order. "I've heard of Stephen King—is he really still alive? But who's this Dave Bartlett guy everybody around here is so fond of?"

"Former columnist for the *Miami Herald*, got syndicated bigtime, and he was supposedly very funny. I never got much past the headlines and the sports pages myself," Phillip said. "Seldom sat still long enough to read a novel, let alone a book of humor columns. I'd do that different if I ever got a do-over."

As the two men chatted at the counter, everybody at the table was playing a game Peter Bloom had called "Shit on your neighbor" with their feet. In the card game, according to Peter anyway, players were routinely required to pass one card from their hand to the person on their left or right, in an attempt to get rid of unhelpful cards by foisting them on someone else. In this game, after sitting down in a predetermined order, everyone slowly slid one shopping bag to the person on their left, and another to the person on their right. Rosie thought it an overly complicated way to buy particular items for one another in the allotted time. But everyone reacted well to Peter's idea, perhaps because it felt so cloak and dagger-ish. Rosie saw that it was getting the job done without drawing unwanted attention.

Linda had made everyone laugh the night before with her response to Peter, something about inventing a similar PG-rated cross-dressing game wherein, under certain conditions, the players exchanged items of the clothing they were wearing with someone else at the table. Both would leave the room and put on each other's whatever before returning to the game. Lou had heartily agreed it was a great idea for a party game, well, except for the leaving the room part.

Rosie loved the new spark she had seen in her team's eyes. They had felt trapped and discouraged for a long time, but never dared hope to undo their decision to sign on at Rad-Corp. Now, because Rosie had trusted them, they had hope—at least for the moment. And win or lose, she had made real friends, something she could barely remember doing, ever so briefly, when she was a child instead of a child prodigy.

"So," Phillip said, sitting down beside Rosie with his roast beef on rye, "did you all quench your shopping Jones?"

"What?" several of the young adults said at once.

"It means did we get it out of our systems," Rosie laughed. "We're showing our age, Phillip!"

As if on cue, everyone at the table seemed to have passed by at least one great deal; and, apparently the repast had allowed them time to talk themselves into splurging for one more crucial item. "I guess we'll be right back," Rosie laughed as everyone but Phillip and Joe rose, several looking at their watches and saying something about just enough time to get back before the South Beach Stompers took the stage out in the park. They disappeared faster than the first time, and Phillip and Joe just shook their heads and took a second bite of their sandwiches.

★ ★ ★

"She walked right by here!" Sherman practically shouted into his cellphone. And her whole team." His homemade clown makeup was surfing down his cheeks on large beads of sweat, and his forgotten helium balloons bounced perilously close to the spiky Palmetto fronds just behind him. Hemingway pulled against his leash, trying to catch the horrendous clown hat on one the pointy spikes there in the shade behind his increasingly irrational human.

"I know," Seth said calmly. "Benny saw them leave the building and gave me a call earlier. I think she wants to help us by having security open the Rad-Corp doors for her when she returns at show time."

"You think? Hell, Seth, what if she doesn't come back? Have you thought about that?"

"I'm trying not to," Seth answered simply, "but if she frees herself, we have more time for the other Rad-Corp employees who might want out."

The line was silent for a second or two before Sherman said: "Jesus, Mary, and Joseph, Seth! Have we fucked this up already?"

"Worst case scenario," Seth answered, "you've got a great fade-out line for your newspaper story."

Seth couldn't tell over the phone whether it was Sherman or Hemingway he heard growling, but Sherman eventually spoke.

"Okay, smartass, I'll bite."

"Ladies and Gentlemen, Scheherazade has left the building!"

This time, Seth knew for certain who was growling just as the phone went dead.

★ ★ ★

Phillip and Joe went way back, and their comradery had become a comfortable thing for both of them. Not in a *Brokeback Mountain* kind of way, of course, but two comrades-in-arms whose lives pretty much precluded a woman's lasting touch. And sometimes the time could slip by unnoticed when war stories followed a couple of beers, but they were on duty now, stone cold sober, hounds in the Rad-Corp big dog hunting club. They had well-honed military instincts, and so at precisely the same instant, they burst to their feet and stormed back into the concourse.

This time, all their little Cuckoo clock figurines were nowhere to be seen.

"We've been played, Gunny, Joe shouted.

"Look!" Phillip replied. Halfway down the mall concourse to the west, they saw Peter Bloom's bright yellow Hawaiian shirt head out through the double doors at a full run.

"Won't be hard to follow that," Phillip said as they took off in pursuit. "And that college boy can't even last ten minutes on the elevated tread mill upstairs. None of them can."

"Yeah," Joe said, "we can catch 'em, Gunny. But then what? We'll have a shitload of nasty paperwork in order to cover our own asses, and that's if we're lucky."

"Damn that woman," Phillip said as they reached the doors and held them open briefly for an unsteady old Jewish bag lady coming their way in a long gray shawl and a dark maroon silk babushka. As they released the mall doors and sprinted out into the sunlight together, Phillip Crowe was exasperated. "Why do I always fall for the smart ones, Joe?"

Chapter Forty-Three

The old bag lady tottered forward at a snail's pace toward the far end of the concourse, where the glimmering brilliance of mid-morning sunlight on Biscayne Bay made the exit doors glow like near-death portals to the afterlife. Ahead of the ponderous senior citizen with the crumpled shopping bag, one-by-one at carefully timed intervals, other oddly attired individuals--their heads all covered-- appeared out of various shops and eateries and made their way through the Sunday shoppers toward those pearly gates. Peter Bloom grinned inside his price-tag-dangling babushka as he slowly and unsteadily herded his coworkers out the east end of the mall. "Damn!" he thought. "I'm not a coward after all."

As each member of Rosie's team broke into the sunshine, items of flowing lightweight outer clothing slipped demurely into the shopping bags they carried. Each walked a different path into and around the large marina. Some mingled with boaters on the various finger docks, others entered and perused the marina store, but eventually, one by one, they all ended up stepping aboard the rattiest looking sailboat in Biscayne Bay.

A half-hour after he had nodded at a polite but hurried Joseph Allen, the Rad-Corp security guard who paused to hold the mall door open for him, Peter Bloom finally ducked his head into the ancient sailboat's cabin.

"What the hell?" he asked as he tried to climb over the fifty-five-gallon drum in his path. "Are you guys in there?"

"Yes, Peter," Rosie said, "all the way up front in the bedroom."

"She means 'in the forward stateroom, Peter,'" Lou Garcia laughed. "You did really great, Peter!"

Everyone applauded as the hero of the moment fell over the steel barrel, dumping the contents of his shopping bag—including his favorite Hawaiian shirt—across the wrinkled silver floor. "Who's the interior decorator here? Alcoa Aluminum? And what's that stench?"

"Oily rags in that barrel," Rosie said seriously. "We're all suspicious about why anyone would dispose of them in here, but at least the owners are obviously aware of the possibility of the rags self-igniting. Come on in here. It's tight quarters, but there are windows, even one in the ceiling."

"Port holes and a deck hatch," Lou corrected Rosie with an eye roll. "Join the party, Peter. It's all in honor of your Oscar-worthy performance."

★ ★ ★

The first tarps, spread out below the newest Banyan canopy paintings, fell free at 1:00 p.m. on Sunday afternoon. Benny's taggers had created a buzz, hinting at the time when the first big reveal would likely happen. And, sure enough, a considerable crowd of festival goers crossed back over Biscayne Boulevard from Bayfront Park in order to be on hand when the time drew near.

Eight of the thirteen concrete columns, the ones facing the four city streets around the Rad-Corp building, were now finished. When Spray Ray Colors wound up the crowd and pulled the tether cord in his hand, the blue and white hanging plastic tarps were released at their corners. Each folded dramatically in half across the nearest steal rigging cable. It was like watching an astonishingly beautiful pop-up book opening down from the ceiling to display a circle of mammoth Banyan trees that held up the sky. The startled sounds of awe turned to mesmerized silence as Spray Ray and the gang moved their ladders inward, pulled the tarps down off their wire clothes-lines, and set to work on the ring of four inner secondary columns.

"Mary, you gotta come down here," Benny said into his cellphone. "And bring Katie! I've never seen anything like it. This will be on TV and in magazines all over the world."

"I thought this was a rescue, Benny," Mary replied laughing at her husband's appreciation for the arts, something he had no talent for whatsoever. "Just kidding. But when the story of that artwork gets told, I hope they're clear about who made it happen."

"That's right!" Benny said. "For the sake of these hardworking homeless people and incredible kids, I hope they do."

"*Idiota*!" Mary said, laughing again. "I meant you, Benny. You made it happen!"

★ ★ ★

It was a hot and sticky south Florida Sunday afternoon when the nondescript little plane rolled to a stop and its passengers disgorged themselves into the bright sunshine. The black ops team's boot steps made little sound as they jogged into the Homestead Nursey's orderly rows of palm trees, palmettos, and pony-tail palms. The man in the suit heard the helicopter before he saw it, but his mind was on his newly polished leather shoes. The decorative trees ended suddenly, and when he saw acres of lush and very damp sod farm spread out before him, he worried less about his shoeshine, and more about whether the soggy run would sink them and spill swamp water into his socks.

"I had to go and open my big mouth," he said as the first of the armed squad bounded through the rotor turbulence and into the waiting chopper, their wide deep-treaded footsteps leaving murky checkerboard puddles. Representative Ellis "Kicks" Keith watched as each team member proceeded him up into the waiting helicopter's side door, and thought: "It's just like stepping into a layup, and I can still dunk with either hand."

Of course, the physics of a narrow leather-loafered foot pushing off a solid oak gym floor is one thing, but in the water-soaked Bahia grass on the edge of the Florida Everglades the well-dressed Congressman's watery divot was considerably deeper than the troopers' wide boots. Ellis' left foot disappeared along with his ankle, and when the chopper crew member caught him and yanked him aboard, the expensive shoe didn't transition along with its owner.

"Sorry," he said to the door gunner, "I gotta go back for that."

Ellis Keith still had no idea whether he was being played. This FBI strike mission he'd been authorized to tag along on as an official overseer could just as well be a carefully designed charade to make him look like a total idiot, a conspiracy theorist gone 'round the bend. Young congresspersons were relentlessly trained to be seldom seen and never heard, but he'd shot off his mouth. Still, he had to see it through.

★ ★ ★

Seth Lowenstein, Navy SEAL to his core, and always cool and calm under pressure, was a mess. He had watched deadly assignments unravel before his eyes, but his team had been trained to turn unpleasant surprises into new paths to victory. He still began each day by making his bed properly. Well, it was Sherman's guest bed, but still. But the best life hack he had learned as a Navy SEAL was that each job, done right, from the time you wake up until the time you go to sleep, leads to success. But success seemed to have wandered off on this particular Sunday afternoon in Miami. Oh, his plan was moving along okay, but the damsel in distress he was supposed to rescue was in the wind.

Sunday morning was gone, and the afternoon was getting ready to ride the Miami Metrorail home. Seth reviewed his plan, critiqued his various assignments to his makeshift team, and reread every correspondence with Rosemary Weathers. "What had happened?" he asked himself over and over. "Why did she decide to go out on her own?"

His biggest source of worry was that the rescue operation was now about what had been only an afterthought earlier in the morning, an assumption that others might want out too. It had all been orchestrated around Rosemary Weathers leading the sheep to freedom. That was looking less likely by the moment since most of the sheep remained inside Rad-Corp, and Little Bo Peep had vanished into thin air. Well, thick, humid air, but still.

And why couldn't he reach Kicks? The Minnesota Congressman was AWOL at the worst possible moment. Everything added up to ABORT. Even the toughest SEAL team knows when to pull back. But to stop now did not feel like pulling back to Seth Lowenstein. And he was pretty sure it wouldn't feel like pulling back to his team and all the volunteers who had signed on to follow them. Pulling back would feel like giving up, and Seth just didn't know how to quit.

Chapter Forty-Four

After helping their fellow Miccosukee tribal members set up their area at the festival in Bayfront Park on Sunday morning, Dan Stone and Grandmother Renee had returned to Dan's pickup truck and trailer. The rig was parked just west of the Rad-Corp building, the opposite side from the park, where it had been seen on most recent days. The only difference was that the trailer carried a full load of eight Space Station individual housing pods and the truck's bed held two fifty-five gallon steel drums and a commercial sized box fan designed to push exhaust fumes out of a large auto repair shop in a hurry.

On the east side of the Rad-Corp building, Benny Lopez had been running an identical fan on low speed for several days. If anyone asked, it was there "to carry away paint fumes." As Sunday crept onward and Grandmother Renee looked on, Dan and Benny set Dan's fan up on the side panel of Dan's pickup facing the Rad-Corp building and secured it with tie-down straps. The big fan was leaning forward slightly, pointed directly at the kiosk mall, and just behind it, the two drums stank of oily rags.

"So," Benny asked his Native friends, "are we just making smoke today, or are there real Indian smoke signals involved?"

"Well, Benjamin," Grandmother Renee smiled ruefully, "we will certainly be sending a signal. But like all fire signals throughout history, the core meaning is always 'peril.' Beyond that, individual translations will depend completely upon those who watch."

"What did she just say, *amigo*?" Benny asked Dan with a grin. "She talks like that every time she has a good poker hand. It's why I usually fold."

"Damned if I know," Dan said with a shrug, "but it must be very wise, don't you think?"

Grandmother Renee sniffed at them, but even a dismissive sniff from Grandmother Renee was so full of love it made Dan and Benny both feel good all over.

Once they got the fan set up, Dan and Grandmother Renee let Benny show them the progress his painting crews had made. The four inner columns were nearly complete, so the intricate Banyan jungle, its looming and tangled canopy, and the brilliant glimpses of blue sky, fluffy clouds and soaring birds completely surrounded them as they approached the metal double doors at the Rad-Corp entrance at the kiosk mall's very center.

Because Seth had successfully hacked the security cameras, his team now knew that the building's central column was inside that high security lobby, surrounded on three sides by a round guards' desk facing the doors. The emergency stairway began just behind the concrete column, bracketed by both a passenger and a freight elevator. That central column was just like the other twelve, but no one would be painting it today. Instead, the outer walls and the doors themselves would become part of the last and largest of the giant Banyan trees.

"This one will be huge," Benny said as, one-by-one, his crew began bringing ladders, tarps, and painting equipment in from the four surrounding columns. "The doors should look like the mouth of a great wooded cave when they're done. The preliminary drawings looked so real I thought I could stick my hand inside."

"These children are incredible," Grandmother Renee said quietly. "I've never seen anything like this in my life. Walt Disney himself never created such a wonder. If I could move my cottage in here tomorrow, I believe I would."

Dan smiled at Benny as he noticed that the blue-and-white patchwork design of the tarps over the past few days was morphing into a bipolar pattern around the Rad-Corp entrance structure. Just as Seth Lowenstein had instructed, the formerly random use of the blue-and-white plastic tarps was now segregated. All the white tarps spread out to the west of the metal double doors, and all the blue ones were being hung across the ceiling of the kiosk mall to the east. Several Rad-Corp guards watched in fascination, but none showed any undue concern. No one seemed to notice that for the first time since the project began, all the tarps' corner grommets were being strung with clear, heavy, monofilament fishing line.

★ ★ ★

By the time Seth Lowenstein closed his laptop, stashed it in his backpack, and got up off Sherman Kanz's sofa that Sunday afternoon, he had done everything he could do. Whatever players he had hoped to have at his disposal either were or were not in their places, instruments tuned, and ready to perform the music he had arranged for them. He left Sherman's apartment, rode down the elevator, exited to Biscayne Boulevard, and turned north up the sidewalk toward the Rad-Corp building two blocks away. This time he was not disguised in order to fool an opponent. He was just Seth, a gay ex-Navy SEAL, trying to accomplish something that he hoped was a good thing.

Of course, since leaving the Navy and getting his private investigator's license in Baltimore, he had always been playing a part. Sometimes Batman or the Lone Ranger or Spiderman maybe, but always he tried to stand up for the proverbial little guy. Little guys (and gals) used to be easy to spot in America. They were poor, often people of color, and they had never quite been able to break into the upper middle class, where the ability to hire a lawyer could make things look good in a freedom-and-justice-for-all sense. As Seth stared up at the twenty-seven floors of the Rad-Corp building, he had an epiphany. The middle class was disappearing in America, broken almost beyond recognition, and unless something radical happened to stop whatever Rad-Corp was, and the power behind shady things like it, the rest of the grand melting pot experiment would never reach the potential men like Thomas Jefferson, Benjamin Franklin, and Martin Luther King, Jr., had glimpsed from afar.

No, this wasn't about Rosemary Weathers (though he fervently wished for her safety and freedom); this was bigger. Or at least he was pretty sure it was.

"You okay?" Benny said, waving the palm of his hand up and down in front of Seth's upturned face. "It's getting real around here, *amigo*."

"You look like you're ready to scale mount Everest," Grandmother Renee said as she placed a gentle hand on Seth's shoulder.

"Are you still with us?" Dan asked. "Don't flake out on us now."

"I'm alright," Seth muttered as he returned his attention to ground zero Miami, "but, well, I sort of have a dream."

Chapter Forty-Five

Rosie's team talked about their next move well into Sunday afternoon. The prevailing consensus was that they would wait until dark. Then they would try to work their way around the marina's security cameras by slipping into the water and easing overhand along the docks to wherever the lighting was poorest, and then straggle on shore in the dark—blocks away from Rad-Corp. Beyond that, talking about their options in the hot cabin just made them all sleepy. They were physically and emotionally drained. They all fell into deep sleep on the old stateroom's canvas-sail-covered bed like a litter of kittens on a warm rug after a hard day of exploration.

They dreamed the boat was moving, a collective dream brought on by the fact that the boat *was* moving. One by one, the groggy Rad-Corp escapees opened their eyes and recognized their dream in the waking world. Water swished along the old sailboat's wooden hull, palm tree crowns moved past the western starboard port holes, and puffy reddish white clouds floated aft when they peered up through the open hatch above them. None of these things was a part of their thorough planning, so the impending flurry of whispered concerns was unsettling.

"What the hell?" Peter Bloom said, rubbing his eyes and taking in the unwanted stimuli.

"We're drifting or something," Linda Ulrich responded, trying to wrap her head around their newest layer of plight.

"There's no diesel engine running," Lou Garcia said with a yawn, "and we're sitting on the mainsail, so we sure aren't sailing." He peeked up out the forward hatch, surveyed the scene to the aft, and ducked back fast. "Shit!" he whispered. "There's a blond dude back there at the helm."

"We're being towed someplace," Rosie said. "I watched them tow this boat to the marina just the other day. I thought they brought it here to fix up. But why would they be towing it again?"

"I don't know," Lou said, taking a quick peek out and forward, "but there's a redhead piloting the tow boat. It's another sailboat, with a diesel inboard churning up wake behind it, and it looks like we're headed for that rocky shoreline at Bayfront Park."

"Well, at least if they're going to sink it, we'll be near the shore," Rosie said, shaking her head in dismay, "but there are several more hours until dark, so we don't want to get out—especially there, right in front of Rad-Corp."

"'Everything that goes around comes around,'" Peter quoted thoughtfully, "but this raises the bar on literal interpretation. I think the smelly barrel is beginning to make more sense. I wasn't interested enough to read the *Miami Herald* article thoroughly, but maybe this is the sailboat that's being restored for the history park thing at the new resort where the old Grand Flamingo Hotel sits. If it is, they could be towing this thing past the festivities at the park, kind of as a show, and then around the corner and west to where the original was docked. That would be a better place to climb out later."

"Of course!" Rosie whispered. "They want smoke to recreate the historic fire on the original yacht. Here, help me cover this old door with canvas. Maybe we can keep the smoke out of this room."

★ ★ ★

Aboard the Hake 32RK sloop pulling Rosie's beleaguered team back toward Bayfront Park, Sean "Mac"

McKnight was on her cellphone, talking to Seth Lowenstein.

"Are we good to go?" she asked. "We're only a couple minutes out."

"Yeah," Seth said. "We're as ready as we'll ever be. We'll cue the mayor that she's up. You put on your show long enough to catch everyone's attention. Then when you see black smoke coming out from under the Rad-Corp building, you can tow our old beauty around the bend and over towards the Grand Flamingo, dowsing the rags while you're out of sight. Our private film crews are geared up for that."

"Gotcha, boss," Mac said. "John's got three fire extinguishers back there with him, so unless he literally chokes, we ought to be good."

"Great! I'll tell everyone we're a go at 5:35 p.m."

★ ★ ★

Meanwhile, over behind the Rad-Corp building, Benny Lopez was pacing when his cellphone rang. "We're ready," Benny said when Seth asked him for an update. "How long do we wait to drop the tarps and start our barrels burning?"

"I'm guessing five minutes, say when Mac and John are halfway past the open space on the waterfront across the park. They should have attracted enough attention by then. Be sure that the tarps fall right before Dan cranks up that fan on the truck."

"10-4, Seth," Benny said. "I'll task someone to crank the other fan facing Biscayne Boulevard to its high setting as soon as Dan revs up his. Have you heard from Sherman? I kept seeing the balloons from time-to-time, but then he disappeared about 15-minutes ago." His voice was strained but determined.

"No, Benny. I'm calling him next. I told Hemingway to bite his ankle if he got sidetracked. My best to Dan and Grandmother Renee. Good luck."

★ ★ ★

Chris Tosh felt the weight of both his fire suits. The one he wore was hot and heavy, and the one folded up as a make-shift backpack—intended to camouflage a runaway Rad-Corp escapee—felt just as heavy. His Miami Heat basketball uniform was the next-best-thing to a swim suit compared to what he and the guys from Station #12 were wearing.

"Seth's gonna call, right?" Captain Jay O'Conner asked Tosh. "I'd hate to be all dressed up with nowhere to go."

"Oh, he'll call," Chris said. "This is high drama, and he's the director!"

"I'm pretty sure there was a gay guy on my aircraft carrier fire crew," the captain said, winking at one of his crew members. "Oh, he couldn't say so back in those days, but he saved all our asses at least twice. I think this Seth Lowenstein guy might be a bit crazy, but if it helps get good folks away from these Rad-Corp goons, let's all be a little crazy today, okay people?"

Everybody smiled, but the fireman Captain Jay had looked at was grinning outright.

★ ★ ★

At the same moment, Sherman Kanz was trying to reconcile a number of unfortunate mistakes during his hot and fruitless morning as a clown recruiter, not the least of which was spurning the blue plastic portable toilets in favor of the air-conditioned shopping mall's toilets at the Bayfront Park's northern border. There was so much going on in the park, he and Hemingway went pretty much unnoticed until he approached someone about following him to his car and climbing into a clown costume. Sure, after a time or two, he began to see the problem, but by that time he had endured several uncomfortable discussions with Miami police officers.

"What are we coming to, Hem?" he said as they entered the mall. "A respected *Miami Herald* reporter stops someone to talk about volunteering, and everybody assumes I'm a pervert? It's disheartening, that's what it is."

Had Hemingway been able to speak to his human, he was all too aware that there were no words to describe the man's lack of good sense, not to mention self-respect. New lows were being recorded on this day that would not soon be forgotten or forgiven. The surly beagle tried once again to brush off the ragged clown hat by dragging his head along the mall's cool glass door, but he only managed to rotate the red and white dunce cap around so it covered most of his left ear. As they passed into the mall's main concourse, the random twitches of his ear made the hat's tasseled point aim this way and that as if it were a hose nozzle watering a flower garden.

Sherman breathed in a deep lung-full of the cool dry air conditioned mall and sighed with relief. That's when he noticed that he and Hemingway were no longer going unnoticed. Several children from both east and west down the concourse were already dragging their mothers towards him. His sigh turned to resignation and he squatted down and opened his arms to the closest of the approaching children. At exactly that second, the little girl's angelic smile turned away from her mother and seemed to really focus on Sherman and Hemingway for the first time.

Hemingway bent forward to sniff her yellow sneakers. His pointy hat poked her shin just as she got a full-on look at his master's face. Her blood-curdling scream set off a chain reaction as the remaining moms and kids realized they were all far too close to a clown who, if not directly from hell itself, was certainly demon spawn of a high order.

As the concourse emptied, Sherman ducked into the nearest restroom, certain—based on recent history—that a police officer was already on the way. When he saw his face in the mirror, he understood why this was inevitable.

Chapter Forty-Six

When Sean Lowenstein's call lit up and vibrated his cellphone, Sherman Kanz was squatting in a bathroom cubicle, his giant red clown shoes on the toilet seat. He was hugging Hemingway to his chest and whispering to the deeply disgruntled dog.

"Please Hem, stay quiet just a bit longer. The mall cop might come in here looking for us. Wait! Maybe that's Sean," he whispered, struggling to retrieve his phone from the old fanny pack he'd dug out of his closet that morning. "Hello? Sean, oh my gosh, you just wouldn't believe it."

"Well, maybe not, Sherman," Sean said, "but it's almost go-time. Are you in position?"

"Not exactly."

"So, where 'exactly' are you? We're going live in about five minutes, and clowns or no clowns, we need your damn balloons. You still have your balloons, right?"

"Yes," Sherman muttered as he looked up and realized that he and Hemingway weren't really hidden after all. The colorful balloons, spread out across the bathroom ceiling, were more effective advertisement than an electronic billboard.

"Well then, get them over here now!"

The line went dead, and Sherman climbed unsteadily down off his porcelain perch. "Well, hell," he said to Hemingway. "We're going to have to hoof it, but not looking like this."

To Hemingway's great relief, the plastic Party City clown costumes both went directly into the trash bin, along with the monstrous red plastic shoes. Next, his human hastily washed off the terrifying sweat-disfigured makeup before ushering them both out the door at a dash. Only the trailing cloud of colored balloons bore proof of the crimes they had been a party to.

When they burst back out into the sunshine, Sherman— now in shorts, sneakers, and a t-shirt—thought much better of the weather. As Sherman and Hemingway ran past the band shell, both Phoenix Rivera and Tito Fuentes Jr. were busy jamming with a Latin jazz big band. Strains of music right out of a 1950's Miami or Havana nightclub made Sherman want to dance despite his present mission of mishaps.

Off to the left, plumes of dark smoke rose from the belly of the old Rena-77 wooden ketch the good citizens of Miami were—thanks to his newspaper articles—now keyed up to refurbish. The billowing smoke was a poignant reminder of Miami's past, but also a sharp prompt to Sherman about the urgency of its present

As Mac and John cruised southward behind a clear plexi-glass podium near the water, her honor the mayor stood reading from various old *Miami Herald* articles about the famous yacht fire and the old Grand Flamingo Hotel. The band played on. The crowd in the park was morphing steadily away from Biscayne Boulevard and the Rad-Corp building, all straining for a look at the "burning" sailboat as it wafted thick black smoke in its wake.

"Well, Hem," Sherman said as they jogged towards Rad-Corp, skirting the shuffling crowds, "It sure looks real from here, and John and Mac are certainly attracting everyone's attention."

★ ★ ★

The blue and white plastic drop cloths suspended around the huge center column of the kiosk mall under Rad-Corp had a dozen ladders stuck up here and there between them. Although the paint job itself was mostly finished, each ladder had the lower half of a human torso sticking out below the adjoining tarps. It was final countdown, but one crucial puzzle piece needed to be fit into place before the paint crew descended for their finale.

So as not to draw attention from the Rad-Corp security booth in the structure's core, both the blue and the white tarps secured side-by-side just above the metal double doors were anchored to the ceiling above the roving security camera and its twin emergency spotlights. From the guard's perspective, everything in the kiosk mall was just as visible as ever. By now, of course, everyone took the plastic tarps for granted. But had anyone paid close enough attention to the paint tarps today, they might have wondered at the odd coincidence which had resulted in all the blue tarps hanging to the east or Bayfront Park side of the Rad-Corp doors, while all the white tarps had been segregated on the western alley side. The former random two-tone patchwork now resembled a great "T" neatly color-coded in half, with its base squarely above the two red doors.

"It's time," Dan Stone said to no one in particular.

"Yup," Benny echoed. "It's time."

Both men stood in the bed of Dan's pickup truck with propane grill lighters in their hands. On the ground nearby, Grandmother Renee placed her hand gently on Seth's shoulder.

"Well, Seth, you are the Red Chief today, and we are ready to follow. Sherman will come."

"Thank you, Grandmother," Seth said, "your faith is a gift." He turned to Dan and Benny. "Light it up gentlemen, but hold off on the fan."

There was a loud "whoosh" as the two barrels, each half-full of oily rags, ignited. Flames rushed upwards seeking oxygen, and a black cloud of smoke began to rise up the west face of the Rad-Corp building.

"The second Sherman shows up, crank up that box fan," Seth said.

"What if he doesn't show up?" Benny Lopez asked.

"We'll give Sherman another few seconds. If he doesn't show, Spray Ray will paint over the camera, but I'd rather not rile up the guards that way."

★ ★ ★

When Sean's text "Now!" lit up both Chris Tosh's and Captain O'Connor's cell phones, Miami Fire Stationhouse #12 came alive. Hot, sweaty, and heavily laden fire fighters jumped into their trucks.

"Remember," Captain Jay called out, no sirens until my lights go on!" With that, he and Chris Tosh climbed into his pickup truck and led the convoy south. Two blocks before they reached Biscayne Boulevard, the chief's lights and sirens came on, and the column split. The pickup and the ambulance turned down the alley, while the two big ladder trucks headed south on Biscayne Boulevard toward Bayfront Park. Ahead of them, thick black smoke was already billowing over the Rad-Corp building, darkening an otherwise perfect Miami sky. Game on.

★ ★ ★

The Miccosukee historical display tent was located about midway between the waterfront where John and Mac were cruising and where the Rad-Corp building sat smoking across Biscayne Boulevard While one tribal woman remained at the display table, the dozen or so costumed dancers and drummers began yet another traditional dance. As the crowds surged steadily towards the waterfront, the dance circle turned into a writhing snake and wended its way in the opposite direction. Thick black smoke signals above the Rad-Corp building seemed to mystically guide the dancers' steps.

★ ★ ★

At that moment, aboard the old wooden sailing yacht, Rosie and her team hunkered in the hot forward stateroom and continued whispering about various escape scenarios they might employ should any number of painfully imminent possibilities occur to further complicate their already farcical escape attempt.

"We can only climb out of that hatch one at a time," Linda Ulrich said suddenly, interrupting three fragmented discussions all happening at once. "Who goes first? Everything else is secondary to that."

"She's right," Peter Bloom added. "I'll go."

"No," Rosie said, "it should be me. No offense, but I'm the least threatening looking, the least likely to garner a hostile response."

Her team looked at one another and nodded. It was a very sensible suggestion, and despite their current dilemma, they all thought Rosie to be the most sensible of them all.

"Okay, that's settled then," Rosie said. "Now, how do we determine whether or when I should go?"

Lou Garcia laughed, almost too loudly, and quickly covered his mouth with both hands and whispered between his fingers: "Oh, I think we'll all know when it's time. If nothing worse happens, we wait 'til dark like we planned. Otherwise, I suspect all hell will break loose, and that will be our clue!"

There were murmurs of accent, followed by a tense silence.

Chapter Forty-Seven

A winded Sherman Kanz and his beagle, Hemingway, jogged toward the Rad-Corp building at a run just as the Native American dancers and drummers were crossing Biscayne Boulevard just ahead, a half block to the south. The reporter watched as one of the Natives paused to adjust the big commercial box fan facing out from the kiosk mall to its highest setting. Then he passed into the shadow under the stilted building. Benny was to crank up the fan on Dan's truck in the back alley, and that front fan was supposed to have been Sherman's job. But nothing about his day had gone exactly as planned. A moment later, as he and Hemingway moved into the shade under Rad-Corp themselves, he focused on his other objective. The remote-controlled video camera above the red metal Rad-Corp doors was moving slowly, scanning the busy vendors and festival goers. As per Seth Lowenstein's suggestion, he paused in front of the red doors, bent to retie a shoelace, and as he rose and walked on toward the alley where Dan Stone's smoke-emitting pickup was parked, he released the great bundle of colored balloons. At last! Something went as planned!

Seth Lowenstein saw the balloons engulf the security cameras and shouted up into the ceiling hung drop cloths: "Now, Ray!" Benny Lopez breathed a sigh of relief and walked up to the big box fan mounted on the smoking pickup's side panel. He lay his hand on the control dial just as the costumed Miccosukee tribal members poured out from under the building and gathered around Dan Stone and Grandmother Renee.

Spray Ray Colors came down off one of the ladders with a small battery-operated bullhorn on a strap around his shoulder. The top half of the rest of his fellow artists descended with him, carrying off their ladders and his, using them to usher certain shoppers aside, and then placing the ladders strategically along a path leading away from the Rad-Corp doors. Ray spoke to the crowd of vendors and gawkers as he herded them along.

"The moment you have all been waiting for has finally arrived!" he boomed. "While this may not be the world's largest Banyan tree, I suspect you are about to be the very first to witness the world's largest and most beautiful hand-painted Banyan tree. I am proud to present you to the grand matriarch of Banyan trees everywhere. Ladies and Gentlemen, in honor of our precious Mother Earth, meet "The Daughter Tree!"

Spray Ray tugged on the cord in his other hand, and all the tarps blocking their view of the ceiling around the largest column fell at once, and the collective sounds of awe from the crowd assured that no one was likely to have noticed what was really happening as Ray immediately led them on a guided tour north around the building's central concrete column. As they passed Seth Lowenstein, Ray winked at him as he continued his crowd-pleasing patter.

Seth motioned to Benny, who turned the fan on the truck up to its fastest speed. Then Seth followed the rest of the paint crew around as they double-checked the blue and white T-shaped plastic tunnel that had suddenly formed around the various ladders, beginning at the red doors. The base of the "T" now headed out from the Rad-Corp entrance, and its top was two color-coded tunnels, one to the east and the other to the west. He watched closely as the paint crew members placed rubber coated hand clamps on all the seams between the tarps. This step, Seth hoped, would keep the smoke out of the T-shaped tunnel, and keep the fleeing Rad-Corp employees in—regardless of whether they ultimately turned left down the blue fork, or right down the white toward Dan Stone's truck, Benny's van, and the Miccosukee Resort & Casino's guest shuttles. From the outside, it looked like a small T-shaped house that was being professionally tented for termites.

At the very top center of the "T," where the blue and white tarp tunnels each headed in opposite directions from one other, Seth unclipped two clamps, slipped inside the plastic tent, and refastened the clamps on the inside. From there, looking down the short stem tunnel, he could see the two red metal doors of the guard house, Sherman's balloons, and the emergency spotlights flickering towards him like strobe lights. To his right, the blue tunnel opened into the sunlight on Biscayne Boulevard. To his left, the white tunnel's end spotlighted the nose of Dan's truck where it sat parked in the alley. Seth reached into his backpack, withdrew a large folded-up banner he'd had printed at a local sign shop, quickly taped it to the tarp wall facing the doors, and headed out through the white tunnel to freedom. The two distinctly different images on his banner were the same he had used in his subliminal campaign. But, here on the tunnel wall, there was nothing subliminal about them.

They were bold and clear. Seth wanted them to be immediately seen and recognized by any employees coming out those doors...even if those employees had no idea where they might have seen the designs before. "Damn, I hope this works," Seth muttered as he threw the duct tape back in his pack.

By the time Seth met Sherman, Hemingway, and the others in the alley, the thick black smoke was blowing through the kiosk mall from west to east, swirling neatly around and over the tarp tunnel, and billowing out onto Biscayne Boulevard as if a great forest fire must surely have been coming along right behind. The weary rescue crew stood together near the front bumper of Dan's pickup with Grandmother Renee, Dan, Benny, and the Miccosukee dancers and watched the poor venders rush to get their pushcarts out towards Bayfront Park. At first, they heard Spray Ray's bullhorn ("Well, folks, there seems to be a fire somewhere, so let's head toward the par..."), but in seconds, the young artist's voice was drowned out by sirens coming from the north along both the front and back sides of the building. By the time the bright green firetrucks came to a stop, black smoke was rising up the east face of the Rad-Corp building as thickly as it had up the opposite side.

"I think you have their attention now," Grandmother Renee said to Seth over the din.

Everyone laughed nervously, and as Chris Tosh and Captain Pat O'Connor walked up to join them, they all stared at the mouth of the white plastic tunnel that opened into the alley a few feet in front of them.

"Hello Seth," the fire chief said, sticking out his hand. "Did you manage to open the doors?" he asked. "I brought this just in case." In his other hand he held up a wicked looking power tool designed specifically for stubborn metal doors.

Seth took his hand and shook it heartily. "Chris said you were Navy too," he said. "I hope we don't need your jaws-of-life, but thanks for bringing them along."

"How long 'till we know?" Chris Tosh asked. "Are those your alarms I hear?"

"Yup," Seth said with a grin, "that's my program's racket you're hearing. Do you all remember what the baseball ghost said to Kevin Costner?" Seth asked as he turned to the laptop open on the hood of Dan's truck. As he typed in a long series of instructions, he answered his own question. "'Build it, and they will come.'"

★ ★ ★

Sundays inside Rad-Corp were typically pretty boring for the guards in the silver sports coats. Sometimes a handful of the big brass might be in the building, but the rank and file never caught more than a glimpse of the real power behind the machine. But the Saving the Grand Flamingo Festival in Bayfront Park was a wonderful change of pace. Had the building been a boat, there might have been dangers involved with having everyone at the east-facing windows all day, but the thirteen mighty concrete columns in the kiosk mall below the high-rise showed no signs of allowing the building to tip in that direction. Throughout the day, no more than one security guard ever manned the front desk and the camera at the ground level entrance. The guards took turns on this lonely, windowless duty so the rest could watch all the excitement in the park from the various vantage points on the floors above. Sure, there were a few diehards watching sports on TV, but even they moved to the east windows during commercials.

With only the one excursion outing on the lobby login/logout screen, there was nothing to do but read or watch videos until fellow guard Joe Allen returned with Phillip Crowe and his 20th floor engineering team. Sure, Eddie Vogel checked the bank of security cameras from time to time, but that was mostly from habit. The cafeteria, the rec floor, and the roof were the only places where much was going on in a group sense, and his infrared apartment sensors mapped out the same thing the cameras showed him. Everyone was watching Bayfront Park through the building's east facing windows.

Eddie had been a foster kid, bounced around a lot before he was given the choice of jail or military service by a Miami judge. He liked the Navy well enough, though the thirty-year career only reinforced how different he was. All the other sailors seemed to have families and friends, but Eddie figured he must just put people off for some reason. He wasn't much of a talker, and never had very strong opinions about politics, religion, or sports. He grew more and more comfortable with himself and his quirks. The Navy had been good for him. He had learned to take pride in a job well done, whether others appreciated his efforts or not. Rad-Corp had recruited him right out of the service, and they paid him well. Well, at least the balance in his personal account suggested he was pretty well off. And nobody minded that he kept to himself. Eddie had learned cherish his quiet, safe, and predictable personal life and space.

But over the past few days, he'd been experiencing unusual feelings about himself, his fellow Rad-Corp employees, and the greater world outside. He'd seen much of the world while in the Navy, but he'd recently been feeling like he might have missed something, something out there which maybe he'd passed by too quickly. Eddie was restless. He had, on several occasions, been in the middle of a movie or a TV show on the in-house cable system, or even just playing a computer game, and found himself staring out the window at puffy white clouds in the bright Miami sky, his mind a million miles away. There were no windows in the ground level guard station, but Eddie found himself staring over at the red double doors or gazing glass-eyed at the entry's outside video camera screen at least twice since coming on duty by himself.

This time, when his eyes refocused, the video screen was a jumble of strange translucent colors and the camera lens was obviously having difficulty focusing as it panned through the sea of...what?

"Balloons?" Eddie said as he took hold of the remote joystick controller and fiddled with the thumb focus wheel on top. As the camera lens turned squarely towards a white balloon, he could briefly see a fuzzy image of the kiosk mall before the balloons shifted and his view was blocked again by a field of stretched red rubber. "Some kid's unhappy," he laughed as he joggled the joystick, trying for another peek through the inflated kaleidoscope which had settled around his camera. He knew he could just step outside and grab the balloons, but the kid was probably already insisting that his mom do that anyway.

Seconds later, his view went nearly black. He assumed he'd rotated into a black balloon until the photovoltaic emergency lights above the video camera came on and he could again see the balloons as they reflected from the double spotlights in odd directions. But there was no light out beyond the balloons to the south where the kiosk mall ended and Southeast 2nd Avenue began. The angles there always let the waning sunlight bounce in off the next building down on Biscayne Boulevard. Eddie looked at the clock. "I might have zoned out for a second," he mused, "but not long enough for the sun to set. And if it did get dark that fast, all the lights out there would have come on. I better go check it out."

Eddie Vogel was halfway out of his swivel chair when whooping alarms attacked his eardrums. The shrill sound came from the public announcement speakers on the wall and from all the computer monitors at once. There was nothing in his training or his history at Rad-Corp about ear-splitting alarms. Suddenly his entire bank of computer screens turned red at once, with a yellow ribbon of words cycling from right to left across all of them: "PLEASE EVACUATE NOW!"

Eddie picked up the house phone, placed it against his ear, and immediately threw it back towards the counter. The screaming alarm sound was coming out of its handset too. "Shit!" he said as he backed up from the large curved counter. The only thing that he wanted to do was get away from that sound, but he wondered about everyone else. Were the elevators working? What about the emergency stairway? He had tried those doors before. They were always locked. And no one had ever mentioned a key. They were supposed to unlock in an emergency. Eddie was greatly relieved when the door knob turned easily and the door to the stairway swing open in his hand.

He stood frozen, covering his ears with his hands, trying to decide what to do next. Running upstairs seemed the noble thing to do, but where would he run? It seemed quieter in the stairwell, but there were 27 floors. That's when he remembered the balloons, the security camera, and the sudden darkness in the kiosk mall. As he turned away, Eddie thought he heard noises coming down from the stairway above, but decided that he might learn more by looking outside first.

Chapter Forty-Eight

Eddie Vogel shoved the push-bars on both red doors at once. The doors swung out easily. A large tangle of knotted white balloon strings hung near the doorway's header beam and he reached for it absentmindedly. But it was the white and blue tunnel before him that attracted his full attention. When he yanked the balloons down off the camera and the spotlights, the strange tunnel lit up and the banner at what seemed like the end ahead drew him like a magnet. Eddie felt like he had seen this before. But he had no idea where or when.

Before he'd had a chance to think through this puzzle, Eddie found himself edging to his right, following the white tarps toward the familiar pictures on the wall ahead. The graphic on the left was a stormy, ominous sky with dark clouds. In the midst of the gloom was the Rad-Corp logo and an arrow to the left. His shoulder actually rubbed the tarps to his right as he moved directly towards the other graphic, a bright blue sky with brilliant white clouds. Here, an arrow pointed to the white tunnel on his right, and Eddie turned that way without hesitation. It just felt right.

When he exited into the light, an elderly woman patted him gently on the shoulder, and spoke softly: "What a strange day, right?"

Eddie, still clutching Sherman's balloons, nodded and blinked against the light.

"I'd like you to meet Chris Tosh," Grandmother Renee said softly. "He plays basketball for the Miami Heat. Have you heard of him?"

Eddie's eyes opened wide with surprise as Grandmother Renee gently passed him off to the tallest fireman he'd ever seen. And damned if it wasn't Chris Tosh himself, leading him toward an odd looking trailer hooked up behind a pickup truck that was billowing a tower of black smoke, some of which was being forcefully propelled under the building from which he'd just emerged.

"So," Chris said as he took Eddie's arm, "we're going to get everybody to safety, and if you'd like, you can wait in one of these Space Station pods." Chris opened one of the eight doors. "Or, if you prefer to stay outside, here's a fire suit you can put on, just in case."

Eddie was staring into the pod, and it was even cooler than the ones he'd seen featured on the TV news. "I think I'll wait in here," he said, handing Chris his balloons, slipping out of his silver blazer, and climbing in to try out the famous "command chair."

"Great," Chris said. "Here's a bottle of water and a trail bar. We're all out here if you need anything, and we'll truck everybody out to the Miccosukee Resort & Casino for free hotel rooms and free dinner when the building is clear and everyone is safe. "Does that sound okay?"

"Wow!" Eddie, said. "Thanks for all the help."

For the next thirty-five minutes, Rad-Corp employees poured out of the white tunnel. Grandmother Renee, Seth, and the gang put them in pods and vans, often disguising them as firefighters or Native American dancers. By the time the white tunnel stopped emitting confused Rad-Corp employees, the pods, the casino's shuttles, Benny's white Filling Empty Houses van, the ambulance, and both pickup trucks were loaded with refugees. Moments later, they were all heading west toward the Miccosukee Resort & Casino on the corner of Chrome Avenue and the Tamiami Trail.

In another five minutes, the tarps disappeared, along with the ladders, the second commercial box fan, and

Benny's paint crews. With the fans gone and the barrels extinguished and heading west, the tower of smoke dissipated in the breeze off the bay. By the time Seth and Sherman walked under the building and out toward Bayfront Park, both ladder trucks were returning to Stationhouse #12.

"Just a little mishap," Spray Ray was saying into his bullhorn in the midst of the busy group of kiosk vendors whose business doubled the minute they had pushed their carts out from under Rad-Corp and into Bayfront Park. "It's safe to return whenever you'd like."

"What a gorgeous paint job, Sherman," Seth said as he tore two pieces of duct tape off the roll from his pack, stuck them over the door lock strikes, and gently closed the dark red Rad-Corp entrance doors on a loud but empty guard office. The doors looked strangely at home amidst the tangled Banyan roots painted all around them. "We may not have saved your damsel, Sherman, but we created a hell-of-a mural for downtown Miami. That's gotta count for something." He pulled out his laptop, opened it on his left hand, and typed in a string of commands with his right. The muffled alarms behind the doors went still.

"I hope Rosie's okay," Sherman said. "I'd like to see her in person! Those folks who came out," he went on suddenly, "did you really know your subliminal video images would send them out like that? I've never seen anything like it, and now I want to research that shit for my story."

"Everything I've read says it works like that on most people," Seth said, "but to tell you the truth, I was wingin' it. Worked a little too good maybe. We'll see. When they've all had a chance to settle down and hear Dan's explanations, we'll find out if I screwed up anybody's brain."

"And where were the angry guards and the mysterious shadow-corporate bigwigs, Seth? It's obvious your subliminal imagery worked wonders on the folks who came our way, some of them were even guards, but there wasn't so much as a scuffle. Look," he said, pointing at a dozen or so Rad-Corp security guards standing across Biscayne Boulevard looking at the empty building with puzzled expressions on their faces. "They're just standing there, clueless."

"Maybe the brass takes Sundays off," Seth said shrugging his shoulders. "And there's nobody here to give them orders. I expected it to get a little gnarly too. This is pretty weird."

As they stepped out onto Biscayne Boulevard, both men looked up at the sound of helicopter rotors far above their heads. The assembled guards in the park heard it too, and they were pointing up at the Rad-Corp rooftop helipad.

"There they are," Seth said. "The rats are fleeing their empty and sinking ship."

"So *they*," Sherman said, "whoever *they* are, just fly away?"

"Well, I probably have video footage of some of them, so who knows? My friend, Representative Ellis Keith, is trying to find out who they are, so hopefully they won't get far. Be nice to know who they were though, wouldn't it?"

"Damn straight," Sherman said grumpily. "That's my Pulitzer Prize about to fly off up there."

★ ★ ★

By the time the two sailboats began rounding the southeast corner of Bayfront Park and heading west, Rosie and her team were relieved to hear the sound of a fire extinguisher blasting away through their stateroom door. Lou Garcia ventured a peek backward out the overhead hatch. He popped back down, whispering, "He emptied one extinguisher, and he's grabbing another one."

"How far to the seawall by the old hotel?" Peter Bloom asked quietly.

Lou popped his head up again, this time looking ahead. "Maybe a hundred yards, or a bit more," he said. "Not far at all."

"It's getting dark faster," Linda whispered. She looked out a starboard porthole window. "Yup, the sun is down behind all the tall buildings now."

"All we have to do now is wait quietly," Rosie whispered as a second blast of fire retardant was being expelled in the old sailboat's main below-decks space. "When it's dark, there will still be lots going on back at Bayfront Park. Who's gonna be hanging out all the way over here, in front of a vacant old hotel and an otherwise empty city block? We've got this!"

Chapter Forty-Nine

The honorable congressman Ellis Keith of the Great State of Minnesota saw the black pillar of smoke in the distance and chuckled. Forgetting that he had a microphone attached to the big ear phones he had been issued, he saw the assault team member's heads turn toward him in unison. "The fire," he said, pointing out past the big 50-caliber machine gun mounted in the open doorway of the helicopter. "I'll bet twenty bucks it's just meant to distract or rattle the folks in that building. My friend, Seth learned that trick as a kid, and used it a couple times as a Navy SEAL."

The squad's eyebrows rose and heads nodded in acknowledgement as the single column of smoke turned into two—one in front of the skyscraper, and one behind. "Look!" Ellis said as the pilot brought them in from the west-northwest and swung out more to the east toward the heliport, "looks like a few of the bigwigs are hoping to slip away before I can chat with them." Six well-dressed men were approaching the other chopper at a run. "You can keep that from happening, right Captain?"

"Damn skippy we can," the pilot said without looking back. "Corporal Higgins? If they ignore my suggestion to shut that motor down, feel free to put a few new holes in that putting green on the roof behind their bird."

"Roger that, Cappy!"

Seconds later, out the big open door, the mini-cannon was pointing right at the plexi-glass bubble-shaped cockpit of the silver helicopter on the rooftop pad. Ellis' pilot and copilot were dramatically drawing their thumbs across their throats while staring directly at the grounded and tense looking pilot at the controls twenty-five yards away. The men piling into the chopper were all shouting at the man in the pilot's seat, but their voices were drowned out by the noise of spinning rotor blades on both birds.

"They're telling him to go I think, Cappy," Corporal Higgins said, "but I don't think he's got the *cajones* for it."

"I hope you're right, Corporal," the pilot said as he menacingly stopped slicing his own throat, shrugged his shoulders in resignation, and cupped his mic with that hand instead. "Just under the rotors, Corporal, when I say 'go!'"

Corporal Higgins brought his oversized cross-hairs right up under the other pilot's chin, flipped off the bright red plastic trigger guard, and grinned like a kid about to light his first firecracker. In the time it took him to shift the gun's barrel up a hair, the pilot in the other chopper had cut the engine and flung himself, face-first and arms wide, out onto the white concrete roof next to his portside skid.

"That's what I'm talkin' about, Corporal," the pilot said with a thumbs-up thrown in. He swung his black chopper in around the silver one, and set it down on the putting green so the Corporal could keep the other bird in his sights. "Hope that's not bullet-proof plexi-glass," he added as the FBI assault squad charged out and ran toward the transparent doorway to the helipad.

"Oh it might stop a couple 50-caliber rounds if it is, Cappy, but 750 rounds will grind that stuff up like confetti."

★ ★ ★

The Latin Jazz band in Bayfront Park had fully engaged half of the crowded park successfully right up until the smoking sailboat went by and the mayor began speaking.

They'd been instructed to play softly while she spoke, even though they were over a hundred yards away. They had done so. When she finished her historical address, and the old ketch disappeared behind the clump of trees at the south end of the park, Phoenix Rivera and Tito Fuentes, Jr. brought the band's tempo and volume back up. Within a few moments, the party was back in full swing. Until it wasn't.

Phoenix and the players in the band shell faced northwest, but the huge crowd spread out throughout the park in front of them was slowly shifting their attention to the southwest, away from the band. When smoke rose into the air over the 27-story skyscraper, a few eyes in the audience began drifting skyward. Then a second column of black smoke rose up in front of the building. Even more folks took notice. Their gazes attracted those of others around them. Soon Phoenix and Tito knew they were losing their audience, but had no idea why. The percussionists both looked up and back, but the concrete band shell blocked their view.

All across Bayfront Park, everyone—including the kiosk venders scrambling out from under the Rad-Corp building—was turning in ones and twos to stare upwards at the twin towers of smoke. Somebody muttered: "A terrorist attack?" Others took up the idea. Over the course of just half an hour, several thousand people—fully engaged in the festivities—became aware that something was amiss just across Biscayne Boulevard. And then, just as the entire crowd seemed to have finally become aware of the non-existent fire, the smoke dissipated. The skies over the Rad-Corp building turned blue again. It was over. Until it wasn't.

Conversations erupted—accompanied by a lot of bewildered head-shaking—and the band shifted into a higher gear in order to regain their audience's wayward attention. It might have worked. But into that already fearful collective consciousness came the sound of helicopter rotors whining their way up to speed overhead. This was followed by a scene right out of war movie. A jet black helicopter, its rotor blades running at full speed and its side door open with a machine gun sticking out swept around the northeast corner of the Rad-Corp tower and hovered just above the rooftop.

Every film crew Seth had put together in the park was pointing cameras upwards, and Sherman Kanz was trying to take notes as Hemingway tugged at his leash while peeking up at the commotion from behind Seth Lowenstein's legs.

"Hope that's the cavalry," Sherman said to Seth as he scribbled madly.

"It's a good bet," Seth said as the blade tips on the otherwise invisible helicopter slowed noticeably. "Shall we go see for ourselves?"

"Oh hell yes!"

Hemingway followed uncertainly. After the day he'd had, he was reluctant to follow his human anywhere. But this other one, he decided, wasn't nearly as unstable. What could it hurt?

★ ★ ★

Rosie Weathers and company waited quietly as their unaware host finished extinguishing the barrel of rags in the main cabin. The redhead tied up her 32-foot sloop first, and then secured the 47-foot wooden ketch. Rosie's team listened while the two chatted amiably about their adventure and speculated as to how everything else was going for the rest of the rescue team.

"She's pretty," Linda Ulrich whispered as she watched Mac tie off the lines through the little porthole window.

"Yeah," Lou whispered back. "No kidding!"

Peter Bloom eased up next to Linda and peeked out the adjacent porthole. "There's a redhead for you!" he said. "You think she's really sold on barrel-fire boy, Linda?"

"Definitely," Linda whispered.

"Is he good looking as me, Lou?" Peter said.

"Only if you consider tall, great smile, and long a flowing blonde ponytail good looking," Lou remarked with a smirk.

Patty Jenkins and Rosie stood in unison and crowded in between Peter and Linda for a look.

"Relax," Peter said as Linda turned to sit down. "The redhead's gone and there's no sign of Barrel Boy."

Chapter Fifty

"Well, Kicks," Seth Lowenstein laughed into his phone, "that was a grand entrance."

"It took bypassing a lot of red tape to make that happen," Representative Ellis Keith said, "so shut up and enjoy the moment, my brother. Any suggestions as to where to talk to these guys? It's hot and windy up here on the roof."

"Yeah, there's a big cafeteria on the next floor down. All those guys will have pass cards for the elevator. I'll meet you there."

"Can you wait down there for the local FBI unit and bring them up with you? They should be arriving any second, barely informed, and likely to be a bit surly, so charm them for me on the ride up."

"Gotcha covered, Kicks. See ya in a few."

The black Ford Explorer pulled up just as Seth and Sherman approached the Rad-Corp doors, and Seth motioned the Miami FBI office agents over as they piled out at the curb on Biscayne Boulevard

"Hemingway," Seth said, scratching the beagle's ears, "make nice to these folks. They're a little tense, and might need some TLC."

Hemingway shook his long ears in frustration. All he needed was a few more hyped up humans to crown off his day.

★ ★ ★

The V.I.P. lounge at the Miccosukee Resort and Casino was bustling with activity. The Rad-Corp escapees were being issued room keys, free gambling cash cards, and the strong drink of their choosing as Grandmother Renee, Dan Stone, Chris Tosh, Benny Lopez, and Captain Jay O'Conner circulated amongst them answering questions. A smart sales rep from Citywide Cellphone service who was staying at the hotel overheard several of the refugees discussing how none of them had owned or used cellphones in years. He promptly called the three closest Miami franchise shops and was selling calling plans and handing out cellphones within the hour. Whatever else might be happening, the make-shift rescue crew was delighted to see that all the Rad-Corp account access debit cards seemed to be fully operational. Former security guard, Eddie Vogel was already sporting a new jacket. The soft deerskin leather Native American designed coat had rustic thong fringes, each ending with a colorful braid, and Eddie looked quite pleased with himself as headed for the casino.

"Well," Dan said to a work team from Rad-Corp's stealth lab on the 12th, floor, "we won't know exactly what happens next until the FBI finishes its investigation, but in the meantime, they say you're free to enjoy the hotel and casino until they're finished here and tell you what's what." FBI agents were already interviewing Rad-Corp employees, and the Miccosukee Tribal Police were charged with shadowing several dozen Rad-Corp employees who were waiting their turns to be questioned.

When the team moved on, Dan caught up with Grandmother Renee. "I told Mac and John that I'd take a turn on boat watch tonight so they can get some dinner. The Bradford Resorts Group and the city are supposed to be working together on a permanent security detail, and promised to have someone there in the morning. I'll drop the pods back off at the factory on the way. If there's anything you need from town, call me, okay?"

Grandmother Renee smiled, nodded, and shooed him off with her graceful fingers before returning her attention to a young woman who seemed desperate to talk ceaselessly about her life at Rad-Corp until her FBI interview time came.

Dan met Seth, Sherman, Hemingway, and the Minnesota congressman on his way out. They were followed by the FBI assault team from D.C., several local FBI agents, and two undercover agents named Phillip Crowe and Joseph Allen. After introductions, Dan asked Representative Ellis straight-out: "Who are they? Are they bad guys for sure?"

"Well," said Keith Ellis carefully, glancing at the reporter and the FBI agents beside him, "at this point, let's just say they're not real Americans, and they're certainly not good guys. I'm sure Sherman will fill the good citizens of Miami and the world in on all the facts as they become available."

"You weren't lyin'," Dan said, smiling at Seth, "he's a politician all right! Thanks for helpin' us out, Congressman. It could have gone lots of different ways."

"Yes," Keith said, "with Seth in charge, that's a given."

"What about the lady we all set out to rescue?" Dan asked.

Representative Ellis turned grinning to the man he'd introduced as Phillip Crowe.

"Gave us the slip, she and her whole team," Crowe said sheepishly. "Made Joe and I look like amateurs. The paperwork and the razzing will be hell."

"You're just upset 'cause you were sweet on her, Gunny," Joe said with a smile, "but she's sure enough slick, that lady. Disappeared into thin air."

With that, Dan laughed, tipped his cowboy hat, and left the casino. As he climbed into his truck and headed back into Miami, he breathed a sigh of relief.

"Hell of a day," he said. "I'm just really glad it's over."

Whenever Dan drove that familiar stretch of Tamiami Trail at night, he got a little bout of melancholy when he passed a small neighborhood called Wrenwood. He had fallen in love with a woman whose folks lived there. They were dying of cancer at the time, she had told him, but she never took him to the house nor introduced him to her parents. She was a nurse at the VA hospital and had tended him when he had returned sick and addicted from Vietnam. They'd dated for only a week when he got out of the hospital, and they had made love only once. After that amazing night, she disappeared from his life forever. His Rosemary—if that was really her name—had become pregnant, it turned out. The child she bore was left outside the entrance to the Miccosukee Museum Village in a cardboard box. That child, his son, was John Ghostwalker. John's mother had broken Dan's heart, but the gift she had left him was beyond all price. Once again as he passed the quiet entrance to Wrenwood in the darkness, Dan thanked all his Ancestors and all of his son's Ancestors for the blessings of his life.

After he dropped the trailer off at the Space Station, Inc. factory, Dan returned to Bayfront Park. He saw the three sailboat masts shimmering in the moonlight, two aboard the wooden ketch and one on Mac's fiberglass sloop. But before he reached the sailboats, he came across his son and Mac. They were sitting near the now-empty park's southwest corner on a concrete bench. The two sailboats rocked gently, twenty or thirty yards away.

"How are they doing?" Mac asked when he sat down with them.

"Really well, all things considered," Dan said. "I suspect they've all got brand new cellphones by now. There was a Citywide rep staying at the hotel, and he's recouping his gambling losses ten-fold by selling the escapees calling plans."

"What about our damsel in distress?" John asked. "Did she ever show up?"

"Neither hide nor hair," his dad answered. "Long gone by now, I'm sure. Her boss in there was an FBI plant, and he was falling for her according to another agent on the inside. FBI's been zeroing in on Rad-Corp for a couple of years, but couldn't hack their computers."

"That's our little Seth for you," Mac said. "It all seems pretty surreal now, doesn't it?"

Three heads nodded together in the night breeze off Biscayne Bay. It was a lot to process.

★ ★ ★

An hour earlier, Rosie and her team had heard their unbeknownst hosts step ashore and walk away into the darkness. The redheaded woman and the tall blonde young man had been talking about where they would go for dinner. Lou Garcia had peeked out the hatch and then reported that while the park festivities were winding down fast, it was not yet safe to sneak out. "But," he smiled, "I don't think we need to get wet. It's pretty dark out there, and unless someone's walking right here on the Riverwalk, we can just step ashore and walk away. As long as we wait a bit longer."

They decided on one hour. It was, according to Barry Cole, "the longest hour ever." But they whispered about their former lives at the Cloisters, they dreamed about life back in the outside world, and they waited the hour out together.

"All clear," Lou reported when the hour had passed. "You still ought to go first, Rosie. Just because you earned it by getting us all out safely."

Chapter Fifty-One

Dave Bartlett was pissed, but mostly at himself. His famous writer friends in the Rock Bottom Remainders' band were no happier. Following Tito Fuentes, Jr. and Phoenix Rivera was to have been the headline spot for their classic rock and roll show, but Dave was slowly realizing that his enthusiasm for the gig had overshadowed his awareness of what effect Seth Lowenstein's escape plans might have on the festivities in Bayfront Park. That, after all, had been the whole purpose of getting the band back together.

"Really," Dave tried to explain back at the hotel bar, "I didn't know the stuff across the street would interfere with the concert! Seth said we were supposed to distract folks."

"Well, Steven King laughed, "that worked out well didn't it?"

"But as long as the drinks are on you, Dave," Amy Tan said, patting him on the back, "We'll find it in our hearts to forgive you."

"Here's a blues jam in Liberty City," Roy Blount, Jr. said, looking up from his newspaper, "let's go crash it!"

"I'll go call a couple cabs," Dave said as he headed for the concierge desk, "'cause I'll be damned if I'm buyin' all the drinks tonight."

★ ★ ★

Lou Garcia created a step with his hands and Rosie pulled herself out of the sailing yacht's forward hatch after looking around in all directions. There was a little light cast by the quaint lamp posts along the Miami Riverwalk that wound through the park and past the seawall where they were tied up. The closest Riverwalk lamp post was twenty feet away. Beyond that, everything was darkness and silence. She propped herself against the cabin and reached in to help pull the others out. In moments, her six former team members stood facing her with eager smiles on their faces.

"We did it!" Rosie said. "If our debit cards work, I'm buying dinner. Otherwise, we eat, the card gets rejected, and we wash dishes. But first, let's walk west and get some distance between us and Bayfront Park."

Rosie had expected an enthusiastic response, but was sorely disappointed. Her team appeared paralyzed, their smiles gone and their eyes big. It took a second for her to realize that they weren't staring at her, but directly past her. She turned around toward the park, and then nearly collapsed as she struggled to catch herself and sit down on the cabin roof before her knees failed her completely.

There on the sidewalk, directly under a lamp post, stood three familiar faces. The first two were the redhead and the tall blond man she'd watched from her bathroom window with her binoculars. Up close, the young man looked strikingly familiar. His face was a face she knew from somewhere else, but in the panic of the moment she couldn't think why that should be. The older man in western boots had removed his black cowboy hat and was smiling at her in a way only one man in her life had ever smiled at her before.

"Can we help you?" Mac asked her calmly. But Rosie couldn't answer. Her entire body had ceased to respond to her wishes. Her team closed around her in concern.

"Let's start with something simple," John Ghostwalker asked gently. "You're obviously not thieves. Who are you?"

"It's Scheherazade, John," Dan Stone said with eyes brighter than the lamp posts. "I'm pretty sure that this would be our famous damsel in distress and her missing Rad-Corp team. And, unless I've gone blind during the past twenty-some years, I am extremely honored to introduce you to your mother. As it turns out," he went on, grasping John firmly around the shoulders with his arm, "her name really was Rosemary!"

Rosie's hand moved slowly to her mouth, her fingertips touching her trembling lips. The young blonde man's face was very familiar because he had her eyes, her nose, and the bright hair she too once had.

Suddenly, John and Mac were both just as stunned as Rosie, and the six young adults on the sailboat were no better off.

"Who'da thunk it?" Dan said, his smile growing bigger. "I just said a blessing on the way by your folks' old neighborhood this very evening. The Ancestors are pleased."

"You?" Rosie managed. "The cowboy hat in the pickup at the Grand Flamingo? And that was you on the other roof that first time, in a yellow hard hat."

Dan nodded. "That was Benny Lopez with me both times. You'll like him."

"There was something so familiar about your walk, but...."

"It's the boots that make me walk funny. And it has been a while, hasn't it?" Dan said with a warm smile. "Now, before anybody faints from shock or hunger, how about we go out to the casino, get you all some free rooms and free dinner? Seth and Sherman are extremely disappointed about not meeting you in person, Rosemary, and there's a very distraught FBI agent named Phillip Crowe out there who has allegedly been pining for you all day. Seems you gave him the slip too," Dan added with a wink Rosie had never forgotten. "He says your secret drone is a work of art, and helped them break the case."

Dan stepped up to the water's edge and extended his hand. "The bad guys are locked up, the other escapees are all safe--busy on their new cellphones by now--and you, my dear heartbreaker, are something of a hero. It's long past time you began enjoying your freedom too."

The End

About the Author

Robinson's been a working freelance writer and novelist since 1984, and though he's been telling folks he's retired since 2004, the evidence doesn't support his claim. He published a series of children's stories called the *Grandfather and Grandmother Bear Stories* in 2012, along with a contemporary novel called *The Ghostwalker File*. Then, in 2014, Robinson wrote a controversial *Pilgrim's Progress*-like non-fiction book called *The Big God Theory: A Layman's Journey in the American Christian Church*.

 The Ghostwalker File--a novel based in the Miccosukee Reservation neighborhoods just west of Miami—morphed into a series when he combined the theme of Native American community with a high-tech escape adventure to create a sequel novel called *The I.M.P. Master* in early 2017, and followed that up almost immediately with a third book in the "Ghostwalker Tribe Series" called *The White Mouse* which is due to be published in late in 2017 or early 2018. Robinson says that *The White Mouse* is something of a return to his Stick Foster mystery series books back in the early '90s, but this time the sleuth is a young

Miccosukee student at the University of Miami, determined to find out who is dumping a new type of deadly pollutant into the Florida Everglades.

Sneak Preview:
The White Mouse

If you enjoyed this adventure in the Ghostwalker Tribe Series, here's a PREVIEW look at the opening of Book Three (coming in 2017): *The White Mouse*

PROLOGUE

Rachel Blackfeather was neither focused nor feeling the fun. She had, perhaps, asserted what Dan Stone called an "unrighteous yes" when she had agreed to help old Joe Walking Fish on this night. Worse, Rachel was just generally out-of-sorts of late. She could not put her finger on the epi-center of her growing disgruntlement over recent months. At any given moment—like this one—her growing frustration was acting like a cheap automobile compass mounted too close to the engine compartment. No matter which way she steered, her internal guidance kept telling her she was still heading "North." She didn't know exactly where she wanted to go, but it definitely wasn't north—whatever "north" meant in her current state of scrambled psyche.

At this particular moment, Rachel didn't like the noise the dozen or so ten-foot pieces of gray PVC pipe were making as they bounced up and down on her right shoulder. Not only did the bundle rattle with every step she took, but stumbling around in the Florida Everglades at night wasn't nearly as much fun as the last time. At around eight years of age, every Miccosukee child got a personal guided tour into the Everglades, always on a dark and rainy night, where Joe "Walking Fish" Lamont showed them that a catfish can and does occasionally walk out of the swamp water and traipse along on *terra firma*.

A decade later, Rachel was a college freshman—a fulltime student at the University of Miami—and it was a little tough being perky with swamp water up to her knees and the inch-and-three-quarters diameter plastic pipes getting snagged on every stalk of swamp grass around her. But, as Rachel stumbled along in the fickle and hazy half-moonlight on this night, it just might have been the outrageous story Joe Walking Fish was going on and on about that pissed her off the most. If the wild rescue tale was true, she was going to be giving her adopted older brother, John Ghostwalker, a serious talking to when she was finished helping old Joe with whatever the hell this latest scheme of his turned out to be.

"This all happened last week?" she said, interrupting the Miccosukee tribal elder yet again. "Are you sure? How is it you got to be a part of this supposed rescue adventure and no one called me?"

"Yes, it is true," Joe chuckled. "Have I made a habit of lying to you little White Mouse? Though, in all honesty, I was merely asked to pass out meal vouchers at the casino when the escaped Rad-Corp employees were driven out to the tribal resort. I assume no one called you because you and Patrolman Stillwater seem to have moved to the city permanently and no longer participate in the mundane affairs here on the rez. Besides that, your policeman boyfriend couldn't very well have participated in all the legally questionable high-jinks that young Sean Lowenstein set up, now could he?"

"Oh, that's right," Rachel said, accidentally poking the old man gently in the shoulder with the front end of a wayward plastic pipe. "That Seth is something else. Did you hear about how he dressed up as a gay mob boss in order to trick a Baltimore enforcer sent down here to kidnap Mac?"

"Yes, my dear," Joe laughed. "Grandmother Renee has pictures of him from that day on her phone, and of Dan Stone dressed up as his chauffer."

"And about our staying in town," Rachel snapped, "of course, Billy and I stay in Miami sometimes. We need to get in more study time and sleep, but no one wants to miss out on an adventure like that! Billy's classes are tougher, but way more interesting than mine," Rachel said as if this last was an annoying afterthought. "And this lady, Rosemary Weathers? You're sure that she's John's biological mother?"

"Yes, child," Joe laughed, "and you will see that for yourself if we finish our work here in time. We're meeting a few folks for breakfast at the Waffle Kitchen in Homestead.

Your parents will be there too. Hell, I imagine half the tribe will be there to meet her."

"No shit," Rachel said to no one in particular. "Well, nobody ever said John Ghostwalker's life was normal. So, she and Dan Stone were, ah, *intimate* back in the day?"

"That's usually how it happens," Joe said, stopping on a small island in a deep stand of swamp grass. "Here, this spot will be perfect! Put that pipe right over here, and try not to knock down any more of the tall grass."

Rachel dropped her unruly load on top of Joe Lamont's, turned to ask what the pipes were for, and discovered that he was already hurrying back towards his truck for another load. The old man had to be at least eighty years old, but it was all she could do to catch up with him before he'd reached the dike where his pickup was parked.

"Here," he said, pulling a rope out from under the front seat of the old Chevy, "let's see if we can tow the rest like an old tribal liter." Joe tied one end of the rope around the end of a bundle of several dozen remaining gray PVC pipes hanging off the truck's tailgate and fashioned the rest of the rope into two large loops, one ahead of the other. "Like this," he said, slipping the forward loop over his head and one shoulder and handing Rachel the other. "Let's knock this out!"

Off he went like a hound on a rabbit, nearly pulling Rachel off her feet as he stalked down the dike and back into the water. If she thought the pipes were noisy before, the sound they made falling off the pickup's bed startled her so badly, she nearly fell again.

"Shit!" she screamed as the weight hit her shoulder and the sound attacked her ears. "That will raise the dead!"

"No dead out here," Joe laughed. "The dead are all eaten pretty quickly in the swamp—especially at night."

"Oh thanks," Rachel shot back. "That makes me feel lots better."

"Come to think of it," the wizened elder went on, "I've heard that gators sometimes stash live prey in their dens along the dike. I've heard tell of unfortunate tourists and fishermen who wake up wet, battered, and bloody inside one of those dark muddy underground caves."

"You're hilarious, Joe," Rachel snapped as she finally got the hang of being a sled dog pulling behind a more proficient lead husky.

"Oh, don't worry," Joe said, "at least one of them must have got out alive, or how else would we have such a great story?"

By the time they reached the little island again, Rachel was as winded as she was curious. While she caught her breath, Joe began pulling supplies out of the satchel slung over his other shoulder. "Here," he said, handing Rachel a zip-lock bag filled with old wine bottle corks, "drain all the water out of as many of those pipes as you can and plug both ends with one of these. I'll be back in a few minutes."

Just like that, Joe Walking Fish Lamont splashed on off deeper into the dark swamp ahead. "You're crazy, Old Joe!" Rachel shouted after his fading visage. "And what the hell are we doing anyway?"

"Yes, Little White Mouse, I am indeed crazy," he laughed back at her. "Joyously crazy! And that's only one of the reasons you follow me with such admirable determination. We, my dear, must discover who, exactly, is poisoning this water. What is water, little White Mouse?"

"Water is life," Rachel called out into the darkness.

"Indeed, it is!" answered the disembodied voice, "But, in order for us to help Mother Earth with the dying water here on our rez, I believe you and I must first divert a few million dollars in research funding!"

CHAPTER 1

The parking lot outside the Waffle Kitchen on Chrome Avenue in downtown Homestead was packed. Cars and trucks filled the lot and lined both sides of the street all the way down to the auto parts store two blocks away. Old Joe Walking Fish pulled into the parts store lot, parked his truck, and headed down the sidewalk with a chagrinned Rachel Blackfeather still in tow—soggy jeans, squishy sneakers, and all. She was clutching an aged and worn hardback book in her hands, trying to thumb through it while keeping up with the Miccosukee elder whose energy and good humor always seemed boundless. Joe had pulled the old tome out of the glove box and handed it to her almost as an afterthought before walking off towards the restaurant.

"This other lady, in this book, Nancy Wake," Rachel said, stumbling where a white oak root had raised a section of the sidewalk, "she's really why you call me 'White Mouse?'"

"Yes," Joe said over his shoulder, "I've told you that before, hoping you would research your namesake on your own, but your incessant curiosity does apparently have some boundaries after all. Mind you, that old book is worth two-hundred bucks on eBay, so tend to it accordingly."

As they approached the Waffle Kitchen, Rachel's mind was running in so many directions at once, she had no room left in her consciousness for disgruntlement. Joe Walking Fish and Grandmother Renee Person (the only other highly revered Miccosukee elder who could rival Joe's age and tribal and historical intensity) both had a way of lifting Rachel out of herself and reminding her that the world was much bigger. The faded black and white photo of Nancy Wake on the tattered paper book jacket stared up at her with a look of such cool intelligence and keen intensity that Rachel was half-tempted to sit down on the curb and start reading the famous spy's autobiography right then and there.

But the overcrowded restaurant ahead was surrounded by a host of vehicles she knew all too well. Each and every one of them had spent time in her backyard. Her father, Nate Blackfeather, was a mechanic, and his shade tree repair shop had hosted a steady stream of their friends' and neighbors' ailing automobiles for as far back as Rachel could remember. Today's mid-morning gathering was a genuine neighborhood event, and her adopted big brother, John Ghostwalker, was once again at the hub of the tribal hub-bub. She wouldn't miss this for the world.

Rachel was glad to be following closely on Joe Walking Fish's heels when they climbed the eatery steps and pushed into the packed house inside the front doors. All the booths along the front windows were full and every table in the restaurant had been shoved up against others to create a massive banquet arrangement. Folks just naturally stepped aside for Joe and Grandmother Renee. In Native tradition, elders were treated with respect in most situations, and as old Joe approached the far end of uni-table where Grandmother Renee was holding court, no less than eight adults and five youngsters seemed to rise as one and offer the elder their chairs. Everyone grew up feeling deeply related to these two elders, and every last soul among them had been taught crucial life lessons by either or both throughout their lives.

Joe had a retired son in Kansas City, but no other actual blood relatives alive in the tribe. Grandmother Renee Person was so old that no current member of the Miccosukee tribe (except old Joe Walking Fish) had ever met one of her blood relatives. Though they were not related to each other in any way, Joe liked to talk about meeting Grandmother Renee's mother from time-to-time when he was a boy. These conversations about their parent's lives sounded like something from the era of Buffalo Bill's Wild West Shows. The turn of that century was a long way back, even for folks who held their ancestry in high regard, but any stories about the time period that spanned the history of the Delaware Cree and their Miccosukee offshoots, to the current age of lasers and cell phones, were always listened to with gracious respect. "Ancestors always instruct," it is said within some indigenous tribes. "And often late ancestors instruct more constructively than living ones...so long as at least one living one remembers."

"Welcome to the party, Joe Walking Fish," Grandmother Renee said with a graceful gesture of her long fingers. "And, you, my child," she said to Rachel, "seeing as your big brother is over there watching from a relatively safe distance, let me introduce you to our newest family member. Rosemary Weathers, this is Nate and Marion's daughter, Rachel Blackfeather. Rachel, as you should see plainly enough for yourself, Rosemary is John's biological mother.

Looking back on that morning, even years later, Rachel never came up with a rational explanation for her behavior. A simple verbal acknowledgement would have suited the situation quite appropriately. But that is not what Rachel Blackfeather did. Though she would never admit later that she had been emotionally overwhelmed, no one in the tribe failed to notice. Rachel barreled over several startled friends and neighbors, wrapped Rosemary in a bear hug, and began sobbing on the poor woman's shoulder.

Grandmother Renee, Joe Walking Fish, Nate and Marion Blackfeather, and even John Ghostwalker himself all shared a moist-eye-moment, and no one present failed to appreciate how that moment enriched each of their lives. For the first time in her young life, Rachel Blackfeather had officially spoken for her tribe—all without uttering a word.

"Life's most important expressions are often silent," Grandmother Renee said with a smile. "Shall we order some breakfast now? I believe we have waited quite long enough."

**Watch for Book 3 in the
Ghostwalker Tribe Series:**

The White Mouse

Available at:
www.Amazon.com

(Coming in 2017!)

Other Books by Kevin Robinson

Visit Kevin at www.backdeck.net

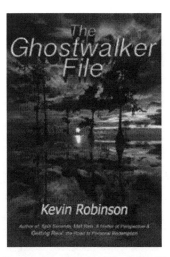

The Ghostwalker File
http://amzn.to/2jnLVvi

GETTING REAL:
The Road to Personal Redemption
http://amzn.to/2jADBaI

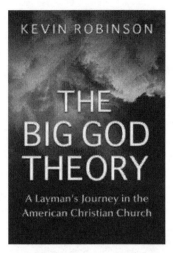

**The Big God Theory:
A Layman's Journey in the
American Christian Church
http://amzn.to/2ikyLNM**

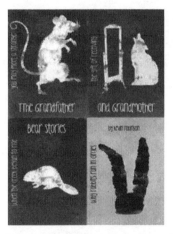

**The Grandfather and
Grandmother Bear Stories
http://amzn.to/2jABSlG**

**You can find all of Kevin's books at:
www.amazon.com/author/ghostwalker**

Made in the USA
Columbia, SC
16 August 2018